Colla
Too Old To

John Walker

DISCLAIMER

Blurb

The pieces have finally fallen into place for the Earth Defense Force. Multiple cultures have come together to form an alliance against the invading Veldon. As they gather to formulate a plan to bring peace to the universe, an insidious inside faction attempts to destroy all they've built.

Meanwhile, Commander Gareth Weston leads his team on a recon mission behind Veldon lines with no idea of what to expect. Patrick Worthing pursues the rogue JTF operative responsible for torturing countless prisoners while the ambassadorial detail of Alfred Chance jump through hoops to bring the Raldor into the alliance.

Each of these missions hold their own dangers which may cause not only the deaths of the operatives but the fragile peace between the benevolent cultures.

Prologue

Klaus took a punch to the face. He found himself surrounded by three men, each of them armed. They didn't try to kill him, though they had the advantage. One of them shouted commands at him, ordering him to surrender. Another two punches to the gut brought the point home.

Two people held him by the arms, clinging tightly to his biceps. They gave the others the opportunity to beat on him, punching him in the face, the chest, the stomach. He took the punishment. He'd been through far worse. But he needed to break free. Sooner or later, they'd whittle down his endurance.

He lashed out with a kick, catching one of his attackers in the knee. The victim cried out, cursing as they moved out of range. A second swing got someone in the groin. Klaus began thrashing about like a feral animal, a creature caught in a trap with nothing to lose. This made his captors struggle to keep a hold of him.

Klaus ripped his left arm free, jabbing the guy on the opposite side in the eye. His thumb felt wet as he yanked it from the man's eye socket. That blow freed him of their grip. He grunted, huffing twice as he charged forward into the nearest man. He slammed the guy into the wall then head butted the swaying man in the face three times.

Blood coated Klaus's forehead. He felt it run down his cheeks as his temples began to throb. But he was free. And unless these maniacs wanted to kill him, they wouldn't have the chance. All of them nursed some pretty nasty injuries, most of them on the floor. They had yet to call for backup as far as he knew.

He grabbed the pistol from the nearest one, turning to execute each of the people walling in misery. As they fell silent, he leaned to look into the hallway. Much as he wanted to make a run for it immediately, he had to find Cole. Without her, he had no way off the ship. Automated piloting wouldn't evade a destroyer.

When the hell did the JTF turn corrupt? When they had boarded the ship at the invitation of Trildair, Klaus had a bad feeling. They were arrested the second they got out of their ship, held at gunpoint and separated. His captives took him into a private room where they set upon him, grabbing his arms while commencing with a beating.

Klaus spat blood on the floor as he took a hard left. He'd pass by the hangar but that was the direction they had taken Cole. If they started in on her as they did him, he had no idea if she'd be useful at all. They might have beaten her into a coma, which didn't seem far-fetched considering how hard they hit him.

What do these freaks want? They hadn't even demanded anything. There was no conversation. Just assault. If they had questions, they could've started with them. But we were cleared showing EDF. So what happened to these assholes? He had always heard the JTF happened to be decent compared to the other militaries.

They were renowned for treating their prisoners with respect. Sometimes more than they deserved.

Maybe we found some pirates... or slave traders masquerading as the JTF. That has to be right. Slavers might start with punishment to break down a person physically. Conditioning later might involve anything from sleep deprivation to sonic torture. They picked the wrong guy for all that shit.

A woman in a JTF uniform stepped out of the hangar. Klaus shot her as she stared at a device. She died without having any clue what hit her. One moment there, the next done. The blast echoed through the open space, attracting plenty of questions. People shouting out questions of whether or not they heard the sound.

Klaus hustled past the entrance then leaned out to see how many might be coming his way. At least four started cautiously in his direction. Since they weren't running, he didn't worry about them. He did pick up the pace though, checking the first door on his left, opposite the hangar.

A briefing room with a dozen chairs and a big screen. Empty otherwise. Next, an office with a desk and three chairs. Also vacant. If Cole was down there, they must have put her in a regular place. Not a cell, nor a holding area. Which also seemed odd. They had dragged him into a large storage closet.

What is happening in this place? I want to talk to this Trildair guy.

"There!" A shout behind him pushed Klaus into a sprint. He hurried toward the end of the hall where he might round the corner. At twenty yards, the guards opened fire. Blasts raced by him. He ducked, evading to the left and right as he neared his destination. A searing burn skimmed his left side.

Klaus hissed as he made it to cover, checking the injury. They got him just at the bottom of the ribs. Fortunately, it was a close one and didn't actually hit him directly. It might've killed him instantly. I guess they're done with me now. Whatever purpose they wanted to put me to might not be worth the effort.

He poked his weapon around the corner, blind firing several times. "Cole!" Klaus shouted, "if you can hear me, tell me where you are!"

Only the sounds of gunfire filled the hallway. Followed by people giving orders to one another about how to advance on his position. They had comms and additional forces. Eventually, someone would come up on his rear. The only thing he had left to do was to find the bridge.

And deal with Trildair.

Catching their leader may well be the only way they escaped the ship alive. Or intact for that matter. He didn't want to think about how they were treating Cole. If they were slavers, and not something creepier, then they might be doing some unspeakable things. Klaus had no qualms about killing people.

Violating them pissed him off. Such acts reminded him of his time under Colm's 'care.'

The pain in the graze brought Klaus back to the moment. He tried to suppress the pain, tensing up to fight through it. They managed to get his device as well as his weapons. Which meant he had no way to map his destination to the bridge. An elevator would work. If he could find one.

Before they mobilize additional forces to put me down. Klaus shoved away from the wall. He stumbled the first few paces before finding his stride. The people behind him continued to work tactically, advancing with caution. That struck him as funny. Had they charged, he'd already be dead.

He checked each door along the way. More offices, conference rooms, storage areas... all empty. Were they operating with a skeleton crew? Why?

Because they're criminals and scumbags. If they were legitimately the JTF, I wouldn't get twenty feet without stumbling over someone. Granted, they'd be rank and file soldiers, likely unarmed. Each of them potential human shields too. People he could use against the others. Instead, everyone's probably armed. Even Trildair.

A door opened, revealing the elevator he wanted. Gunshots flashed near his face. He hopped aboard without a second thought as volleys filled the hallway. Enough firepower to take down a squad. That was lucky. Had it been a regular room, they would've cornered him. Then they wouldn't have even had to come in after him.

Just lock the door, sap the air, and leave him to suffocate.

Instead, he tapped the top floor button then aimed his weapon at the door. His heart hammered in his chest every time the digital readout showed the number change. The last three got him bouncing on the balls of his feet. Anticipation made him chew the inside of his cheek until it went raw and ached.

The door opened.

Klaus blasted the first figure he saw. The body dropped forward before he could grab it. As he stepped out, a heavy blow struck him on the side of the head. Dazed, he stumbled into the wall. He fired his weapon though he didn't bother to aim. The shot splashed on the deck as someone cuffed him again, this time with something metal.

His vision turned black, his tongue seemed to swell in his mouth as he fell to his knees.

"Disarm him, you moron." The voice sounded distant, as if from the end of a metal tube. A hand grabbed Klaus's hair, forcing him to look up. He saw a figure approach through blurred vision. "You're passionate, hmm? And here I thought you were disposable. An EDF grunt to be killed."

"Fuck you..." Klaus muttered. The words slurred together, but the message was clear enough.

"Yes, you have the fire I need." The man chuckled. "I'll find great enjoyment in ending your defiance. Channeling it to something we can all use. Maybe you'll find value in your new life under my command. A chance to be part of a cause. A great machine bent on changing the course of galactic civilization."

"Might... as well... kill me... now." Two people grabbed Klaus's arms. This time, he didn't have the energy to squirm or fight. Blood poured from the side of his head, feeling hot and sticky at the same time. It made him sneer. "I... won't give... you won't... there's nothing... you can... do to me..."

"Don't talk like that." Trildair came into focus. He touched Klaus on the face, caressing his cheek before dipping his fingers into the head wound. The contact brought out a hiss. "There you are. You still feel things." He brushed his fingertips over Klaus's lips, coating them with blood. "Believe me, if you feel, then I can do things to you."

"Won't... matter... I know... how to... how to suffer."

"Not yet." Trildair drew close so their noses touched. Their eyes were inches apart. The man's icy blue eyes lacked any shine at all. They were completely lifeless... hollow. "I'm going to have such a joy breaking you. Piece by piece over the course of the next several hours. You and your friend."

"Leave her alone!" Klaus growled. "I'll rip your face off and crush your—"

"Sh..." Trildair pressed his fingers against Klaus's mouth. "No need to make threats. But I appreciate your confession. You care about the girl. That will go a long way. Progress is much easier when you care about something. Undoubtedly, you don't care about yourself. But if you can muster the strength for her..."

"It won't help you. I don't care about her like you think."

"We'll see." Trildair stood. "Take him to the medical lab. We've got our next candidate."

The men began dragging Klaus toward the elevator. "You should kill me!" he shouted. "I'm telling you right now, you're making a huge mistake! If you don't, I swear to God, I'll tear you to pieces! It'll be far worse than anything you've done, you pile of shit! This is your last chance!"

"You know..." Trildair followed them to the elevator. He stopped it from closing. "Fascinating that you've got so much fire about dying... so many threats... you should really pick. Beg for a quick end or tell me you'll kill me. Offering me a choice makes you sound a bit foolish. But you've got plenty of time to consider these things. Goodbye."

Klaus slumped as the doors closed in front of him. The two men holding him didn't say anything. They barely moved on the way the down. He wondered if they were alive at all. This is what he's promising to do to me. Trildair knew how to make people pliant. He'll find I'm a little harder to condition than his other victims.

He didn't know why he went off the way he did, carrying on about murder or death. But he intended to make good his promise. As long as it took, he'd find a way to end the man. Or die trying.

***

Cole asked a dozen questions of the men as they led her away from Klaus. She demanded to speak with their superior, the person who invited them aboard the ship as a friend. He made no indication they'd been guilty of a crime, no statement that they would be detained.

He offered them help then arrested them?

"Is this just to check out our stories?" No reply. "Are you verifying our IDs?" Nothing. "Do you not trust Klaus? I can vouch for him. He's okay." Silence. "Come on, guys! You have to give me something. I'm an EDF representative, an officer, and I demand you give me the courtesy of at least telling me why I'm being detained!"

When none of them said a word, she finally stopped moving. "I'm not taking another step until someone gives me an explanation."

"Hurt her," one of them said.

"What? What do you mean—" A blow to the kidney interrupted, making her hiss. She started to fall but they held her aloft. "Sons of bitches! What is this all about? Neither of us did anything wrong! That fuel depot situation was—" Another blow, this one to the ribs. "Jesus! What is this? When did the JTF turn into thugs?"

They began moving, dragging her at first before she got her footing. Her side ached, throbbing from the punches. They kept their weapons in the holsters at least. That gave her some hope. At least they don't intend to execute us outright. Though whatever they had in mind may be worse.

Okay, let's draw back on the hyperbole.

Cole tried to yank her left arm free. Her captor's grip didn't budge. They pulled her to the right through a set of doors into a room with a medical chair in the center. Restraints on the arms and legs would hold her wrists and ankles. She started struggling as they brought her closer to it.

"Let me go! God damn it, I have no idea what you think you're about to do but let me go! Right now! I'm EDF, did you not hear me? I'm not a criminal! I don't need... whatever this is! Please! You don't have any right!" They picked her up. She kicked at them. One took two blows before he got her legs contained.

None of the struggling helped. They managed to get her in position, locking her in place. She strained at the straps, thrashing her head about before they managed to lock it in a vice. Her ears pressed against her skull, muffling her hearing. One of them came forward, moving slow.

He held a knife. Cole tensed up thrashing in an effort to get away. The man's dead eyes met hers. "If you struggle, I will cut you. Stop moving."

"What... what're you doing?"

"Stop moving. Or I will cut you."

Is that all he can say? Cole closed her eyes, biting her lip not to move. He cut away her clothes, stripping her down to her underthings. He had to pull them out from under her before backing away. God, what are they going to do to me? Why'd they have to take my clothes like that!

"We will commence with the procedure shortly." His monotone voice chilled her almost as much as what he said. The lifelessness of it, the near computerized method of speaking, impacted her hindbrain. It was so alien and terrifying, she doubted even the Raldor would put her off so completely.

They might even have more humanity.

"What procedure? Who are you people! Just… answer my questions! Please, god damn it! Now!"

"You will feel horrible pain," the man replied. He continued speaking in that dead voice. "And when you do, you will understand the world better. You will see it clearly. And you will obey."

The others intoned, "You will obey."

"What kind of freaky ass cult shit are you guys into? What happened here? Where is Captain Trildair? He invited us. He's a JTF operative… who are you… who are you people?"

"We will begin." The man paced slowly to a console on the far side of the room. Cole's heart raced until she felt light headed. She started thrashing, screaming for help. None of the people around her appeared moved. They stood motionless. Impassive. "The process starts now."

He touched the panel.

Waves of agony rushed through her, pain like she'd never experienced before in her life. She screamed until her throat went raw. Convulsions danced through her nerves. Her eyes rolled back in her head. Time seemed to slow then stop. And when the pain ended, she slumped, tears flowing though she didn't have the energy to sob.

Gunfire in the distance gave her hope. Klaus... he's free. He can't leave me here either. He needs me to fly the ship. He'll come back for me. I know he will.

"You sacks of shit are dead! He's coming for you and he's not remotely merciful. I'm telling you... every single one of you sick piles of shit are going to die!" Cole slumped, laughing hysterically. Sweat coated her whole body, soaking the chair as well. If not for being secured both hands and feet, she might've slipped right off.

Gunfire rose to a crescendo. Dozens of shots, maybe a hundred. They grew distant.

"No!" Cole shouted. "Klaus! I'm in here! Please, I'm here! Come back! Don't leave me!" Tears flowed until her eyes burned. She finally found the strength to sob uncontrollably. Just half a second before the current started again. All that horrifying pain came back just as strong as before.

There was no relief, no acclimation. It seemed to go straight to her nerves firing them up. More screams, and it seemed like she might never let it go. She couldn't drift. Her mind remained hyper focused, experiencing every single second without pause. They had no mercy. She felt their presence as they stood there, unmoving.

You could at least enjoy it!

The pain stopped. The door opened. Cole struggled to see who came in. Any hope she had for rescue faded. A tall man paused directly in front of her. He put his hands on her bare knees, sliding them up to her inner thighs. He stopped there, staring at her face with a twisted little smile on his pale face.

Icy blue eyes met hers but he lacked all humanity, any sense of being alive at all.

"Welcome to my ship. My name is Trildair."

"Fuck you..." Cole spat on him. "We didn't do anything... we didn't... you don't..."

Trildair slapped her leg, though she barely noticed. "Have some respect. You're the property of the Uldarn now. It's time you start acting like it."

"You might as well kill me," Cole said, "because there's nothing you can do to make me be someone's slave. How did you get this JTF ship?"

"Because I am with the JTF," Trildair replied, "or I was. But it doesn't matter now. The game is over. I've got what I wanted. Now, we change the universe. And while we prepare to do so, you and your friend will join us. Painfully, I'm afraid. In ways that will leave your personality broken. Frayed. Gone."

"Why?" Cole asked. "Why me? Why... do this?" A chill hit her. "Did you kill Klaus?"

"Oh, no." Trildair smiled. "He came to do so to me. Or perhaps he planned to bargain with me as a hostage. He didn't realize no one here would have cared. But also that I had plenty of people on the bridge to keep me safe. I had intended to test him for viability. He passed with flying colors… on his own terms."

"I don't know what that means."

"Only that those with drive can be changed," Trildair said. "The more passion they show, the more of them we can keep. Shaving off the parts that defy, but allow for creativity and problem solving. Some…" He gestured to the people standing around him, "don't require that to be effective. Others… well, we need operatives."

"Like you?" Cole asked. "Did you let them shave parts of your brain? Is that why you're a sick bastard? Or were you always like that? Just a pathetic piece of trash happy to hurt people all the time. I bet you got brought up on charges within the JTF. Probably looked at being discharged. Maybe even prison before you underwent your 'change.'"

Trildair laughed. "I see you're feisty too. Perhaps we'll have to alter the plan somewhat. I need an EDF person. Someone I can trust to get work done." He turned to the man at the console. "Alter to condition forty-three delta." He looked at Cole. "You'll like this much more, my dear."

"Go to hell."

"I'm sure you'll understand," Trildair replied, "that I've been there. When you come out the other side, we can compare notes. Until then, do enjoy your stay. I'd like to tell you I'll be back to give you some kind of encouragement or even to chat. But there's no point. This process takes time, you see. It's better not to be interrupted."

"You won't break me," Cole said.

"You should keep that to yourself," Trildair replied. "You and your friend made it quite clear. I wonder if it's a threat, a promise, or an empty boast. Probably a little of all three, don't you think? Challenging your captor is such an old notion. Humans have spat in the face of those who bested them many times. I wonder why?"

"Human spirit?"

Trildair clicked his tongue. He shook his head. "No. Empty bravado. Idiotic pride. The better path is to feign subservience. Allow them to believe you have given in. Surprise them. Of course, in your case, feistiness may have saved some of your personality. Your very being. So in this one case, it helped."

"You won't get away with this. I hope you know that. You're on borrowed time. Whoever you're working for, whatever you think you've got, it'll end. There are way too many people to stop you."

"As if we haven't infiltrated their ranks," Trildair said. "For my part, I have some ambition still. The sort that involves rising above my situation. I want control. Power. I've come to enjoy it. Taking things from people." He smiled. "And I enjoy pleasure still. You will as well. Forty-three delta will make you pliant."

Cole scowled. "What exactly does that mean? What're you talking about?"

"Don't worry about it." Trildair stepped away. "When this ends, we'll talk again. You know... I typically began these sessions with deprivation. A little hunger, isolation, no talking, nothing. Then we moved into this. I've been testing which is best. Today, we're starting with the conditioning. We'll move to the other later."

"You can still stop this! Trildair!" Cole shouted his name twice more before he turned to look at her. "I can help you get a deal with the EDF. If you tell them what you know, if you turn, we can help you get away from their clutches. I know you don't want to be a puppet so let us give you a chance to do something else."

"Imagine the things you'll be willing to do for the pain to stop," Trildair said. "And the other miseries to come. Think about all the bargains you'll make and the parts of yourself you'll give up for it all to stop." He gestured to the man standing nearest him. "This one sobbed uncontrollably for three hours straight. The one over there clawed out his own eyeball."

"And I'm sure you loved every second of it."

"It's fascinating, what a person will do to save themselves. Or to make something stop." Trildair waved. "Goodbye, my dear. I'd love to stick around, to chat with you some more but you know how it is. Duty calls. We'll talk again. When you're feeling less... defiant."

Cole opened her mouth to shout after him. The pain turned it into a scream. An agony that would not stop this time. Klaus was not coming.

It was over.

***

Trildair left the room, smiling as the sound of her screams echoed through the hallway. Her torture filled him with joy, an adrenalized rush that made it nearly impossible not to take her immediately. But he wanted to wait. He knew what it would be like after her conditioning. Some part of her would remain a prisoner in her mind.

And it would be fully aware of his violation, even as her body accepted him.

Several parts of him had survived the conditioning. He'd always hidden a cruel side of himself, a dangerous aspect that nearly got him in a great deal of trouble with his JTF superiors. He let it out when he could. On suspects no one would believe or civilians on the verge of death.

The Uldarn had freed him, allowing him to extrapolate his desire for horror. He took it to the next level with the conditioning, amplifying the process to ensure it inflicted unimaginable pain as well as forwarding the appropriate agenda. Some of the victims didn't have enough willpower to satiate his desires.

Others, like Cole and her friend, were ideal. Had he been able to hold on to Chelsea Weston a little longer, he would've seen her face contort in agony. Their work on the station started subtle. On the ship, he had no such concerns. Nor did the Uldarn necessarily have much sway over him out there.

After all, his activities ensured he needed to go on the run. Until he had enough people like Cole under his sway. Then he could alter his identification, appear as someone else, and ultimately ingratiate himself into whatever organization existed. Bring them down from the inside, assimilate their highest ranking people, and control the universe.

Trildair was not content with his standing within the whole of the empire. He knew a group existed beyond the conditioning, the ones who started it. They were his peers, they simply didn't know it yet. Their choice to leave his mind mostly intact, allowing him to scheme properly, made such thoughts possible.

If they didn't want me to think that way, then they wouldn't have let me. Which felt like an invitation. If he proved himself, then they would allow him into the inner circle. Providing they get over their obsessions. Trildair did not agree with their search for scientists. We can develop our own breakthroughs later.

Though even as he privately felt disdain toward their actions, he wondered what drove them to the hunt. He understood the conditioning process. Perhaps they worried that it hampered the creativity of the genius. Trildair disagreed. At least on a personal level. Though he could not speak to true discovery.

I wish they would've put me on the hunt. I would've found them all by now. Trildair had the hunters. The entirety of a JTF station until recently. This is why I must belong to their inner circle. When I join, they'll reverse the process. I'll be entirely myself, ready to rule whatever piece of the galaxy they hand me.

Trildair paused at the door where Klaus underwent his version of the conditioning. Unlike Cole, they started with neglect. The man needed to cool off anyway. He was prepared for pain, so they gave him the opposite. By ignoring him, he would sit there wondering when it would come.

Whatever it happened to be. The next beating, torture, or even execution. His mind would do a great deal of the work toward the conditioning. The process itself came easier if the person had been broken down a bit. Cole was an exception. Not really for a good reason. Trildair wanted to see her suffer.

It made him happy.

The Uldarn seemed to be just as horrible, just as cruel. Otherwise, they would not have slaughtered countless millions. They would not have pushed so far into the galaxy and the universe, infringing on innocent colonies. These things didn't bother Trildair. He privately hoped they decided to commit genocide against the Raldor.

Disgusting creatures. They have no value.

Trildair made it to the bridge. He turned on the comm to listen to Cole's constant cries, turned hoarse. She would not be allowed to pass out for a while. The machine knew when to stop. Long before death. But at a point where she would be sufficiently tarnished. The next step involved building hope. Playing games.

Both people represented a different challenge. He so rarely had the opportunity to stretch himself or the technology given to him. Until then, he needed to focus on staying ahead of any pursuers. Those who might be earnest in tracking him down from the JTF base. When the Korlas arrived, he had no way to silence all the necessary voices.

Fortunately, the Uldarn had yet to contact him. Somehow, they would know about the failure. He didn't think it would impact his ambitions, not considering what he had to deal with. Or the fact he'd operated directly under the noses of so many authorities for such a lengthy period of time.

And he had so many successes. Would they be fair? Of course. I'm one of their favorite operatives. They will treat me accordingly. He knew they wanted him to walk amongst their highest echelons. They only needed a little more time. Which he'd fill with some of the finest resources he could muster.

"Take us out of here," Trildair ordered, "be on the lookout for more distress calls." They may not all be catches like Cole. But he had need of replacing some of the people he lost to his new guests. Not to mention those on the surface and at the station. Nihkal in particular. Perhaps Cole can replace him.

He had high hopes for her. In so many ways.

□

Chapter 1

Korlas intelligence reports spilled in from all over the galaxy. They observed that the Veldon had ceased their advance, spending their time searching the various worlds they already waylaid. This proved true of the Zitha worlds as well, though their own corrupted former military scoured those areas.

After a week where no other colonies were destroyed, no additional ships attacked or ambushed, Captain Harold Kensington finally felt like he might take a deep breath. They'd been in a constant state of high alert, waiting for the other shoe to drop when the Veldon discovered their fleet or the new colony for that matter.

Things had changed considerably in the ten days since Earth fell. Humanity found themselves surrounded by allies, bolstered cultures either on the verge of assault the victims of internal strife. Their new home, a hub world occupied by all of them, they found themselves working together smoothly, without any appreciable issues.

The cultures agreed to call the planet Sentinel One, though some of the humans referred to it as Eden. Harold preferred the secular designation. He wondered what the Zitha and Likari people referred to it as. They hadn't volunteered the information and though many of them worked together with the humans, the name didn't seem to come up.

Not when he was around at least.

Multiple military bases sprung up across the surface, one for each of the cultures represented. The EDF moved from their position in the center of those places, turning that settlement into a communal space for collaboration and negotiation. There, the various military leaders sent their officers to form plans for taking back their territory.

And freeing those places already under the rule of the Uldarn.

Everyone knew the true enemy they faced and they had a good idea of what they were after. Multiple scientists from different places across the universe had been identified as targets. The Uldarn wanted to capture them, though the exact reason remained a mystery. Many of the scientists appeared to be safe.

Only the Raldor had yet to sound off on their person. But supposedly, Ambassador Chance had made contact with them. At least the last time their transponder went off, they'd been in that general vicinity. They should have come back already, or reported in. Some were growing pessimistic.

I have to trust Lieutenant Hale. Franklin Hale knew his business. If anyone could keep the ambassador safe and accomplish the mission, it was him. He'd been through far worse than a little negotiation pain. I wish I could send Commander Weston and his people to check on them.

Sadly, the Pytheas was needed elsewhere. Harold planned for them to visit Veldon space, to determine what happened there. They were to probe the enemy's defenses for a chance to cut their supply chains at the source. If they mustered a strong enough force, they might wipe out the Veldon's primary base of operations.

Then mop up the rest while they languished without fuel, food, or reinforcements.

Much as they wanted to hurry, the Pytheas crew needed to take care of some things. Most of them did. Since returning from the JTF station, they took some downtime on Sentinel One, recovering from the ordeal. Technicians studied their ship along with the project plans they took from a secret base founded by multiple factions.

Harold thought their efforts at bringing the cultures together would be the first time they worked together in earnest. The Pytheas proved him wrong. Some part of the Korlas, EDF, and Zitha worked their way into the designs. Likari officials suggested they might have had something to do with it as well, though they seemed allergic to straightforward conversation.

Many of the advancements they discovered seemed ideal to fight back against the Veldon. Defenses capable of fending off their weapons, offensive tools ready to tear through their superior shields, armor, faster drives… if only the findings had been released a year earlier, Earth might not have fallen.

Which made Harold wonder what had happened. No one found the answers in the databases, though with so many files, an explanation seemed likely. Whoever made the decision to keep it to themselves stood responsible for the deaths of millions. Perhaps billions. Likely over an arrogant decision that they knew best.

He knew enough 'brilliant scientists' to make the claim.

Commander Weston found himself the subject of one such man. Doctor Augustus Keppler made a name for himself in the medical field only to be disgraced for the deaths of several people during an experiment gone awry. They had yet to brief Harold about the specifics.

So he called it a fountain of youth shot and moved on. Weston looked better than he had thirty years ago. He'd retired due to old age, but his vitals proved he had the body of someone in their middle twenties. And not just any young person, but a top athlete. The best of the best and then some.

Whatever the drug did pushed him beyond the normal limitations of humanity. Into a realm Harold hadn't seen before. A soldier of incredible prowess and endurance. Providing he didn't pass out from it, as he had when he arrived to help his crew with the JTF situation. That made the application questionable.

Weston assured Harold that there'd been no other way. When he found Keppler, he'd been so badly injured, he wouldn't have lived without the drug. Once he started down the path, there was no choice but to follow it to the logical conclusion. Life, or death, it bought him some time to bring together his crew.

Including his daughter Chelsea Weston. She'd been with the JTF until recently, now fully reinstated with the EDF. After a corrupted branch of the other organization imprisoned her, she had no interest in going back to them. Not until their people had been fully vetted and the criminals charged.

They were looking for Captain Trildair Kayse, though Harold didn't have any illusions. No one would find him anytime soon. Except maybe Lieutenant Commander Patrick Worthing, a JTF detective. After what he experienced, he seemed determined to track the man down at any cost.

He hadn't given up his rank within his own organization, though Harold wished Patrick would've reconsidered. The Korlas considered the JTF to be compromised. The report from their own operative suggested revamping from the ground up. Which seemed like a knee jerk reaction.

Not my problem. Harold had no intention of getting involved outside of offering advice if someone asked. The situation with Chelsea put him in a difficult spot. One of his best teams rushed off to deal with a situation which may have resulted in a lot of death not to mention losing the Pytheas.

Fortunately, most of the data had been transferred from the project databases or else it would've been an even greater risk.

Captain Rowell sent a message regarding the promotion of Marsha Silva. She took over the small corvette previously commanded by Captain Madden. After he was murdered by his own first officer, she fixed the situation herself while at the same time earning the respect of the Zitha commander.

They needed more people willing to go above and beyond the call of duty. Too many of his officers spent their time lamenting the losses they experienced. Every day they received news of more human colonies that survived the purge, other people making their way to the safety of Sentinel One.

Harold wanted people to take heart in the heroics of people like Silva and Weston, to embrace the fortune of so many people joining them. He admitted it was difficult. The days directly after the attack proved hardest of all and the death of Admiral Gaston sent him into a real despair.

They still didn't have any leads on who killed the man, though the investigation team wanted to pin it on Madden's first officer, Aevers. If he had been willing to risk the alliance with the Zitha to kill their administrator, if he had the ear of enough soldiers to turn them to his cause, then he had the means for murder.

Harold didn't buy it. The whole thing felt too convenient. Pinning a crime on a dead man was a cop out for the investigation team when they didn't turn up any leads on their own. After they heard about what he did, they probably threw a party. It didn't even take them a full twelve hours to present their findings.

Facts twisted perfectly to support the conclusion.

He let it go for the time being though he asked Reggie to keep an eye out for any evidence which might warrant re-opening the case. Gaston deserved justice. Unless they found something specifically implicating Aevers, a politically motivated murderer remained at large.

Someone willing to risk the fate of the galaxy for a grudge killing. Harold knew plenty of people so single-minded and selfish that they couldn't read the room. Murdering Gaston hurt humanity as a whole. Yes, they recovered and things proceeded on target. But it could've been horrible.

If they wanted to cause actual chaos, they needed to kill me too.

How many people agreed with the murder? Harold had no idea how to uncover such a truth. He worried there might be plenty of military personnel who thought it was a good idea. They backed Minister

Bracknel's right to lead them, though they lacked the information Gaston had when he blocked the politician.

I can't release anything like that without risking serious backlash. After agreeing to work with Bracknel, he had painted himself into a corner. The only path forward was to do his best to keep things civil and ensure they continued in the same direction. Politics in the face of oblivion. At least we have allies now.

When the Korlas finally started honoring their agreement, a sense of hope washed over the EDF forces. Their people had a civilized culture to fall back on, a place they could look to for refuge and help. Then their ships arrived, providing security for the civilian ships, and at the same time, restoring trade.

The colonies still standing after the Veldon's initial strike continued to put out their commodities while under the watchful eye of several combat vessels. The added peace of mind meant the workers didn't have to worry about how they might evacuate during an assault. Soldiers stood by for them.

A report came in letting Harold know the embassies for the represented cultures opened on Sentinel One. They coordinated so they might all start providing services at the same time. The gesture probably didn't matter too much, but as a tool for boosting morale, it did the trick.

The Zitha occupied an area around their deposited forest biome. The station released it, their mechanism for landing the vast section kept it safe through the descent. Once there, they left the dome up to keep it safe while they established a perimeter. Their complex formed just outside though the plan was to wrap around their little patch of home.

Harold had never thought of their culture as particularly sentimental. But they sure displayed it in full color when they arrived at the colony. He met their military leader Ghrenda Hauv and found someone he immediately admired. A person who cared about his people and the universe.

The combination meant they might just keep things on track for surviving the assault.

If only the Veldon hadn't stopped on their own. If they came squealing to a halt because of some line of military vessels, or a culture capable of holding them back, that would've been one thing. Every military advisor warned they could start the assault again. Even the alliance might not be enough to stop them.

Which meant refitting their military with advanced weaponry. Taking the EDF Patton's work on weapon and defensive improvements. Ensuring all captains and soldiers used their equipment to the absolute fullest. Anything they managed to pull off might be the thing giving them the necessary advantage to win.

Reggie stepped into the room without knocking. "Sorry, sir. I've got some reports."

"No problem." Harold smiled. "I see you've gotten comfortable enough to barge in without asking? You're lucky I'm not the type of man to get involved in a scandal."

"I did have faith you'd be decent." Reggie joined him at the desk. "Did you hear about the embassies?"

Harold nodded.

"We've got over a dozen civilian ships showing up today. Not just EDF either, but some Zitha too. They'll be taking up residency on Sentinel One. Korlas security forces are providing some additional support to ensure we don't have any problems. Keeping the peace. Plus, our administration center comes online in two hours."

"What's the first agenda item?"

"Establishing a council," Reggie said, "that's what Bracknel suggested at least."

Of course he did, Harold thought. He wants to be the head of that council. I'll bet the Korlas take the duty. Though if Bracknel plays it right, he might be able to claim responsibility for bringing us all together. If that happens... well, it'll be very interesting. Definitely take some grandstanding. I don't know how much the Zitha will like it.

"They should be talking about pushing the Veldon out of our territory. And the treasonous Zitha."

"Well," Reggie continued, "it seems that some people are hoping we'll hear from the Raldor prior to making a definite plan of attack. Then there's the point of getting the Pytheas out to Veldon space. The intelligence we hope to gain from that may change the plan of attack. Right?"

"It's possible," Harold said. "We might even find ourselves in a situation where it would behoove us to hit them at their home rather than take back various planets. There are two ways to think of it. One, we might tip our hand by launching assaults for lesser targets. Or two, we could gain a great deal of morale saving people."

"Wouldn't it be better to save the attack for something that matters?" Reggie asked. "Like... like maybe Earth?"

Harold sighed. There it is. That's what everyone is probably talking about. Saving Earth as quickly as possible. So they can scour the ruins, pray for a resistance, hope beyond hope that our last sweep didn't show the real story. I wish they understood the danger of holding on to that dream.

"I'll be honest," Harold said, "Earth isn't likely well guarded. We could probably wipe out whatever forces are there right now. Today, even. But while that might gain us some small sense of victory, it's not the way to reach an endgame. A better course of action would be to hit the main Veldon fleet, wipe out as many of them as possible, and bail."

"Hit and run?" Reggie nodded. "I could see that leaving a mark. Be a powerful message too."

"I hate to say it," Harold replied, "but at this point, we should be fostering a sense of vengeance. Not that I want our armed forces looking at genocide as a viable solution to our problem. The way to win is to eliminate the enemy's ability to make war. Taking territory is lovely, it might even save some lives in the short term."

"I get it."

"Yeah?"

Reggie lifted his brows. His expression turned sad. "Yeah, I do. If we take a colony, we have to defend it. That thins our ranks. If we go on the offensive, start hitting them, then the fleet can remain as strong as possible to push them back. Maybe even eliminate them as a threat. One means we can win, the other might lead to a stalemate."

"Exactly. And honestly, I don't want the Veldon to have another crack at us. Or the Uldarn. Whatever faction is responsible for this senseless assault. We need to eliminate their ability to make war for all time. Crush their industry. Force them to make amends and ultimately, join us on our terms."

"You think anyone will accept them after all this?"

"I don't think anyone is willing to commit genocide. I know I keep using that word. It's important to ensure we don't lose sight of the fact we cannot be the culture that utterly wipes out another one. There has to be some code, some standard we hold ourselves to or we'll be no better than them."

"May I ask... why does that matter? They killed our civilians, wiped out colonies, all while searching for something. We thought they hit us for vengeance over the war, but we've proven that's not the case now. I'm not sure why we care about standards when they have none. And our allies won't care either."

"It's about living with yourself, Reggie. About waking up tomorrow and knowing you did the right thing."

"Or," Reggie countered, "we can look at it as taking one for the team. We make the hard choice so our children don't find themselves in the same position. Mark my words, we leave the Veldon alive after everything they'll have to do for contrition, and they will be war ready within two generations."

"You don't think we can prepare our people for that eventuality? That we might be able to guide the Veldon culture to avoid such a thing? And don't forget, we know the real enemy now. I've made the mistake too, but we have to keep the narrative on the Uldarn. They started this. They'll be the ones to pay."

"But—"

"Wait." Harold held up his hand. "We have the Veldon to blame for our attack. What about the Zitha?

The Uldarn made that look like a civil war. How do you propose they stop the situation from happening again? They don't have the ability to stamp out the threat on their end because it might be fostered in the hearts of any number of their soldiers."

"I see what you mean."

"They can never feel entirely safe... if we believe the only path to victory involves the annihilation of aggressive forces. No, the real way to come out the other side is to make the people we're fighting with see the light. Have them join us again for a fruitful future. One where we all make prosperity instead of violence."

"Maybe you should be heading down to talk to the council, sir."

Harold chuckled. "Yeah, I'll be there remotely. We can't all be there together in case of some sort of insane plan, I guess. We talked about it earlier. Despite all the precautions, the defenses, even that shield network we put up, there are still concerns someone might try something."

"Surely, not Aevers' buddies."

Harold shrugged. "I don't believe the first officer of a starship orchestrated all that violence. I just don't."

"You think the investigation ended prematurely?"

"Of course."

Reggie sighed. "I wanted that to be the answer."

"Just because it's convenient," Harold replied, "doesn't mean it's right. Whoever did it was already aboard the ship. And knew how to scrub comm data. Among other things. The investigators primarily gave up because someone covered their tracks too well. But I think the right investigator with an inch would've turned up some real information."

"I'm sorry about them then." Reggie shrugged. "I genuinely believed they'd do a good job. I didn't think we'd come away with a vague answer."

"They sure did make it clear they believed Aevers was responsible. Maybe not directly, but one of his agents. Unfortunately, that leads to the suggestion that Aevers was some sort of mastermind. A man with a whole crew of dissidents willing to do crazy shit for his hatred and prejudice."

"I see your point. Gaston represented a lot more than working with the Zitha."

"Exactly. So if this theory is true, they put everything on the line for one issue."

Reggie asked, "Do you want me to put people on it? A different set of investigators? Someone with more curiosity maybe."

"Not right now. Sentinel One is more important. I'm afraid if we put someone on the case, they might end up causing drama with the embassies. We'll let it go for now, but like I said, I want to keep an ear out for more evidence. You seem like you might've put it aside entirely."

"No, I took what you said to heart. I just... I didn't anticipate we'd find anything. Until now."

"Good. Keep thinking like that. Have you heard from William?"

Reggie scoffed. "He's practically living with Marsha now. I think they're having an affair, but I can't prove it."

"Not the most professional choice, given how closely they work together. I don't see the harm right now if they're getting their work done. His new work he managed to snake into. How did you pick him anyway? I thought he was your choice for breaking into Bracknel's inner circle. Now he's off working with the Zitha and totally out of our influence."

"I don't know, I thought so too, sir. I genuinely did. His record made it clear he was the right call. But then he had all those qualms. Captain Rowell got his hands on him and put me in a shitty position. I either had to accept the request or come up with an excuse as to why he couldn't do it. And that might've seemed suspicious to Bracknel."

"I agree. Rowell should've come to us first. But then again, he was in a difficult position. The Zitha leader likes William so that makes it tough to argue." Harold laughed. "I don't know. In a way, I find it hilarious. We're trying like hell to gather information and everything around us conspired to keep us in the dark."

"Even our own guy," Reggie said. "Because let me tell you, he sure was twitchy about it."

"I don't even think trying to embed someone else makes sense. It'll be too obvious this time." Harold leaned back in his chair. He rubbed his eyes. "No, we've got to do this another way. Hopefully, it'll all work out. But Bracknel... I don't know. The last time we talked, he seemed relatively sane. He made sense."

"So you're feeling more confident with him?"

"Yes... and no. I'm suspicious. But some of that came from Gaston. They knew each other much better. As a captain, I didn't have as many dealings with the Minister of Defense."

"He must like you," Reggie said. He stared at his device. "Looks like he intends to put you up for grand admiral of the EDF. The consensus here is that it'll pass too. You'll be in charge of all military operations."

Harold laughed again. "Well, there you go. Now he's trying to buy me with that. I guess if he makes that gesture, then I'll be confident he has no intention of messing with us too much. The guy wants power. Maybe he sees the civilian side of things offers him greater influence than trying to take charge of us."

"Or," Reggie said, "he's not confident he could do better. I looked at his track record when he served. Before becoming a politician. He didn't have the best mission success rate. Those that he did pull off could be argued to have been the result of excellent subordinates.

So I'm not sure he's in a position to take over without some scrutiny coming down."

"Which would in turn call into question his ability to lead the civilian sector." Harold nodded. "Good point. He's not an idiot. Though I suspect that aide of his has too much influence."

"Olav? I agree. They're definitely lovers."

"Great." Harold rolled his eyes. "He's got someone close to him that has the chance to whisper things in bed. That's never a good combination. How'd you find out?"

"It's obvious," Reggie said. "Body language, mostly."

"You're sharp. I didn't notice."

"You can thank William for me scrutinizing them. When he ended up reassigned, I started watching closer."

"Glad you did." Harold sighed. "That's the hand we've been dealt. I'm not sure there's much else we can do about it." He stood. "I'm going to the conference room to be part of this meeting. You should come with me. If they give me grand admiral, I'm elevating you to captain. Give you my old job, basically."

"Whoa," Reggie held up his hands, "you sure about that? I feel like I've been making plenty of mistakes."

"So did I. And you're not one of them. Yes, I'm sure. I don't want someone else. I've confided in you too much to transition to a different officer." Harold checked the time. "Look, we've got about forty-five minutes before the meeting happens. I want you to reach out to Captain Carmine on the Patton."

"What about?"

"Let him know that he should start prepping for an assignment. I believe his ship has already received the upgrades and the refit."

Reggie nodded, "Yes, sir. They sure have."

"Good. They seem like the best choice to check on our ambassadors. They've been off comms for too long. I trust Franklin, but now's the time to find out what happened. Plus, they can act as a secondary ambassador with the Raldor. They need to get on our side so we can proceed with some action."

"Right away, sir." Reggie offered a quick salute. "I'll meet you in the conference room then?"

"Yep." Harold watched him hurry off. I really hope Franklin pulls off a miracle and shows back up, he thought. We'll be in a shit situation if he and his people have died because of the damn Raldor. I don't want them starting a second war. They'd have to let the violence slide too. At least until the Uldarn were dealt with.

Unless the Raldor happened to be corrupted already. That possibility hadn't escaped him. He'd been worrying about it every day his people didn't get back to him. They tend to be strange creatures. Our ambassador may be outside of comm range while working on them. That's the best possible scenario.

He didn't want to consider the alternative. Not when so much rested on bringing everyone together. At least the alliance would survive one culture staying out of the fight. Longevity came into question. Could they stick together if one civilization stayed out? But that was a worry for another day.

Harold had plenty to occupy his mind at the moment.

***

William flopped on his back, struggling to catch his breath. Marsha panted beside him. They held up in her private quarters to take advantage of some downtime while they waited for the council meeting to take place. Their part in the gathering took place hours before the gathering.

They had found themselves with some time to kill while they waited for new orders.

"Have you worried…" William muttered, "that maybe… maybe this isn't ethical?"

"What?" Marsha asked. "Are you talking what you did with your—"

"No," William interrupted. He felt his cheeks burn. "I meant the fact we're working together so closely."

"People do it all the time." Marsha rolled on her side to kiss his cheek. "It's fine. There's only a problem when command structure comes into play. Then there are regulations against fraternizing. Gotta love that word. But I'm EDF, you're basically a civilian contractor. No one's going to complain. Especially these days."

"Yeah?"

Marsha nodded. "We're fine. Why? Do you want to break things off?"

"God no."

"Then stop worrying." Marsha patted his chest then rolled out of bed.

William watched her as she walked naked across the room to the bathroom. Her confidence still embarrassed him, but she deserved it. She wasn't the flashiest woman he'd been with, yet she got him going like no one he'd been with before. Their connection was obvious, and it worked.

"What's the deal with your friend Margaret?" Marsha asked. She splashed water in her face.

"Do you mind putting on a robe or something while we're discussing this?"

"Why? Do I distract you?"

"Obviously."

Marsha smiled. "And you don't like talking about other women? Have you not been in many relationships?"

"C'mon, it's just hard to be all business with you flashing… everything."

"Tough." Marsha stepped into the bathroom. "Come stand by the door. If you get in here, we won't talk."

That wouldn't be a terrible thing. William crawled out of bed. He leaned against the wall as she started up the shower. "So what about her?"

"Just thought we'd see more of her. What's she been up to?"

"Working with the minister, I think. Or Olav, maybe. One of the two."

"Ghrenda doesn't like her," Marsha said. "Thinks she's too… meek, I guess."

"I never would've considered her meek," William replied. "But I can see why he'd think that way. The Zitha aren't exactly gentle."

"Nope. Maybe that's why she's been spending more time in orbit than down here. Think she'll be at the council gathering?"

"Why so curious?" William asked. "Do you know something I don't?"

"You always know more than I do. I'm just making conversation."

William considered the situation for a moment. "If I had to bet, I'd say she's prepping for good news from the Raldor. Though that might be insanely optimistic given what they're like. If we haven't heard from the ambassador yet, they might be in real trouble. In fact, I heard we're sending a ship to check on them."

"The Patton," Marsha said. "Going out that way to make sure our people survived at the very least. Maybe start up negotiations if a problem kept the ambassador from arriving."

"What kind of problem?"

"An accident," Marsha replied, "something like that."

"Shit. I didn't think... I mean, they're so capable, but then I guess it doesn't matter if there's a disaster. Something beyond their control. Man. Well... here's to hoping they made it."

"Do you know the ambassador they sent? The one who made friends with the Likari? Because he sounds like something else."

"No. Krayna spoke well of them though."

"She's not easy to impress." Marsha got out, wrapped in a towel. "What're we going to do now? How long before we have to throw ourselves back into work?"

"Dunno. I kinda need to get in there too."

"I don't know, seeing you stand around like that is inspiring. Maybe you can bask on the bed while I go through reports."

William chuckled. "That won't keep you focused on the task."

"Some people have images of their favorite holiday location. I could have you physically lying on my bed naked. I think it's pretty close to the same thing. Only I can't have you doing that while I'm on the bridge."

"What a shame, huh?"

"Unless we do something genuinely unethical by going up there while everyone's away. Though I think Kim would know somehow."

"He's got cameras all over that bridge," William said, "at least that's what I think."

"Such a voyeur." Marsha toweled off then started dressing in her uniform. William paused to watch. He particularly liked how tight the pants were. "And you're staring."

"Uh... sorry?"

"It's fine. I like it. But I also like when you blush." Marsha finished getting dressed. "All put away. You can focus now." She pointed down. "Unless that's going to stay... well..."

William cleared his throat and disappeared into the bathroom. "Maybe we should be on the bridge during the actual assembly. We've still got about forty minutes before it takes place."

"Ugh. I thought we had the chance to avoid that nonsense."

"C'mon, if we're not..."

"What?" Marsha prompted. "Were you going to say if we're not having sex, we might as well be working?"

"No, of course not. I was going to say if we don't have something else to do right now, it might behoove us to be involved. We've done a lot to ensure the success of what's happening there."

"I dunno." Marsha came closer. "I feel like it's premature. We should've waited for the Raldor."

"Any more delays risked the Zitha and the Korlas having trouble. I trust the Likari to keep calm. They're the most relaxed people I've ever heard of. But we've gotta start collaborating." He washed his hair. When his head wasn't underwater, he asked, "Do you think the Raldor would be put off?"

"God knows. They're bizarre."

"No one's said anything yet. I get the reason we're moving forward quickly though. What if the Raldor do not come around? Then we're waiting for no reason. The Veldon might start their push again. Before we're ready to repel it."

"Yeah, they need to start military operations to take back our territory. It's imperative." Marsha sighed. "Not only for morale, but the people trapped in those systems we can't reach. Or haven't tried to visit because there may be enemy activity out there. So much is riding on us taking action and so far... we haven't."

"Not entirely true. Look at all the civilians we have here. That's got to count for something. Besides, you're not volunteering to get out there to fight."

"Whoa. Be careful there. Just because I accepted this assignment and honestly wanted it doesn't mean I'm trying to shirk duty. I hope you weren't implying that."

"I'm sorry, I wasn't. Or at least, I didn't mean to." William got out. He wrapped a towel around himself to come out. "Seriously, that wasn't an attack."

"Kinda was. But we can let it go." Marsha tilted her head. "You don't feel like we're not moving fast enough?"

"We're doing what we can," William said. "If that means taking our time to get it right, then so be it. I'm all for it. I just want to be sure when we get ourselves out there..." He paused. "I don't know. That we have a solid plan to ensure as many people live as possible. Military and otherwise."

"War takes people," Marsha replied. "No matter how much you plan and hope. You've got bad luck, poor timing, accidents, and any number of other random things. Funny thing... I know all that mentally. But it took a long time to believe it. Before the Zitha station, I thought I had it. Now... it's different."

"Why?"

"Because I had to kill Aevers. I saw Madden dead. He was my mentor. A friend since I left the academy. You look into someone's vacant eyes, someone close to you, and the point drives home. I felt it in my bones then. The fact we might die in this job.

And it doesn't have to be from an external enemy. It can literally happen any time, anywhere."

"Sounds horrible."

"You should have it too after what you went through on the station. Saving those Zitha."

William shrugged. He put on his pants. "I tried not to think about it."

"Better if you come to terms, honestly. Then you're ready for the inevitable."

"You sure about that?" William asked. "Because for me, it seems like it might be a distraction. Something that might make you hesitate at a crucial moment. For me, I want to think about living first and foremost. When I'm in combat at least. I think I've done a fine job of putting it out of my head."

"It's about peace, I suppose." Marsha waited for him to put on his shirt. She helped him button it. "When the moment comes, there may be nothing you can do about it. Shout, scream, cry. In the end, you'll meet your fate. And how you do it in those final moments matter. At least, they do to me."

"I was going to say, we could have a debate about the afterlife if you'd like."

Marsha shook her head. "Not interested." She stared into his eyes. "I'm falling for you."

"I hope so." William smiled.

"Dead serious right now. If you don't want this to go anywhere, if this is just something for you to pass the time while we're planning or before things get back to whatever the new normal is, then we should probably cut it off right away. Otherwise… what we have is big to me. It's something I want. Very much."

"Me too." William put on a sober expression. "But I've already fallen. I love you, Marsha. Maybe it seems quick, but after spending every waking hour and just about all the sleeping ones too, I'm certain. I can't imagine not being with you. So… there's that. And if you feel the same way, so much the better."

Marsha kissed him. Just a quick peck. "Good. Then we should run off to the bridge like you suggested, right? Get to work and all that?"

"Whoa… hold on…" William pulled her close. "We do have some time before that's necessary."

"Not according to you." Marsha squirmed away. "Hurry up! Don't forget your shoes, by the way. Might look a little suspicious running around without them. Oh!" She got to the door, pausing to look back, "and be sure to brush your hair. I'm pretty sure everyone aboard knows we're having sex, but might as well not rub it in their faces."

"Right." William waved at her. "Go away before I break out in a rash." He waited for the door to close. That's something. He couldn't wipe a stupid grin from his face. I never imagined… hell, I should thank Margaret. And Reggie for that matter. Had he not put me in the position to spy on Bracknel, I never would've ended up here.

Meeting Marsha changed his life. More than fighting for the Zitha or befriending Ghrenda. Before the Veldon conflict, he had struggled to make any meaningful connections. This made it seem possible. Like he deserved a chance with her. To take a relationship as far as possible. All the way maybe.

One step at a time, idiot. William finished getting dressed. One step at a time.

□

Chapter 2

Lyra felt anxious. Days of downtime seemed bizarre, almost impossible to fathom considering how fast they'd been moving. Before the attack on Earth, she and Barty had kept running at full speed. Their raid on the remote colony leading to her encounter with Alfred Toombs and Chelsea had kicked off constant motion.

Then after the JTF station, they returned to the EDF where they were given a chance to take a deep breath.

Barty needed it. They moved him and Eliza to one of the battlecruisers for medical treatment. Both of them remained in critical condition for three days. Their doctors kept them sedated for the better part of their time there. Lyra struggled to remain optimistic over the first forty-eight hours.

Lyra received word they'd be fine at the end of the third day. She happened to be at dinner with her sister at the time. The relief she felt was like having a heavy blanket pulled from her head. If Barty died because she insisted they rush off to rescue Chelsea, she doubted she'd forgive herself.

She didn't have the opportunity to visit them for another full day. When she did, she discovered Barty moving through some basic physical therapy. Nothing too crazy, since the majority of the healing had been done. Doctor Keppler insisted he go through some paces to ensure he'd be fit for duty again.

Eliza was in a similar boat. She wore a sling for her left arm over the course of two more days before they cleared her for duty again. Unlike her partner Patrick, she renounced her JTF rank in favor of stepping into the EDF, though she'd never worked with them before. She entered with the rank of lieutenant.

Lyra didn't see much of Commander Weston during their rest period. He seemed to be on the job, working with Captain Kensington on some kind of operation. When he wasn't there, he spent time with Keppler, allowing the doctor to perform various tests to ensure the serum was operating correctly.

Even Chelsea didn't see her dad much during those days. Lyra introduced her to Mary. The three of them helped out around the colony where they could, and when there wasn't something immediate to do, they hung around with the landing crews. Those people remained on standby for any cargo ships coming in, but mostly, they stood around bored.

The night before Lyra was to report for duty again, she hung out with her sister on the edge of the colony, staring out toward the towering trees on the horizon. Those represented the forest the Zitha brought. Everyone with an ounce of colony experience worked together to ensure they found a way to keep them alive.

Lyra asked, "Do you have any idea why they were so intense about those?"

"They wanted some piece of home," Mary said. "The Zitha culture values the homeworld above all else. That's one of the reasons they didn't colonize many worlds. In fact, they call them outposts and the people working there tend to want to get home as quickly as possible. It's a big deal to them."

"Funny that we spread through the stars," Lyra said, "took to planets where multiple generations of humans lived and died without ever seeing Earth. Then, when the origin point gets attacked, everyone goes up in arms."

"What did you expect?"

"I didn't think anyone would care all that much, honestly. I mean, I knew they'd be upset about the people who died, but the planet itself? It's barely a symbol for some of those places. Especially the self-sufficient ones."

"Oral history," Mary explained. "People pass down the importance of Earth to their children and so on. So they've been raised to think of it as this... mythical place. Something to be revered. When it was attacked, it hits close to home. Like way back when a monument would be hit. People didn't have to visit to be offended."

"I hadn't thought of it that way."

Mary patted her shoulder. "And just so you know, there are plenty of colonists that don't give a shit about Earth. You're just noticing the ones that do because they're loud about it. They've got passion. The others, those apathetic to what happened, know better than to speak their mind since it might lead to a fight."

"I guess so. How do you feel about it?"

"I'm less concerned about the place," Mary said, "and more upset about the people. That's where I'm at. You can rebuild a city. All the lives lost… those are gone forever. When we have Earth back, we can clear away the rubble. Bring the homes back. Restore it to some semblance of its former glory."

Lyra nodded. "Sounds hard though."

"Maybe. The Veldon must not have obliterated the whole thing though. Not if they wanted to find something. Keppler, right?"

"And his research, I guess." Lyra shrugged. "Which I don't understand. Though if Commander Weston is proof of concept, it should be a game changer. Providing the subject survives the procedure. From what I understand, it causes unbearable agony. Enough to kill most people."

"Check please." Mary smiled. "In all seriousness, I'm not sure who would volunteer for that. I heard that's why he found himself exiled from the scientific community. He killed some people who put themselves up for the procedure. I also heard the experiments weren't all that ethical."

"Probably not," Lyra said. "I've been around him. He's got zero bedside manner and probably didn't even think about the implications of what might happen if they didn't make it. In fact, I'd be willing to bet Keppler thought for sure his serum wouldn't hurt anyone. And that he'd walk away with another major success."

"Oops." Mary sighed. "This place is nice, huh? I kind of don't want to ship out tomorrow."

"You're off too?"

Mary nodded. "We're checking with the ambassador. Trying to find out what happened with the Raldor."

"They've been gone for over a week without contact. Don't you think it's time to assume they didn't make it?"

"Not my decision," Mary said. "We've been ordered to check so we're off. What about you?"

"Rumor states we'll be heading into Veldon space for an intel run. Probably won't be all that exciting. I think they're all going to be busy scouring the galaxy for the scientists or their research. The Uldarn have them acting like errand boys. Or hound dogs, I guess. Likely more accurate given all the fur."

Mary snorted. "Wow. Well, I think we both might need some good luck, huh?"

"I hope not. Especially for your sake. Has your ship been updated sufficiently to fight off the Uldarn equipment? Or will you need us to come help your ass again?"

"C'mon, of course we've done the upgrades." Mary nudged her with her elbow. "You think we're totally stupid?"

"Yes."

"Thanks a lot! This coming from the woman who made her living stealing things."

"That was a choice," Lyra said, "not a necessity."

"And how does that make you intelligent? Seriously, Lyra. You could've done anything with your life. Command track, even. I wouldn't have been surprised if you made commander by now with your talent. Instead, you got relegated to some shit duty then just bailed on them. Ended up in prison. I don't understand."

"Really?" Lyra asked. "Are you serious?"

"Yes, I'm very serious. Why?"

"Because I hated taking orders," Lyra said. "I hated being in a position where my life was being wasted constantly sitting around waiting for someone to come up with a task for me. I needed to be in charge of myself. If I didn't do anything for two days, it needed to be because I made that call. No one else."

"What's the difference?" Mary asked. "At least with the EDF, you made a difference."

"How?" Lyra asked. "What benefited from me checking in cargo ships for the military? Nothing I cared about. Did turning to crime make sense? Yes, at the time, it sure did. After what's happened, I..." She bit her lip. "I guess I feel like we're making a difference so... it's frustrating that I needed a war to give service meaning."

"Like I said, if you had applied yourself, you would've been doing a lot more than checking people in. Your insubordination got you in that position, not your talent."

"Which is why I left. Mary... can we please stop talking about it? I don't want to argue."

Mary nodded. "Sure..."

"Good. Especially since this is the last time we're going to see each other for a while."

"Not entirely true," Mary said, "you could join the Patton. I can pull strings. Get you on the same ship. We could work together. I think we'd do well. You've got a tactical mind, great with weapon systems. We might—"

"I can't do it," Lyra interrupted. "I can't leave them after everything we've been through."

"Come on, you want to make a difference, come with us. It'll be a safer mission too, I promise."

"You don't know that. In fact, you guys are going into a situation totally blind. The Raldor could be on the warpath, killing anyone that gets close. If that's the case, you'll find out the ambassador's dead and you guys will have to fight your way home."

"I don't think so," Mary said. "I know Franklin Hale. If anyone could survive an ambush or something like what you described, it'll be him. He's a great officer."

"Doesn't matter how badass you are when the enemy blows you up before you have the chance to say hi." Lyra put her hand on her sister's shoulder. "I love you. I don't think it's a good idea for us to work together directly. And in all honesty, I don't think I could take orders from you."

Mary laughed. "Are you serious?"

Lyra nodded. "Absolutely."

"Why not?"

"Because... I dunno. I'm too prideful? I'm a jerk?"

"Yes." Mary shoved her. "You totally are."

"Yet I'm not the one assaulting other people."

"Please. You want me to wrestle you to the ground the way I did when we were kids?"

"God no." Lyra looked around. "People will think we're incestuous lesbians or something."

"Well, you're still twisted."

Lyra chuckled. "Some things never change. What can I say?"

"Oh." Mary cleared her throat. "We've got company. Looks like Chelsea's finally caught up to us."

"Hey!" Lyra waved. "What've you been doing?"

"Talked to my dad," Chelsea said. "Hi, Mary. Good to see you. I don't mean to interrupt."

"We're just hanging out," Mary replied. "Do you need a few minutes? You look like you've got something on your mind."

"I do. Is it okay? We can talk later if necessary."

"Nah." Mary waved her hand. "I should get back to the ship soon anyway. I've got a lot to do before I can get some sleep." She hugged Lyra. "I love you. Be safe out there. Think about what I said though. If you change your mind before we leave, you can still make it happen."

"I won't, but thanks." Lyra watched her go. She shouted, "Love you too!" After her sister left, she turned to Chelsea. "Why so glum? You look pretty miserable."

"I'm not. Just... Dad was undergoing those tests from Keppler. I still have a hard time trusting him."

"He saved Barty and Eliza," Lyra pointed out. "That should count for something."

"Oh, it does. I mean, I'm glad he's on our side, for sure. But..." Chelsea sighed. "I don't know. That isn't even why I'm here."

"So what's up?"

"We're heading into the heart of Veldon space. Only a few ambassadors have gone where we are. Straight to the homeworld. We're expected to gather intelligence on what's been going on there. See if we can make out any sort of..." She shrugged. "I don't know.

Activity, I guess. Something to help us decide if we should attack them there."

"That's harsh," Lyra said. "Not that they haven't spent the last ten days earning it. Anyway, what're the parameters? What do we do?"

"Recon," Chelsea replied. "Straightforward. Except for the fact we'll be light years behind enemy lines without any chance for backup."

"Hey, when we came across the Pytheas, we had no idea if we'd ever see an EDF ship. It'll be more like old times, right? Just us against an empire. Besides, I'm pretty sure your dad won't let us go, take a look, and leave. We're going to do something out there. Perform a miracle mission to smack them back for what they did."

"I guess." Chelsea turned to her. "I've got a bad feeling about it."

"Why? Rather, do you think it's founded?"

"I don't know. Probably not. I've been thinking... maybe I'm worrying because of what happened on the JTF base. I didn't have a lot of time to think about it when we got aboard the Pytheas... after being jettisoned from the hangar. Then we came back here, I got busy. Everything was a whirlwind."

"But now you've had time to think about it?" Lyra asked. She understood. After the brief time floating in space, she had nightmares every time she slept. Bad enough that she thought about talking to one of the psychiatrists, but they didn't have time to do much more than introduce themselves.

Though she knew it was inevitable. When she laid down, she got a sense of weightlessness and it made it queasy. Sometimes, she had to sleep in a chair. It had been bad. Someone she talked to in the bar suggested it got better. They'd been through a scenario where they had to float around for a couple hours.

Zed did mention he had started to feel better in the last few days. That gave her some hoe.

"Yeah," Chelsea answered. "I've been thinking about sitting in that cell. Trapped. And I started out feeling pretty good about it. As in I knew I'd get out. But then despair settled in. I didn't feel like myself. When you showed up, it took a lot to believe you were there. Your voice brought me back."

"You don't think you were gassed or something, do you?"

"Maybe. Yes, actually. I do. But Keppler couldn't find anything. Of course, I didn't tell him about it for a few days. It may have already left my system. But how could it if they intended for me to end up like... like those others? The brainless thing walking the corridor. Or that guy Ithila killed on the surface."

"Someone capable of thinking for themselves but still being forced to work for them." Lyra put her hand on Chelsea's shoulder. "You're fine now though, right? You don't feel any overwhelming urge to help them? Or you know… betray us?"

"Don't be ridiculous." Chelsea looked away. "Just… since then, seeing what they wanted to do first hand… it made me sick. Now I have to deal with the aftermath while we head off to see the heart of the empire willing to turn people into puppets. How could they do that? What sort of disgusting, amoral society does that?"

"Slavery isn't new."

"This is beyond that. This is… conditioning. Outright alteration of the mind so the person is pliant. And there are levels, obviously. Because we've seen them. It leads me to ask the question about Trildair. Had he undergone a different type of treatment? Was he one of them? Or…" She sighed. "Was he just a sick piece of shit happy to help?"

"Probably a little of both," Lyra said, "don't you think?"

"See, I'd rather be hunting for him than going to Veldon space."

"That's the cop talking."

Chelsea shook her head. "No… that's vengeance talking. It has nothing to do with the law. I want to put him down like an ailing pet. I want to see him die." She met Lyra's gaze. "And I've never felt quite so passionate about wanting to kill a man before. But there it is. I guess it's finally come to that."

"After what he did to you, it's not a wonder." Lyra stepped directly in front of her. "But you're tough enough to get through that, right? At least, I think you are."

"Why did you risk your life and freedom to save me?" Chelsea asked. "Seriously."

"Because you're my friend."

"You steal a ship and travel to a place you were told not to for friends?"

"Okay, you're more than a friend."

Chelsea tilted her head. "How much more?"

"I don't know. You tell me?" Lyra pursed her lips. "Do you even go my way?"

"I..." Chelsea narrowed her eyes. "I chased you down as a criminal for a long time, Lyra. I wanted to arrest you so much. I couldn't believe how long you'd managed to get away with your crimes. Then we finally met. And you weren't a file anymore. What you did for me... for my father... for Barty..."

"Hey, I'm not a monster, that's all. You still needed to chase me down. I did commit crimes."

"That's... not my point. I guess I'm trying to say, I didn't think I'd be your friend. Even when we worked together, I figured we'd get along. For the sake of the mission. Then... it changed... a lot. And fast."

"Do you want to answer my question?"

"I am," Chelsea replied, "in my own roundabout way."

"You're going to be tired from beating around that bush."

Chelsea smiled, but it faded fast. Her brow furrowed. "Yes. I do. I've... been with..." She shook her head. "That doesn't matter. Yes, I'm attracted to you."

"Good?" Lyra smiled. "That's good, right? You think so, I mean. Cause I do." She put her hand on her chest. "I'm like... totally for it. And in fact..."

Chelsea kissed her, hard enough to knock Lyra back a couple steps. It lingered for a good minute before she pulled back. Their eyes met. Both eased into breathing again.

"Wow..." Lyra muttered. "Unexpected."

"Good?"

Lyra nodded. "Yeah... very."

"This... isn't probably a good idea," Chelsea whispered. "Working together... getting to be like this..."

"Screw that, there's nowhere I'd rather be than standing with you. Well..." Lyra grinned. "Maybe there's one place."

"Hmm?"

"I know there are some private quarters where no one would bother us for the next few hours." Lyra motioned with her chin to the left. "You want to grab that shuttle... head over to the Pytheas..."

"Is anyone onboard?"

Lyra shook her head. "Zed's in the command center helping them go through the downloaded files.

Barty's still in Medical. You're dad's in the medical bay on one of the big ships, isn't he?"

Chelsea nodded. "With Keppler."

"That only leaves Ithila, and we both know where he is." Lyra took her hands. "So what do you say?"

"As long as we can somehow silence Zoe... I know she's an AI, but she's got my mom's voice. That would be weird."

"I'll shut the whole damn planet down for a night with you." Lyra pulled her away. "Come on, before someone decides it would be a fantastic time to take a tour of the ship."

Never thought I'd get to this point. Lyra's heart throbbed in her chest. She had developed feelings for Chelsea while they were in the embassy on the Korlas planet. Their time together made her realize how much they had in common, despite the fact they were on opposite sides of the law. That barrier's gone. We can pursue something now.

If it lasted past the war, they'd have some things to figure out. But Lyra had no intention of worrying about the future just then. The past demanded her attention and she planned to make the best of it.

***

Gareth felt better than he ever had before. Twenty-year-old him still suffered from aches and pains, mostly from rigorous training. Yet sitting in the medical bay with Keppler, he firmly believed he could take on any challenge. This despite passing out from a serum crash while operating a starship.

Which equated to a lot of tests to ensure it didn't happen again. Though he doubted he'd find himself completely alone for a while. Their next mission involved going into enemy territory with little chance of taking off on their own. Providing he kept Lyra under control, they'd remain a group.

Keppler made a number of grunts while he leaned over a computer screen. Gareth didn't bother to watch. He didn't want a lecture with a bunch of terms he'd never heard before. And the doctor didn't stop to define anything. If his audience understood, so be it, but if not, that was on them.

Kensington sent a message asking if he'd be available in the next hour. Gareth wrote back to say he had no idea. They needed to go over some last minute points about the mission. With the brand new council about to meet, Sentinel One became a hotspot for activity. Security measures had been elevated by all parties involved.

I kind of want to see it. They all stood on the verge of opening a new chapter for galactic politics. One where multiple cultures, some of which dedicated themselves to war, promised to find peace. Which offered so many amazing possibilities from colonization efforts to exploration.

If they could get over two major hurdles.

The first involved their own prejudices. Some of their people continued to harbor bad feelings for one another. That actually didn't seem so bad this time around since they found commonality in loss. Other than the Korlas at least, and they generally didn't express their disdain for others.

Most of the cultures took it for granted.

The second came from the Uldarn, the Zitha traitors, and the Veldon. Those three enemies may put an end to everything before it began. Though Gareth's confidence had been bolstered recently over the quick updates the EDF made to their weapons and shields. Not to mention the fact the Veldon slowed their attack.

It didn't make much sense for them. Without the context of knowing they'd been influenced or allied with the Uldarn, Gareth would've thought they were planning something special. Instead, they paused. With humanity and the Zitha on their heels, the attacking forces didn't bring home victory.

Which granted hope of turning the tides.

They'd moved to a larger medical bay with more room and tools. Keppler requisitioned the head surgeon's office, which caused a stir. He didn't seem to notice. He needed somewhere private to conduct the tests, and said they should've done it on the Pytheas. They still had yet to find the final piece of the sixth injection.

Which made the doctor nervous. Gareth shared his concern. If the entirety of the EDF fleet, all the Korlas, and the Zitha couldn't provide something, then what were the chances they'd locate it? He still didn't know exactly what they were after. Some bonding agent or other. The explanation involved more confusing nonsense.

"We'll have to find this missing piece," Keppler muttered. "If we don't die on this idiotic errand you're insisting we attend to. Why we'd go behind enemy lines with a single ship is beyond me. I don't care if this is the best ship in the fleet. In fact, it seems to me, we're making a grave error risking it."

"It'll be fine," Gareth said. "When we're done, we'll do what we can to find what we need for the last shot."

"It'll be important," Keppler replied. "My calculations were wrong. Mostly because I never got to this point in the process. So we should really focus on ensuring you stay alive before we worry about much else. My research will change the course of human history. And if the Veldon have stopped..."

"No one believes they stopped. They slowed down."

"We don't know that. War is always the pastime of humanity though. So I suppose I shouldn't be surprised all of your colleagues would rather get back to killing than work toward the betterment of our people. That's what happened to me, after all. Cast out because it didn't have enough of a military impact."

"You were exiled," Gareth said, "because you ran an unethical experiment that killed people. The military shouldn't be blamed for that part. They could've put you in prison but let you go off to the mountain. And just because you ran out of subjects when you went there doesn't mean you weren't able to forward your cause."

"It would've been a lot easier with resources." Keppler sighed. "On another note, you're doing well. Totally stabilized. If you must go on this assignment of yours, then you'll be more than safe enough to do so. I recommend leaving the heavy lifting to the younger people though."

"Yeah? Because I'm not feeling my best?"

"No," Keppler turned to scowl at him, "because it seems stress and punishment sap you quicker. Until we've made the process permanent, you're in jeopardy of burning out. And we can't afford that without the proper ingredients for the last shot. And I've got some bad news about that."

"Great. What?"

"It seems the mixture might be personalized. I've had plenty of time to study your body chemistry so I'll be able to make it happen. But if I want to replicate this, I'll need someone with basically Zoe in their head too. She can get me the data I need much quicker than I can come up with it myself."

Zoe spoke in Gareth's head, "I'm glad I can be of some use to the arrogant bastard. Did you hear admiration in his voice just now? I think I did. And I really kind of enjoyed it, if I'm honest."

"Well, I guess we'll have to..." Gareth paused as the door opened. Patrick Worthing stepped in.

"This is outrageous!" Keppler pointed at the man. "Don't you know how to knock! This is a private office! Granted, I requisitioned it but that doesn't make it any less sacrosanct! I am with a patient and he has the right to—"

"Calm down," Gareth interrupted. "It's fine."

"Thanks," Patrick said. He stared at Keppler for a long moment. "Commander, can we speak in private? Just for a few minutes. I promise."

"Sure. We can step into a conference room so the doctor here can work on his bedside manner. Or whatever it is he's up to." Gareth pulled Patrick outside. They left the medical bay then entered one of the conference rooms. "What's on your mind?"

Patrick locked the door. "I'm about to take off soon. I'm... I'd like to ask you for a favor. It's... kind of important to me."

"I'll see what I can do."

"No one's going with me on this mission," Patrick explained. "I'm going to find that Trildair piece of shit.

Take care of him. I think Eliza would try to go with me, despite the fact she joined the EDF. I'd like her to go with you instead. I think I can trust your team to keep her safe rather than—"

"You know they left the JTF station in a destroyer," Gareth replied. "They've got some serious firepower. You alone might not have much of a chance against them."

"There's always a way."

"Yes, but usually it involves larger ships and a lot of people. Not one angry guy with a smaller ship that he requisitioned from the EDF. What's your endgame here? How do you intend to infiltrate the ship to take him down?"

"I don't know. The opportunity will present itself."

Gareth sighed. "Son, I know how you feel about what happened. That guy tried to kill you. He damn near succeeded in getting us all. I want to see him brought to justice just as much as anyone. But what you're talking about is suicide. I really have to insist you pick someone to go with you."

"Since your team won't," Patrick said, "I'm not sure who else I can trust."

"There are any number of other soldiers here I'd trust. Will you let me find someone? Someone I can vouch for? That should satisfy your trust issue, don't you think?"

Patrick frowned. He turned away. "Just one?"

Gareth chuckled. "Starting to think you need a squad or something?"

"Honestly, no. The more people, the greater chance of discovery. I want…" He paused. "I want to infiltrate the ship. Find him, get him out of there. Gather evidence of what they'd done. Maybe save the other people he brought onboard. I know the Korlas saved some. Or at least gave them to us to put under observation."

"What's the deal? You think they don't have much in the way of firepower? By now, they might have picked up some reinforcements. Which means you'll find yourself—"

"I've thought it through, Commander. I'm sorry, I don't mean to be short. Yes, I would appreciate you recommending someone. I may not take them up on the offer, but I'd like to have some options. And as far as what I'm expecting…" Patrick shrugged. "I've done this kind of thing before."

"These guys are different," Gareth said. "I'm just reminding you of what you already know. They've brainwashed their people. Chelsea talked about feeling a sense of despair in the cell. That should tell you something about how they do it too. Deprivation and possibly an inhalant. We didn't have time to test her."

Patrick nodded. "Now, if you'd let me take her…"

Gareth smiled. "I can't afford her. Why don't you want Eliza?"

"She's not ready for what I have to do."

Gareth tilted his head. "You don't intend to bring Trildair back, do you?"

Patrick didn't respond.

"You can speak freely. I won't say anything."

"It probably won't be possible, sir."

"I see." Gareth leaned against the table. "You know, I've run a lot of operations in my day. Hundreds probably. We pit ourselves against some of the nastiest customers the EDF faced. Some criminals, sometimes Zitha. During the war, it was Veldon. I've even skirmished with the Korlas."

"I'm familiar with your past... what... begging your pardon, but what's your point?"

"Just that all those times I went out there, it was never personal. We could keep emotion out of the equation. Now, with Earth, I think we've got a lot of people feeling otherwise. They want revenge. And that's why we're taking the attack part of things slowly. Because it's dangerous."

"You think I'm only interested in payback."

"Only?" Gareth shook his head. "Of course not. You want to bring him down to save other people. But the motivation to go alone, or with one other person, that's revenge talking. Because you plan to be reckless in your pursuit of this guy. Which is why Eliza can't go along with you. She'd be a voice of reason."

"Maybe. I'm also pretty damn good on my own. I've gone undercover with some seriously—"

"Stop." Gareth waved his hand. "Seriously, I don't need to hear your CV. I get it. You're tough. You've been through a lot of shit. I'm not here to be sold. But you need to think long and hard about the situation you're putting yourself in. Because if someone here found out your motivation and your plan, they'd think you're suicidal."

"That's ridiculous."

"Is it though?" Gareth asked. "Seriously, Patrick, you don't have to chase this ghost. He'll be caught eventually. We've put out a warning. Anyone who encounters the guy will either run or kill his ass. You could put your skills to better use right now if you wanted."

"Like how?"

"By joining me and my team. Come with us. Help find out what happened to the Veldon."

Patrick shook his head. "I can't. Eliza can help you with that more than I can."

"Whenever we go on a mission," Gareth said, "we end up leaving a skeleton crew behind. I need people capable of hitting the ground with us. You've got what it takes. The things you survived on that planet make you ideal. But I won't push. I've only got one more point to make."

"What's that?"

"Vengeance can drive a man to do extraordinary things. You can learn a lot about yourself while you pursue it. It might even tax your skills to their absolute limit depending on the enemy. But if you succeed, it's an empty victory. And if you fail, you died for a vendetta you could've easily walked away from."

"You really think that?" Patrick asked. "That the victory would be empty? After what he tried to do to Chelsea?"

"We don't do anything for only one reason. There are always things we can use to justify our actions. But yes, taking Trildair off the board alone will be an empty victory when you put it against what it'll cost you. I've seen it plenty of times before. That look in your eyes isn't new to me."

Patrick sighed. "If I don't try..."

"What?" Gareth asked. "You'll kick yourself? Be angry? Feel empty? You could say the same thing when you don't immediately answer a slight. Some asshole at a space station throws shade and you don't pop back. That's kicking yourself. Going out to hunt and kill a man is something else."

"No one here is prioritizing him."

"Nope. You're right about that. They sure aren't."

"So we're supposed to what? Just let it go?" Patrick slapped the table. "I'm not able to do that! There's a reason I joined the JTF. That was so bad people didn't get away with things. We pursued them to the ends of the galaxy. No matter what, they went down. Now, the organization is in disarray, sure... but I can still do my job."

Gareth nodded. He extended his hand. "Then I'll wish you good luck. I'll make sure Eliza stays safe. And I'll send my top picks for who should go with you if you decide to make it happen with a partner."

Patrick looked at his hand for a long moment before shaking it. "Thank you, sir. I'm sorry to get so passionate. I genuinely do not want to—"

"Say no more." Gareth took a step back. "I understand, son. I really do. I just hoped you might see the folly of it. But I also know when someone has to address a problem. I've been there myself. Not necessarily vengeance, but close enough that I get where you're coming from. Do this smart. Try to survive. And don't become the next victim."

"I won't." Patrick turned to the door. "Commander... when you're out there with the Veldon, do you think some of your crew might have the same feeling I do right now? That they might be interested in exacting some vengeance against the Veldon for all the things they've done? Say you find them in a weakened state."

"We don't regulate feelings," Gareth said. "We rely on discipline. No matter how you feel you do what you're told."

"The way Lyra Vahst did when she went to save Chelsea?"

Gareth chuckled. "I'm sure you know who she is."

"I do. So I'm concerned about what might happen out there."

"We've had a long talk," Gareth said, "and we've come to an understanding. We're going to communicate better going forward. That was the failure last time. Neither of us talked enough before she took action. And if you want to know, I don't blame her. The gut feeling she relied on proved better than mine."

"But that's not discipline."

"Not yet." Gareth clapped him on the shoulder. "But we're always improving, aren't we? Mistakes are made. And we're at a time of war. Having my daughter alive helps the cause more than me punishing Lyra for her decision. One that I'm sure either of those women would do again if it came down to it."

They stepped into the hall. Patrick nodded. "You've given me a lot to think about."

"Maybe it'll help." Gareth watched him go. I hope you figure it out before it's too late.

"He's dangerous," Zoe said. "I think he's going to find himself in more trouble than he can get himself out of."

"I don't know," Gareth muttered, "it may be that he's got the drive to see it through. Who are we to judge? In fact, he might just surprise us all. If he finds a way to get that Trildair guy, then that's one less problem for us to deal with."

"Or he'll be calling for help," Zoe said, "diverting resources to save him from his fool's errand."

"Nah. He's not the type." Gareth sighed. "Time to get back to the tests."

"Oh good. More time with Keppler. I can't wait."

Gareth chuckled. "Yes, well. He's better than some."

"Who? Who is he better than?"

"Uh... recently promoted field medics. Anyway, hush. I need to think about the upcoming mission." And how I'm going to convince Eliza to leave Patrick on his own. She won't like it. Not after what they survived together. We need the extra hand. I'll have her transferred. Keep her busy.

Like the rest of his crew. So they don't think about the danger they're about to face. Because it would be out there. Even if the Veldon found themselves waylaid by the Uldarn, they wouldn't be waiting for a quiet chat. No, this is going to be rough. But I think we're prepared. As much as anyone could be at least.□

Chapter 3

Security around the new council building tightened up considerably in the hour before they were meant to start their meeting. William and Marsha started out in orbit, but ended up landing the ship at the starport. They each took up positions in the surrounding blocks to coordinate with the ground forces.

Before they left, they donned armor, though their helmets hung from a hook on their belts. Marsha made the suggestion to avoid having civilians look at them like they were crazy. Or worse, be afraid of them and cause unnecessary chaos prior to the start of the event. Most of them had been through enough trauma already.

We don't have to contribute to it.

William leaned against a wall, listening to the comments from the various soldiers positioned all around the area. They kept a close eye on traffic, particularly pedestrians. Every so often, they'd ask someone to check someone out. After half an hour, no suspicions panned out to something dangerous.

The council delayed their meeting for a variety of reasons. Some of them couldn't get from their ships in time, and they all wanted to arrive roughly together. That decision put extra stress on the security forces.

William listened to the groans during the briefing, and he understood. It meant holding the area for much longer.

A second channel lit up, requesting his attention. William flipped over. "This is Nesmith."

"Hey!" Rivo Dess shouted into the line. "Just what exactly do your people think they're doing? You're turning the square here into a fascist zone! Have you guys forgotten what happened to everyone? This is almost as bad as when the Veldon hit their colonies, man! It's not remotely okay!"

"First off," William said, "we haven't shot anyone. So right there, we're better than the Veldon were. Second, we're keeping the area safe. No one's being unnecessarily detained. They're going about their business. But before you complain too much, you should realize I pushed to clear the area."

"Why didn't they go for it?"

"Because the people in charge wanted all civilians to feel like their leaders trusted them. While I appreciate the thought, this isn't exactly the time to be lax. Speaking of which, how the hell are there so many people here anyway? You can practically still smell the paint on some of these buildings."

"They moved in to create commerce around the council." Rivo sighed. "But I guess I see your point. We should've known it would be rough."

"Leaders are hard to come by, my friend. You can't just expect much less."

"Just try to make sure your security friends are gentle with the people, yeah?"

"No one's even been arrested," William said. "What exactly do you think is going to happen? That we'll get bored and start tearing people up for fun? Maybe drop some gas canisters? We're not even wearing our helmets yet. Which you know is against the standard protocol."

"Okay, okay... I get it. You're doing everything you can."

"I appreciate you recognizing that. You know, you and your buddies could help us keep an eye out. You probably know what's out of place better than we do. Let me know if you catch anything. I'll be discreet with the information."

Rivo grunted. "I know you will. What about whoever you bring with you?"

"You trust Marsha?"

"Yes," Rivo replied. "For the most part. She's still a soldier."

And I'm pretty much a spy. I wonder if that would change his perspective on me.

"Okay, so I'll bring her. We'll deal with whatever. Get to it. Call me back if you find anything." William switched back to the regular channel. The light flashed indicating Marsha reached out on their private comm. He switched. "What's up? You okay over there?"

"They were asking for you," Marsha said, "on the tactical. So I should be asking if you are fine."

"Yeah, I was dealing with Rivo."

"I knew we'd hear from him. Complaining about the tactics?"

William smiled. "He compared us to the Veldon."

"Wow. That guy's middle name is Hyperbole."

"Probably, yes." William paced to the edge of the alley to get a look down the street in both directions. The prefab units included a decent road for bringing ground vehicles through. If he hadn't known better, he would've been fooled into believing it had been there for the better part of a decade. "Maybe we should get back to the tactical channel."

"I doubt anything's going to happen."

William felt a chill rush through him. "I thought the same thing when we arrived at the Zitha station. Look how crazy that got."

"Okay, fair point. But Aevers is dead. Intel thinks he was the mastermind behind that. Anyway, I see your point. Let's hop over now."

They switched over. The same sort of conversation went on. Calling out status on different corners, drawing attention to specific pedestrians, and even talking about distant ships flying around. Command control provided information about the shuttles carrying goods to different parts of the colony.

Everything's totally fine, William thought. I'm probably being paranoid. Rivo's right. We're probably being too intense on the normal people. How many of them had the capacity to do anything? They didn't have access to weapons nor any of the heavy ordnance in the armories.

Anyone can get a weapon. And bombs are easy to build.

The representatives were set to arrive in the next ten minutes. If anything might happen, it would likely be when they entered the building. Afterward, a would-be assassin would find it difficult to do much to the outside of the structure. Getting in would be part near to impossible as well.

Every member of the building's staff had to undergo strict screening. Which seemed like an unnecessary step since they didn't have much of a pool to draw from. They were EDF people primarily, with a few civilians working the less intense jobs. Primarily running the operations of keeping the place tidy.

Aevers did a number on us. We're afraid of our own people.

"Hey!" A voice from less than twenty feet away startled William. A man coming down the alley. "You there!"

"What?" William tensed. He let his hand rest on his weapon. "What do you want?"

"Why are you here? You think you're some kind of hero or something? Hanging around here in all that armor, you want to intimidate us? You want to make us feel small? You little bitch!"

"I don't..." Arms wrapped around him from behind as his captor shoved him deeper into the alley. The other man drew a pistol.

William threw himself to the left while twisting away from the wall. The man holding him slammed his back into the concrete, loosening his grip.

"Grab him again!" the armed one rasped. "Hurry!" He brought his weapon up. "Don't do it!"

William spun, grabbing the guy languishing against the wall to use as a shield. He drew his weapon in the same motion. "I don't know what you two jokers want, but this isn't the time for any bullshit. You know what's going on out there? What this could mean for both of you? The security guys around here are twitchy and they don't want prisoners."

"You drop your gun," the armed one said. He looked young, his brown hair a mess around his head. Dirt covered his face, but it could've been mistaken for a beard in the wrong light. "Give us the comm channel security clearance."

"Or?" William asked.

"You're going to die."

"What's going on?" Marsha asked. "Who are you talking to?"

"Couple idiots attacked me in the alley," William said. "They want in on the comm. Put everyone on high alert. Right now." He tilted his head. "Not sure how good of a shot you think you are kid, but it doesn't matter if you put me down. I've just let everyone know what you're up to. My advice? You surrender now."

The man William held on to squirmed. William slid his arm up to the man's neck, tightening around his throat. His shield happened to be an inch shorter than him, but seemed to have a lot of muscle. He might be capable of wriggling out of the grapple. The key was to choke him enough to keep him from thinking straight.

"We can't. We won't!" Dirtbeard grumbled. "We can't allow the EDF to form an alliance with the Zitha. At all cost we have to stop that."

William sighed, "C'mon, man! They've got a military base and a town barely twenty miles away. They've been nothing but sincere with us, working toward making a safe world for dumbasses like you. And you what? Want to start a fight? With the Veldon still out there? I don't know who you're listening to, but they're going the wrong way."

"We..." the man William choked grunted out the words, "we know... what they do to... to people all the time! They're... dangerous..."

"Everyone is dangerous," William said, "given the right circumstances! Now please, for the love of God..." Gunfire down the street interrupted him. "God damn you both. Whatever you've decided to do, you're putting all of humanity at risk. Literally every single person left alive."

"Better than joining those murderers!" Dirt beard shouted. He fired his weapon, striking his friend in the chest. The miss made his eyes bulge. "Oh my... no!"

William shot him in the head. The body jerked back before hitting the ground hard. His shield slumped. He let him fall but put one in the back of his head just to be sure. I can't risk you playing games. Not when we've got a full-blown attack going on. He moved to the edge of the alley, peering out.

"Report," William said. The comm channel went silent. What happened? He switched to Marsha's. "What's going on? Why am I not hearing the security people?"

"They're switching to eighteen," Marsha replied. "Some kind of jamming on the primary. Get over there."

William flipped to it. Chatter instantly filled his ear, calls of action all around the plaza near the center of the settlement. A quick glance up and down the street revealed no civilian activity. They must've fled. Taken cover in the buildings. Whatever the case, I shouldn't have to worry about getting to the others.

His helmet had fallen off his belt during the struggle. William snatched it off the ground then pulled it on. The HUD showed up a second later, giving him a scan of his immediate surroundings. Two major battles took place with tiny skirmishes on every street. The big ones consisted of more than five people on either side.

"Who needs support?" William asked. "How should I proceed?"

"Take the smaller ones," a voice called, "clear the battles in the alleys before those attackers can group up to be a major problem."

William shoved away, hustling down the street toward the nearest activity. He slid to a halt before entering the mouth of the next alley, peeking in. One of the security forces took three shots to the chest, convulsing backward before falling to the ground. They stopped moving immediately as three men armed with rifles charged toward the street.

A quick burst took the one on the right down. William remained in cover as he sprayed the other two, cutting into them as they turned to look at their dead companion. Black marks marred their torsos. A garment caught fire as they slumped.

"I've got a man down in sector three," William said, "request immediate medical assistance to that area. It's secure with no more assailants. Do you want me to stay or continue the fight?"

"Keep going," the same voice from before told him. "We have to clear these guys before the ambassadors arrive."

You've gotta be kidding me! William moved away, but he asked, "Why haven't we aborted their arrival?"

"Local comms are the only thing functional right now," Marsha said. "I'm working on clearing them up. Shouldn't be much longer."

They had less than seven minutes before the various cultural representatives arrived on the scene. Their bodyguards will see the flashes of weapons. They'll abort before they land. God, I hope they don't try to land with all this action going on. William figured even if they took out the attacking forces, the building might've been compromised.

William made it to the next alley. Security forces got the better of their opponents there. Several civilian bodies sprawled out next to their weapons. He lifted his hands as he approached when they took aim at him. "Whoa, guys. It's Nesmith. You can relax, huh? I'm with you."

They lowered their guns.

"Thanks. Form up on me. We'll get this work done."

Four people fell in behind him. William checked for the next action. They'd have to cross the square where the worst of the fighting took place if they wanted to continue putting down smaller brawls. That didn't seem practical so he led them straight for the worst of the conflict.

Their point of entry brought them down another alley. When they reached the end, they had limited cover but a good line of sight on their opponents pinned down in a small park. Someone erected a wall around the grass, which acted as a decent means to keep from being shot by the larger security force to the left.

"Lay into them!" William shouted. He opened fire, the rest of his people doing the same. Their volley sliced into the enemy force as they crouched, killing at least half their forces in one go. Those that survived hustled to find a new place. They were torn apart before they even made it out of the square.

"Marsha," William said, "we're making progress. Looks like we don't have much left before we can call this—"

An explosion cut him off. One of the buildings to his left began to collapse. "Move!" He shouted, hustling out from the mouth of the alley. He ran toward the others as they withdrew as well. Stones fell all around him, massive chunks of debris from the fabricated building as it collapsed.

A particularly large one struck his shoulder. It knocked him off balance and he stumbled for a few yards before finally going down. Panic gripped him. If he stayed down too long, he knew what would happen. As a result, he tried to roll out of it. He made his knees before scampering away from his current position.

Something crashed directly behind him where he'd just been. An eight-foot piece of the structure half burying itself in the ground. Two of the men following him hadn't been fast enough. They disappeared under hundreds of pounds of rubble. He came close to his destination, the next alley which represented some semblance of safety.

A hit to the back knocked the wind out of him. He hit the ground, trying to crawl. Hands grabbed his wrists, pulling him toward the alley. His helmet couldn't drown out the noise around him, the crashing of the building as it continued to come down, impacting those structures around it as it leaned into them.

Glass shattered, the high-pitched clatter seeming to echo above the low rumbling boom of tons of stone crashing all around them. William coughed, struggling to breathe. His vision dimmed… then he realized he struggled to keep his eyes open. His limbs felt weighed down, as if his muscles quit working.

Marsha's voice shouted in his ear. He thought she might be asking for a status update… or she just wanted to know if he was alright. Answering seemed impossible. He opened his mouth. Closed it again. Tried a second time. Nothing came out but a wheezing gasp. The people pulling him didn't stop.

Darkness fell around him then the sun reappeared. They got him at least a block away. Blood filled his mouth. He let it drool out, hot and sticky against his skin. Gunfire brought back some awareness but he couldn't focus for long. Not before he lost track of the world moments before passing out.

***

Ghrenda waited for his shuttle to break atmosphere. He looked forward to the discussion. The key points he wanted to discuss involved hostile action against not only the Veldon, but the Zitha traitors that took his homeworld. Scouts were on the way to find out what sort of damage they could expect.

And if they might salvage the major cities. Building had never been the Zitha strong suit. He hoped they might learn from their allies, enlist their aid, make their culture stronger through diversity. The difficult part involved convincing the hardline members of the benefits. Which included many of his officers.

Even the man closest to him.

Riut sat beside him, observing comm traffic. He seemed particularly sour, mostly because he made his disdain for the meeting clear earlier in the day. His personal feelings had started to become a problem, enough that Ghrenda wondered if he might need to take some kind of formal action.

The prospect felt wrong after they'd served together for such a long time. But the future didn't have room for those unwilling to change their perspective based on new evidence. Though what that meant specifically remained in the air. Execution was not a possibility but what else did they have?

"Sir," Riut said, "comms are down. We cannot reach the surface. And I'm picking up some kind of conflict. A building was destroyed."

Ghrenda lifted a brow. "Really? You don't think it might've been an accident?"

"Negative. I'm picking up weapon fire. We should send down at least five shuttles to pacify the situation. We can nullify the attackers, put an end to whatever this is, and still arrive at your meeting on time. I can still reach the ship, so we still have time to receive this backup if you'll just—"

"Stop." Ghrenda put his hand on the man's shoulder. "We will do no such thing."

"Excuse me?" Riut turned on him. "And why not?"

"Because that is how you act when you are in the business of war and violence. We are now in the business of trust. The security forces we have in position down there are working to ensure our safety. We need to give them the opportunity to perform their task without our interference."

"But we have forces down there," Riut countered. "Do you want to leave them to the whims of that rabble?"

"Yes." Ghrenda nodded. "Because I know where our people are. They are in the building waiting for us. They aren't in any danger at this time. And if they are, then they'll be forced to work together with the human soldiers. So be patient. Calm. This will serve to help our cause."

"Unless all our people die," Riut said. "Then we'll see how our people view the situation. I do not believe they'll be favorable to an alliance."

"The humans will have lost people too," Ghrenda replied. "We can focus on that. Bring our sides together over commonality. That's how this works, my friend. Maintain altitude. Keep our people from intervening. The moment you can get me through to William Nesmith or Marsha Silva, do so."

"Those people." Riut scoffed. "As you wish, sir."

"Please don't be so bitter. You have had plenty of time to see this for yourself. The fact you haven't saddens me. I'll try again when we have time to speak alone. Until then, you'll just have to trust me." I hope he can. "Do you agree?"

"You're my commanding officer," Riut said, "and you haven't led me astray yet. Though I still find it hard to see your perspective. Allow me to get back to observing the scans."

"Of course." Ghrenda settled into his chair with a sigh. Come on, William. Reach out to me. Find a way to tell us what's going on. He knew the young man understood the importance of communication during such a difficult time. If anyone had a chance to find a way to fix the situation, it would be him.

If he has the opportunity to make it happen. The fate of the alliance seemed to rest in the hands of the Sentinel One security forces. I placed my faith in them. They now have the chance to prove me right. Or wrong.

***

Marsha tried William on the comm four more times. He didn't answer. The tactical channel was in total chaos. She dialed them in, sending three pings to clear the chatter. They needed to rally if they hoped to figure out what happened. Scans made it difficult to determine how many enemies they faced.

Unless someone started shooting, they looked like civilians. No armor, no comm signals, they somehow managed to coordinate their strike ahead of time. But that came at a disadvantage. They didn't have the flexibility to make changes. Nor could they call for reinforcements at any specific location.

"Alpha leader," Marsha spoke firmly, hopefully loud enough to be heard over the remaining chatter, "give me a sitrep. How many attackers are we looking at? I also need a casualty report. Over." She waited for a moment before someone started shouting. They started out too loud for the microphone.

When it finally settled, she came in after their introduction.

"Ten dead. Three unaccounted for. Number of attackers is hard to say. They aren't wearing uniforms. People just start shooting at us. This is a coordinated attack but they don't have any defensive equipment. We should have this situation pacified in the next few minutes. Ten at the most."

That's too long. The exploding building should've given him more respect for the enemy. Marsha had no clue why he didn't bring that into account. "Can William Nesmith please sound off?" Her heart thumped in her chest. The mention of ten dead might've included him. When he didn't answer the private comm, she feared the worst.

And no one replied to her request.

Damn it, William!

Marsha put on her helmet then grabbed a rifle. "Listen up, I'm leaving the command post for the field. Coordinate on this channel with me." She ran a scan for personal transponders. William's remained functional, roughly four blocks from her current position. The layout of the settlement as it was, that meant a half mile.

The security post where she stationed herself sat at the top of a small hill just beside the starport. It wasn't quite at the center, but close enough for everyone to rally there if necessary. Though she set the largest building as their rendezvous point—the place where the various representatives would meet.

An open field spread between her and the nearest building. The structure she'd been sitting in was just big enough for five people comfortably. Which is why they ensured they had room for everyone to stand for a briefing outside. A set of stairs led to a path with a barrier on each side.

I'll have everyone head to the rally point soon enough. Once I've got a better idea...

A blast hit the ground to her left. Marsha dropped to the ground, hitting the path hard. She crawled until she had an incline provide some cover to the right. The attacker had to be in that direction. Quick footsteps made it clear they decided to charge. She rolled on her back, taking aim.

The first person's head came over the small ridge. Marsha fired, melting half their face. They gurgled as they died, tumbling down to land only a few feet away from her. They had a companion, someone following at a discreet distance.

Marsha took a knee, then fired over the hill at the first sign of movement. She got the person in the shoulder. As they spun, they fired back, going wide. Throwing one more, she narrowly missed.

Scans showed other lifeforms in the immediate vicinity as well. One behind her, another two on either side. If they had been together, they must have planned to hit the command post. Not that it would've done them too much good. The security forces relied on the local tactical channel at the main structure in the center of town.

Though they had managed to cut them off from orbital comms.

Someone knows what they're doing, Marsha thought. Far too well, in fact. Why? Aevers is gone.

The injured person didn't get up. They moaned out there, calling for help, but they did not stand. Marsha repositioned, staying low as she hustled along the path toward the structures. Movement on the left made her pause. She took aim as an armed man came into view. His eyes went wide half a second before she popped him in the chest.

He went down though a second one opened up fully automatically. He didn't have control over his weapon, though, so the shots went high. One grazed her helmet, causing an alert to appear in her HUD, a warning about proximity. She stayed low, moving to get a better angle on the attacker.

The man kept shooting, screaming as he did. The way he strained with the weapon, he clearly hadn't fired one before. When he grabbed the top to pull it down, he screamed in pain, dropping the rifle.

Marsha braced hers, aiming at his head. He went for his sidearm. She put him down.

A blow to the back made her huff, but it wasn't a shot. She turned, watching as a person threw a second rock in her direction. The projectile went low, bouncing off the ground before scattering across the path. When she focused her attention on the young man, a teenager it appeared, he ran with his hands in the air.

What the hell was he thinking? Marsha continued on, hurrying into a sprint. The remaining forces trying to take the command center could have it. They'd be busy for a while, though she doubted they had a clue what to do when they got in there.

"Switch to channel eight delta," Marsha said, "secure with code foxtrot, niner, lima, four." She waited until she made the first building before adjusting her comm to the same. The conflict was only a few blocks away. Gunshots echoed through the streets. She saw flashes occasionally, blasts fired into the air.

A shuttle circled high above the surface. Marsha wondered which of the leaders knew to stay out of the fray. Her money was on Rowell or Ghrenda. The others may not have the same awareness of what conflict looked like. She checked her long-range comm. It remained offline.

Someone managed to block just that. Probably because they had to do it from afar. If they'd come down here to cause that kind of trouble, we wouldn't have had any comms at all. Marsha wondered why the mastermind behind the attack didn't bother to give their agents some equipment.

Maybe they know this is doomed to fail. They don't want anyone to figure out who started this mess by tracing the lost gear. Marsha pushed away from the wall, heading toward the nearest conflict, a battle raging in a clearing only two blocks from the embassy tower. That's the point we have to keep at all cost.

Chatter returned to the comm. The enemy forces intensified their numbers. More civilians seemed to be in on the fight. Marsha glanced behind her to ensure she was clear in the alley. Once she knew she wouldn't be shot, she crouched, leaned against a wall, and reached out to Rivo.

"What's up?" Rivo asked. "What're you people doing out there?"

"Fighting for our lives," Marsha said. "I don't know if William's even alive. What do you know about this attack?"

"Nothing!" Rivo shouted, "come on, you know I wouldn't start shit with you guys! You've been nothing but good to us once we started working together."

"They're all civilians!" Marsha snapped. "You have to know something! You wanted to be in charge of them all, so talk! What have you heard that you didn't bother to tell us about? I want to know everything. Now!"

"Look, I can ask around. I have no idea what they're on about! They shouldn't be. I've not even heard any grumbling about the Zitha. But that's what this seems to be about. A bunch of civilians getting worked up because we're forming an alliance with the raiders. Maybe they're just bent out of shape over—"

"Cut the shit!" Marsha interrupted, "and get out there. Find me information. I want to know who started this nonsense. I want their name and location as soon as possible, Rivo. Don't screw around. Find out. Right away. Everyone's life depends on it."

"How do you figure that?"

"Humanity can't afford another war," Marsha said, "we can't fight on two fronts. Honestly, the Zitha can't either. So we'd be condemning two cultures to annihilation. So if that doesn't get you passionate, then nothing will. You with me?"

"Yeah! I'll do what I can, Jesus Christ!" Rivo cut the line.

He'd better follow through. Marsha moved again, preparing herself for a terrible sight. She assumed there would be a lot of bodies. Dead civilians, dead security, wrecked streets... after the building exploded, they put themselves in a bad position. One she didn't know how to recover from easily.

Or if they even could.

***

"Trivak!" Rivo shouted from his office. He didn't bother to get up from the desk, mostly because he had no idea what to do. Marsha and William had always been straight up with him. Far more than the other military leaders. Doing right by them wasn't a hardship, but finding the appropriate way to help eluded him.

"What?" Trivak leaned in. "Why the hell are you yelling?"

"You hear the explosions?"

Trivak shrugged. "Yeah?"

"And they didn't strike you as odd?"

"I thought someone was doing some demolition. Maybe getting rid of the eyesore buildings to put up something nicer."

Rivo blinked. He didn't say anything for a good thirty seconds. "Sorry, I was giving you a chance to tell me you were kidding."

"Why?"

"Because that's idiotic!" Rivo stood. "God damn it, man! A bunch of people are shooting out there. Killing security personnel. Fighting in the streets."

"I ask again, why?"

"No, you ask a second version of why... but... okay, fine. I'll bite." Rivo rubbed his eyes. "You do know we're having the leaders of multiple cultures meet today, right?"

"Nope. I was busy."

"With what? Finding a shovel for all the sand you've buried your head in?"

Trivak frowned.

"I'm sorry, man. But you've gotta admit… look, we don't have time for this. You need to move your ass. Find out who started this nonsense. Get some data."

"Who are we getting the information for?"

"What's that matter?"

Trivak shrugged. "I like to know who we're working for."

Rivo rolled his eyes. "William and Marsha. Does that help? You feel motivated now?"

"Sure. You don't have to be an ass. I just wanted to know." Trivak stepped back. "I'll head over to the hall. Plenty of guys over there still. I bet they heard something about all this. Maybe they got approached about it."

"Good. Make sure no one leaves either. It's not safe out there."

"What're you going to do?" Trivak asked.

"See about getting comms back online." Rivo pulled on his coat. He checked the pistol he'd taken to wearing at his waist. The battery was fully charged. He was ready to rock. Not that he had a whole lot of experience with the thing. Certainly not the practical kind. "Hopefully, I can do it without being shot repeatedly."

"Who do you think would shoot you?"

"Anyone with a gun at this point." Rivo shrugged. "Don't worry about me. I'll make it happen. Reach out to me on the comm if you find anything out. Or better yet, just call Marsha directly. She's running around out here too trying to make this place safe again. I swear to God, we've got some serious assholes on this planet."

"True of anywhere, isn't it?"

"Yeah," Rivo replied, "but these dumbasses want to bring about the end of our species. Genocide is a higher form of being trash." He waved. "Be safe out there." He felt a tingle of fear when he touched the door panel. It slid open, and he found it was quiet. A couple people milled about, most of them watching the horizon.

Rivo stepped outside. He looked up, watching a shuttle circle high overhead a few times before heading off toward the action. The saboteurs could only have taken comms down at a few locations, though his bet was on the power planet. The colony put it roughly in the middle of the settlement, making it easier to connect the various buildings.

Plus, it tended to be lightly guarded. If civilians could take anything, it would be there. Won't be the case after today. Rivo started jogging. Maybe I should've stuck with Trivak. If guys with guns are sticking around that place, I'll probably get my ass blown away. He tried not to think about it.

The security personnel probably need reinforcements. If I get ahold of the ships above, I can make that happen. None of them will put people down right now. The powers that be wanted things to go smoothly. Dumping a bunch of soldiers on the situation held the potential of causing more chaos than it solved.

A group of Zitha and human soldiers had been training together in an effort to bridge the gap between the two groups. He wondered if he might get them in on the action. That would probably be for the best. Then they could both take credit for saving the day. Rivo hadn't worried too much about the politics going on around him.

Not until buildings started coming down from the violence. And civilians started it. He worked hard to ensure the military treated them with respect. If they all fell under suspicion, forced to endure checkpoints and 'random' stops, their lives would become all the more tedious.

If risking his life to get the comms back online fixed that, then it might be worth it. Providing it was only a risk and not a sacrifice.□

Chapter 4

Patrick boarded an assault vessel. The EDF hesitated to provide him with a vessel at all. Commander Weston and Captain Kensington both made it happen. His JTF ship hadn't been nearly as advanced. This one carried some stealth potential, defying scans. That would be a big deal along with enough weaponry to stand a chance against a destroyer.

The JTF fleet was just shy of military grade, which gave him an advantage. He could handle several shots from Trildair's craft, which might save his life. But the key was to get aboard before any shooting started. Every single one of the people he encountered needed to die.

Command structure's down. I can't trust anyone. But at least I can remove this guy from the board.

"Were you going to tell me?" Eliza's voice made him stiffen. "Before you took off, were you going to say anything?"

"Better you not know," Patrick said. "You've been in Medical. I wanted you to recover."

"So you planned to abandon me."

"This is a one-way trip." Patrick turned to her. "And after you fought for your life, I think you deserve a chance to live."

"Who are you to make that choice for me?"

"Your commanding officer," Patrick said. "First, at least. Then your friend. Besides, you're EDF now. I heard you renounced your JTF status."

"Which means you shouldn't be telling me what to do!"

"You've got an assignment," Patrick replied. "Commander Weston's crew will take you with them. That's the safe bet. And considering where they're going, that should mean something to you, don't you think?"

"Are you bringing the guy back?" Eliza asked. "Do you intend—"

"No. I'm killing him."

"That's not you!"

Patrick shrugged. "It is today. What he was doing? What he's probably doing to other people right now? He's going down."

"You're not an executioner! Why even stay with the JTF then? And how did the EDF authorize you to go off on this mission? They gave you a ship to be an assassin? Come on!"

"They don't know."

"God damn it, Patrick!"

"Stop." Patrick approached her. He put his hand on her shoulders. "Please."

"Are you going alone?"

"Weston gave me some options. I picked one that seemed appropriate for the job. So no, I won't be alone."

"There's that at least." Eliza backed away. "I'm sorry you don't trust me enough to make this happen."

"I hope you know that's not the case. I'm protecting you. Look, how about we wish each other luck and call it good, huh?"

Eliza looked down. "Okay… We were a team though. For a long time. I wish you'd come with us instead."

"Don't sound like Weston. He couldn't talk me into it." Patrick escorted her to the cargo area. "If I make it out of this, then I'll talk to you again."

"Please try to survive. You sound like you're about to commit suicide here. And I don't get it."

"Between what Chelsea said," Patrick replied, "and what I saw, I knew what I had to do. And I'm not going to kill him immediately unless that's the only way. He's got intelligence about our real enemy. So he's going to spill his guts before I finish him off. I doubt anyone else on that ship will know what he does."

"Okay." Eliza nodded. "Be safe then, detective. I thought I'd use the title to remind you what you do for a living. Not assassin. Someone who uncovers truth. Maybe if you remember that on the assignment, you'll come to your senses and realize it's not worth your life. Trildair is not worth it."

"I'll keep that in mind." A form appeared at the bottom of the ramp. "Uh... hi."

"Hey there." The man waved. He stood six feet, brown hair, civilian clothes. A duffel sat on the ground beside him and he shouldered a larger bag that nearly touched the floor. "Is this a bad time? I was told we were about to ship out so I came as fast as I could. But I can hang back if you—"

"No," Patrick said, "you're cool. Come aboard." He looked Eliza in the eyes. "My friend was just on the way out to her assignment."

"Sure am." Eliza backed away. "Keep each other safe." She left without another word.

I'm so sorry you don't get it, Patrick thought. It doesn't matter if she's angry as long as she isn't here. He turned to the new guy, who had to be in his twenties. What the hell, Weston? Shit, I should've paid closer attention to the dossier. I don't need a newbie. If anyone's coming with me, they need to be ready to rock.

"Name's Esher," the young man extended his hand. "Rhett Esher."

"Patrick Worthing." They shook. "Welcome to my crusade. Um... did anyone tell you what we're doing? And have you done anything like this before?"

"I worked as an MP," Esher said, "tracking down people that went AWOL and convicted fugitives. Seems this is pretty much that, only the guy defected from your division, didn't he?"

Patrick nodded. "JTF captain turned to shit. We're going to bring up his file en route. I think I know how we can track him. At least to his next destination after leaving the base. The Korlas provided me with all the recent traffic from the FTL buoy. That'll be our starting point. From there, we hunt."

"Think it'll be difficult?"

"No." Patrick led him through the cargo area to their small lounge. He gestured to the locker. "You can put your stuff there. And I'm pretty sure the guy we're after is an arrogant piece of shit. He probably thinks people are looking for him, but all that means is he'll be in motion. We follow the buoys, we'll get him."

"Then what? He's got a destroyer, right?"

"JTF destroyers don't have the same sensors as an EDF combat vessel. So yes, he's got some firepower, but we should be able to attach to the ship easily enough then infiltrate. Make no mistake though, anyone we encounter is a target. There'll only be one prisoner and that's Trildair."

Even then, I don't intend to keep him alive for long.

"They're all targets?" Esher lifted a brow. His brown eyes almost looked black in the low light. "May I ask why?"

"Because Trildair is guilty of conditioning people in such a way that they lose not only their will, but their self-preservation... or at least most of it. They'll do whatever it takes to kill us and stop the attack. So in order to defend ourselves, we'll have to be on it. If you have a problem with that, we may need to part ways."

"No, I get it. Commander Weston told me this might get rough. He talked about some moral ambiguity as well."

"That depends on how you feel about putting people out of their misery. Because they aren't there anymore."

"None of them?" Esher pressed. "Because let's be honest, we don't understand the process, do we? It could be reversible."

"The EDF is not committing forces to this. They gave me this ship and you. So we don't have the luxury of disabling the vessel with a cruiser then boarding with a few platoons to knock everyone out. I'm afraid they're collateral damage. And if we find out they could be saved, well… I'll take responsibility."

"Seems like a harsh burden." Esher lifted his shoulder. "But I'm here to do what it takes."

"What's your rank?"

"Lieutenant," Esher said. "A few years now."

"Why no promotion?"

"I like what I do."

Patrick smiled. "I know what you mean there. Going to the next level may have cut down on the action. You certainly wouldn't be chasing people around out there." He headed to the cockpit. "If you're ready to go, I'll get clearance. We can move out. While we're departing, you can go over the data."

"Sounds good. One of the best parts. Finding the trail left by the target."

Okay, good show, Weston. This guy seems perfect.

"May I ask how old you are?"

Esher took a seat in the copilot's chair. "You didn't look at my record?"

"Skimmed it, honestly."

"I'm twenty-seven."

"How many fugitive have you tracked? How many people go AWOL on the EDF?"

"Oh..." Esher considered the question. "My part? You know, we're faced with just over twenty-two hundred counts of AWOL every year. Probably higher, but that's the report I've seen. I either help or track down more than twenty people a month. Fugitives are on a task force basis. I've done a lot of those."

"Wow. Why so many?"

"All kinds of reasons. Everything from boredom to frustration to feeling trapped to wanting a good time." Esher logged into the computer. "When people get desperate, they do crazy shit. I guess the bottom line is, we're not sitting on our hands. The military police genuinely are busy all the time."

"Got it. So of all the people you've tracked, how many have you had to shoot?"

"Depends on who they end up with," Esher said. "Most are easy enough to find. They're hanging out at some stupid bar or hide out with a relative. Others end up with criminals. Sometimes even pirates. Those situations often end with violence. Though we have a track record of at least bringing our people back alive."

"What's the common punishment?"

"Dishonorable discharge… sometimes prison. Never really goes beyond that for a basic count. If they get together with pirates, they find themselves in a world of hurt. That goes well beyond the general court-martial. I've seen a man get life in prison after he went AWOL and helped a group raid his home colony."

"Jesus, are you serious?" Patrick tilted his head. "Man, I thought the crooks we chased were bad."

"What did you do before you left the JTF?" Esher asked.

"Infantry," Patrick said, "spec ops, mostly."

"Ah. So you've done the fighting, but you didn't have to track down the enemy. Generally speaking, someone told you where they were and you took them out."

"Yeah, that's a fair assessment."

"My job's more investigation. Like what you did for the JTF."

"Then I guess we'll both put our efforts to use on this op, huh?"

"If I may," Esher said, "I hope we err on the side of my job than your old one. Not that I'm shying away from throwing some beams downrange. I've had my fair share of conflict. But if we can do this in a subtle way, we're more likely to get information out of this guy. Unless you have another thought on the matter."

"Only that he's hurt a lot of good people," Patrick said, "including a friend of mine. Chelsea Weston."

"Commander Weston's daughter?"

Patrick nodded.

"Wow. No wonder he seemed hot about it." Esher rubbed his eyes. "Okay. Well, I'm a hundred percent with you, sir. Whatever it takes to make this happen, whatever I have to do to bring this person to justice or help you with your task, you've got me. And I won't let you down. I promise."

"Right on. Well... I look forward to working with you." Patrick got on the comm for clearance. Alright, Trildair. There's really nowhere you can go we won't find you. Though he worried the man might have run straight for the Veldon border. Back to his comrades and the people who started the aggression in the first place.

This conflict began long before the attack on Earth. They infiltrated the JTF. God knows what other organization fell prey to some conditioned asshole. I hope the EDF takes it seriously as they investigate their own. Patrick encouraged them to run people through psych evals. He got the sense no one felt like they had time.

If they don't make the time, they'll regret it. But that seemed to be the way of every organization in the galaxy. Hope for the best then feel guilty when it fell through. Not this time. If we can make anything right, it'll be disposing of this piece of trash. One small victory. That's what I want right now.

They lifted off, taxiing out of the hangar. Time to grab it.

***

Franklin fired his weapon down the hallway, flinching away as a blast struck his cover near his face. Sparks splashed across his helmet. He gestured for Sean to stay on his side, out of the line of fire. The two of them pressed hard into the station, taking the first three rooms easily enough.

After that, the resistance intensified. Five people did a reasonable job holding down the corridor. They brought mobile cover into the middle of the room. Two of their number crouched behind it with two more at the corners. A third provided overwatch, which Franklin nearly discovered the hard way.

The person's aim surprised him. Up to that moment, most of the shots didn't come close. A few hit the ground near their feet during movement. But otherwise, they weren't all that good. The initial defenders had been caught off guard. The way Franklin brought their ship into the hangar, the rapid deployment meant the opposition had no time to respond.

Even mowing down the initial defense force didn't buy them enough time to make the command deck. Not before the best of the enemy got their bearings. If he had Ethyl and Tesh, they probably would've had no problem. Just the two of them made it more than a challenge. It was probably a suicide mission.

"Nah." Bjorn seemed to be standing beside him, leaning against the wall. "This is good times. Don't you remember how many times we were outnumbered? Doesn't matter. Just kill them all."

"Easier said than done," Franklin muttered. He crouched, poking his weapon around to take a couple shots.

Sean did the same. They couldn't make progress without taking a risk. Which meant pressing to the next bit of cover. But their opponents seemed to have the corridor well defended, throwing constant volleys in their direction. Enough firepower to take down a couple squads.

"Cover and move," Bjorn said. "Like the old days. You can even be the brave one. Go first to show the boy how it's done. Little piss ant likes to talk so much shit. Give him some inspiration already, Franklin."

"That's easy for you to say. You're already dead."

"What's the point of living if you don't take a chance? That's what I did back on the station."

"And look where you are now!"

Sean replied, "I'm right here. What're we going to do? If we stick to this spot, we're dead. We gotta move or withdraw."

"I know." Franklin sighed. "Get ready to move. Lay down fire. Keep your shots to the right. I'll go left the second I can." He took a deep breath. "You ready for this? It'll be the worst part of the raid."

"Ready." Sean dropped low then leaned out, rapid firing down the way. The volleys lessened considerably. Those that did come down range went toward Sean.

"Moving!" Franklin dashed out, staying crouched. He let off shots too, driving the enemy to cover. He made the next corner, hopping through. A couple energy blasts came far too close for comfort, scorching his armor. He pressed his back to the cover, waving at Sean to get back. "Give me half a second to set up then you can go through."

At least one of the enemy died in the advance. A body rested face down in the corridor. Oddly, they didn't bother to communicate. No one tried to talk them down or convince them to surrender. They had superior numbers and refused to charge either. So what exactly was their problem?

"They're cowards," Bjorn said, "or they've got the same thing going on as the bitches the Veldon messed with. Why don't you show some glory, man? Just get down there, rip their asses in half. You can do it. Let the kid go first if you're feeling like a damn coward. But do something."

"We just took ground!" Franklin growled. "What the hell do you want?"

"Really? Your little shuffle is taking ground?" Bjorn scoffed. "Screw this. I can't watch this BS."

Good, I don't need the distraction of going completely insane.

"Move!" Franklin shouted. He leaned out to lay down fire. Sean called that he was moving next, hustling past him. The next bit of cover was an alcove, only barely big enough to take any cover in. Shit! "Press! Keep going!" He shoved away from his cover, aiming as he went.

A blast got his shoulder, another hit him in the hip. Franklin continued on, stumbling against the wall. He put another three people down. Sean got another then dropped to his knees. There was no stopping though. If they did, they'd be done. The pain cut through him, throbbing out from the impact points.

The opponents took their cover, firing blindly. Franklin put on a burst of speed then threw himself to the ground. He fired to the left first, putting two more down. Someone kicked his back. He rolled with it, blasting the others. They got him on the right side of his chest. He hissed… a body fell on him.

Son of a bitch!

"Sean!" Franklin grunted. "You still alive, man?"

"Yeah…" Sean coughed. "That was stupid!"

"Didn't really have a choice." Franklin sat up. "We're almost there. Next door… whatever techs they have in there… we've got it."

"Goddamn Raldor." Sean crawled over to him before getting his footing. He helped Franklin up. The two of them leaned against the wall. "Why'd we agree to this again? And why didn't we make that fat bastard come with us? Or the freak? Could've used the numbers. Especially just now."

"No point in complaining." Franklin gestured for the door. "Get a scan on that, please."

"Good job," Bjorn said, "see what I meant? You nearly pussed out and here you tore through this shit. That's what I'm talkin' about."

Why does he keep coming back? Franklin dreaded seeing his old friend nearly as much as he hoped for it. Probably from Deina messing with my head. I probably need to tell someone I'm losing my mind. Though I'm not sure what would happen besides being taken off duty. Or maybe they'd tell me to suck it up.

Bjorn nodded as he walked backward in front of them. "Probably right. They don't have time for officers to lose their shit right now. They'd tell you to get it under control. Besides, how distracting am I? My inspiration pushed you to attack when you could've stayed behind. All the way back there, waiting to die."

I can't even tell him to shut up.

"Sure you could," Bjorn replied. "Let the kid know. He's already an insubordinate little shit. Let him give you a hard time."

Sean got the door opened. He grunted while lifting his weapon. Only two people stood inside. A woman and a man, both probably under twenty five. They aimed pistols in Franklin's direction. Their hands shook, the barrels dancing as if they were having a seizure. Neither of them spoke, they just stared.

Franklin circled to the right while Sean took the left. Flanking the others meant they had to decide who to keep their guns on.

When they hesitated, Sean shot the guy in the head. As the girl twitched in his direction, he put her down too. Both collapsed, finishing off the mainstay of the enemy forces. More people supposedly held up in the lower levels. They weren't Franklin's problem. The Raldor could deal with them.

"Go for it." Franklin gestured vaguely to the consoles while he leaned against the wall. His body felt numb. "This better be all they want." Goddamn jelly looking pieces of shit.

"Never liked them either," Bjorn said. "Damn, your kid proved dangerous, huh? Just blasted those children. Pretty sure you could've had them stand down. They would've surrendered after two guys charged through every security officers, slaughtering them all before getting here."

I'm not giving him a hard time for what he did. The objective is to take the station back.

"At all cost," Bjorn replied. "I like it. You always turned me down when I offered solutions like that."

Those were different times, I guess.

"Not really." Bjorn sighed as he leaned against the wall beside Franklin. "Just different tactics. Different levels of desperation. You know, if we wouldn't have been such a bunch of pansies, we could've taken the Veldon out a long time ago. Finished them off so we didn't have to worry about an attack on Earth."

We know now the real enemy used the Veldon, Franklin thought. It could've been any culture. They were convenient.

"Yeah, I guess." Bjorn yawned. "Is he going to do his job or will you have to do it for him?"

"How's it going?" Franklin called.

"I've found the equipment," Sean replied. "I've initiated the Raldor's program. They'll be able to board in ten minutes."

"I guess we wait." Franklin closed his eyes.

The Raldor sent them to take back a key station from what they called criminals. The way the men fought, the lack of anything but screams and the occasional grunt, led Franklin to believe they might be dealing with more of the drones. These individuals didn't fall into the trap leading to a dead world.

Instead, they conquered a station, and probably leaked a lot of information to their superiors. Once those criminals boarded the station, they killed the Raldor in place then installed a device fatal to the former occupants. Letting off a high frequency vibration, it surrounded the station like a shield.

Franklin didn't even feel it, but a Raldor would've shaken apart.

Buying themselves time to steal all the information stored here.

"Good plan," Bjorn said. "Too bad these trash bags didn't think about dropping a device like that on the Raldor homeworld."

No one knows where that is specifically anymore, Franklin thought. They'd be guessing.

"Hit their colonies then. And when they turn up, fly too close to their battleships. If the Raldor are that fragile…"

It doesn't work like that. It would have to be on the ship to hurt them.

"Oh."

Even in my head, you don't think everything through. If you're in there, why don't you know everything I do? This is stupid. Why am I even talking to you like you're a person?

"For all intents and purposes," Bjorn said, "I'm exactly as you remember me."

Why you? Why not someone else? A family member... something like that.

"Because you feel guilty about my death. Which is stupid. I screwed up. My fault on the station. Not yours. I'd say you should probably let it go. But then I'd be gone. I'm not necessarily ready to leave yet. Especially since we've had so many excellent conversations. Sometimes one-sided."

Franklin had tried to ignore him several times. It didn't work. His voice was too loud, too pronounced, too real. He thought about talking to Deina about it, to find out if they had some way of dealing with the visits. The thought scared him. Much as he didn't want the distraction, he didn't want to lose Bjorn a second time.

"Done!" Sean shouted. "Can we please get to the medical center now? Find out if we're in serious trouble?"

"Pretty sure we'd already be dead if we were." Franklin pushed away from the wall. "The armor protected us for the most part. Probably got some severe bruising or a couple burns. It won't be all that bad." He limped toward the door, bringing his comm online. "Alfred? Come in, you lazy bastard."

"Whoa," Alfred's voice came through with too much treble. It made Franklin's head ache. "I'm not sure that's fair. I've been working my ass off back here after you crashed us into the station. Which, Ethyl would've loved, by the way. She's all about that kind of thing. Seriously digs it."

"Fantastic," Franklin said. "Glad to know she's a thrill seeker. We're on our way back. Sean let the Raldor know we succeeded. Can Tesh and Ethyl move to their quarters? Because we need their beds in Medical."

"Uh... I'll ask Deina while you're on your way back. Was the opposition rough?"

Franklin laughed. "No, they kindly surrendered and let us waltz in to turn their shit off. What do you think? Is this all they wanted, man? Because I don't even know how long we've been playing games for those tentacled pricks."

This had been the first bit of violence they had to commit. Deina and Alfred performed most of the work before that. The diplomatic process took days. During that time, Tesh and Ethyl remained on their backs, which proved all the more how lucky they were to have survived the drone attack.

Though both complained about being confined to the medical bay for the most part. Deina wouldn't clear them after explaining the long-term side effects of moving too soon after taking so many projectiles.

Franklin backed the decision, keeping them off duty. Though he regretted it with the space station.

"I'll find out," Alfred said. "We've done everything they've asked. They should at least open the FTL buoy to us. Deina can't even hack it. We've tried to get through several times without causing grief. The Raldor don't trust us yet. But this should be enough. It'll close the deal. I'm sure of it."

"No you're not," Franklin replied, "but nice try. Just make sure Deina's in Medical when we get there. If Ethyl and Tesh can walk, they're discharged. I don't care anymore." He killed the comm. He turned to Sean. "The bastard's sure. Can you believe the nonsense coming out of that guy?"

Sean nodded. "Yeah. Of course I can. He's a windbag. We should've brought him with us. Between his girth and his mouth, we might not have had to fire a single shot."

Franklin laughed. The act rewarded him with a shock of pain. "God, this is terrible. You know that moron won't get us off that easily, right? Somehow, we're going to have one more Raldor hoop to jump through."

"Something slimy," Sean replied. "Dripping with sacrifice you guys so we don't have to get hurt mentality. Why are they total cowards? Don't you think they should learn to fight for themselves? In fact, why do we care if they ally with us? They sure as hell won't fight. What're they going to do?"

"Share their tech?" Franklin shrugged. "You don't think their faster than light travel option will be worth it?"

"What we've gone through? I dunno. I'm struggling to say yes."

"Well, you should." Franklin noted they were nearly to the hangar again. "Took longer to get back to the ship than it did to leave it."

Bjorn seemed to be walking beside him, opposite Sean. "Because you're slow. And that ambassador prick is about to call you again. You know he's already failed to talk the squid down. The question you gotta ask is what check has he written for your ass to cash? Will this be the one that ends you?"

Probably. Franklin glowered. Ethyl and Tesh can help with the next one. If we're mostly in good shape. Sean seemed to be walking okay. Was he that tough? Maybe. I don't feel like I am anymore. This one did me in. The rushing through enemy fire, the stress of the landing, the first half dozen guys they killed… the whole event weighed on him.

"You got a lot more to go, bro," Bjorn said. "You can't be a pussy now. It's time to man up again."

You are beyond offensive. You always were. How did you manage to stay in the military for so long when you literally could not censor yourself? Franklin remembered a time Bjorn insulted a female commander when he talked about her privates in a vulgar way. She turned so red, it looked like she popped a battalion of blood vessels.

"Stuck up prig," Bjorn muttered, "she could've had a sense of humor about it. But nope. Had to be a cow. Whatever. If they can't take a joke, they shouldn't be in charge, you know what I'm sayin'?"

"Franklin?" Alfred came through the comm again. He sighed.

Bjorn laughed. "Here we go."

"What is it?" Franklin asked. "You'd better have good news."

"I... kinda do? But not really. The Raldor do have one additional task they need our help with."

"Of course they do," Franklin said. "You tell those squid looking piles of—"

"Slow down," Alfred interrupted. "We're going to have some help this time."

"What do you mean?" Franklin asked. "How? Who? When?"

"Seems the EDF Patton is looking for us. The Raldor are going to... invite them to assist."

"The way they invited us? Without the Likari, won't they be screwed?"

"They're going to warn them," Alfred said. "We'll have a battlecruiser on our side. So whatever they want will be a piece of cake by comparison, right?"

"Not if we need it!" Sean yelled. "You dumbass!"

"Cool it," Franklin said. "What do they want us to do? What have they said?"

"They'll... tell us when we rendezvous with the Patton."

Franklin sighed. "God damn it, Alfred..."

"What can I say? This is how it's working out, man! Come on. Just... relax. We've pulled everything else off. And this will pay off. You and I both know they've got plenty to offer us, so let's go with the flow. Right?"

There's no point in arguing. Command would want us to make this happen no matter what. Franklin hadn't intended to become an errand boy for other cultures though. That offended him. We should've negotiated for resources. Supplies. Territory. Not our asses and whatever else they could extract.

"Whatever," Franklin said. "It better not be too bad. This is rapidly exceeding any value we might garner."

"But think about the—"

"I don't have to," Franklin snapped. "Just... prepare to get us out of here. I don't want to see what the squid plan to do with this place." I just want some pain relief and a damn nap. Tesh can do the flying. He reached the ship, taking the ramp slowly. Maybe I'll be less angry after I've woken up.

He doubted it, given what they went through already. With more to come. That was the rub, and he couldn't do a damn thing about it."

***

Mary Vahst leaned forward, straining her safety belt as she stared at the screen. They arrived in the area where the ambassador's ship had last been seen. Comm traffic ended shortly after. Common sense suggested an accident or an attack ended them. She expected scans to find debris soon.

Instead, they found nothing. An abandoned space station with massive chunks missing, a couple planets without any sign of life or structure, and some natural satellites. Not even the FTL buoy the ambassador used to contact the EDF. Which offered an unlikely explanation that their signal had been hijacked and tossed to this place.

Leading a rescue party astray.

Mary had heard of Zitha using such tactics. She doubted they were out there, or that their culture attacked the ambassador. Not considering he's the one who put together the alliance with them. So what could've happened? And how long would it take Milton to give them the go ahead to leave the area?

"Raise the shields," Captain Carmine gave the order. "Do it now."

"Aye, sir." Mary wondered what the hell he saw. Milton didn't say anything, and he'd been hovering over the scanner without moving. Must be a hunch. She knew he had them, but was he being paranoid? She brought the defenses online. "We're good to go. Everything shows green. Weapons?"

"Standby," Carmine said. "Milton, give me a status update. What's out there?"

"A whole lot of nothing, sir. Like… seriously, nothing. I don't even have anything on scans that might have bounced a signal."

First Officer Alistair McKinley asked, "What about debris? Any forged metal at all? Raldor or otherwise? Maybe this is where our people… lost it."

"Negative," Milton replied. "I'm serious, this is an empty system. The planets here have enough resources to make it a decent find. I'd like to mark it on the star chart for later investigation. But beyond that, there's no reason anyone would come here. Unless they met someone and went somewhere else."

"This," Carmine said, "is the location for where we've met the Raldor in the past. Unless there's a serious mistake."

The pilot, Heather Stiles, spoke up. "Checking coordinates and our positioning now." She paused. "We're dead on target, sir. This is where everyone's listed their destination for all the other diplomatic missions out this way."

"Maybe," Milton offered, "they moved the station that was here. Like the Zitha did."

Carmine replied, "I doubt they'd get too far with the thing, considering. We'd probably still see it."

"After a week?" Alistair asked. "I dunno. Maybe we should check the adjacent systems to see what we can find. Won't take too long. Better part of a shift for each direction. Test the theory that they made a mistake with the coordinates. Or somehow bounced far enough away that we can't detect them."

"Sir," Mary said, "they might be crashed somewhere and need assistance too. If their beacon went out..."

Carmine nodded. "Alright. Milton, get me a listing of all the neighboring systems. Prep a temporary buoy so we can perform a long-range scan for any others. I'd like to check the civilized systems first. If there are any. If not, then we'll have to do this the old-fashioned way. Like explorers."

That's going to be boring, Mary thought. Why do I want it to be exciting? She had enough of that when they fought the Veldon while evacuating colonies. I wonder what Lyra's up to right now. Did they get behind enemy lines already? Or are they still in transit? Looks like she does have it harder than me this time.

"Whoa!" Milton slapped his console. The viewscreen changed, showing a bright purple flash. Three large vessels came through the light, their weapons blazing. Beams struck the starboard bow before any of them could so much as speak. The vessels broke formation, two veering off for flanking maneuvers.

"Heather," Carmine ordered, "full reverse. Evasive maneuvers. Mary, return fire! Milton, warn those ships off and tell them we'd like to negotiate."

Who the hell are these guys? Mary didn't recognize the ships. They were squat, short but bloated in the center. Similar to the Raldor vessels, but the hulls were dark gray. And they had a lot more weapons than she ever remembered them sporting in the past. Shields held though. That's the important part.

She brought each of the ships up on the targeting computer before unleashing three separate volleys. Their enhanced weapons put serious strain on the generators, even with double the normal amount. But it paid off. The attacks all hit home, a dozen shots for each. The enemy shields dipped below forty percent in a second.

"Direct hit!" Mary clapped her hands. "Prepping for another round." Another solid hit held the potential to finish their targets off. I hope they realize that if they have any inclination of talking. Otherwise, we'll be sifting their remains for the better part of three hours. The power meter rapidly climbed past sixty percent, racing toward ready.

"I'm getting static," Milton said, "and they're firing again!"

All of their attacks struck home, blasting the Patton's port and starboard bow as well as dead on the nose. Shields dipped to sixty percent, but it wouldn't matter in a moment. The enemy fired a third time, putting them below fifty.

That was unexpected. I didn't think they'd be able to shoot again so fast. Well, it doesn't matter because it's our turn.

"Ready, sir," Mary announced. "Permission to fire?"

"Fire at will," Carmine said.

Mary tapped the console. They unleashed another assault. The first one broke through the enemy defenses, obliterating their armor and turning them to a molten, red globe. The second suffered a similar fate, though their reactor must've gone up. Bits of their vessel scattered in all directions.

The final ship attempted to evade. Only half the attacks got them, but it was enough to bring down their power. The ship drifted a moment before something popped inside, tearing out the center and top. Fire didn't consume them. They simply... stopped functioning. The attack force was gone.

"Get me a full scan on those," Carmine ordered. "I want to know what was onboard and why they pulled that nonsense." He looked at Alistair. "We need to get that buoy out as well. Coordinate with the Engineering team to make that happen. Mary, let me know when defenses are back to full."

"That won't be necessary," a voice came through the speakers, raspy and high-pitched. Mary recognized the species immediately. The Raldor had come. Or at least they found a way to talk from afar. "You have passed the test, Captain Carmine. Congratulations. You may assist us with our problem for your diplomatic efforts."

"What are you talking about?" Carmine asked. "Identify yourself! Why did you attack this ship? That was an act of war!"

"I am Sslan, a Raldor ambassador working closely with your Ambassador Chance. They have been running errands for my people, but this final one will be more than they can handle. You will assist them to secure our alliance. Then we will share our hyperspace technology with you. And defy the Veldon."

"Slow down," Carmine said, "are you saying you've had our ambassador this whole time? Why hasn't he checked in?"

"Because he is very far away and we have been keeping him busy. You will be too. Soon. A portal will open. A hyperspace wormhole, you might call it. This will take you where you need to be. There, you will rendezvous with your people and perform a final mission. After you've debriefed, then I will give you the task."

"We're not your errand people," Carmine replied. "You can't give us tasks like we're servants here. Now put my people on the line immediately!"

"That will not be possible. And we all know how much you need this alliance. Comply and it will happen. The portal will open shortly. When it does, you will decide if you want to help your people, save them, and this alliance... or not. Then you can go home with the tragic news that you left the few to handle a job of the many."

"You must think we're insane," Carmine said. "To go into some bit of light that on your word happens to take us to our people? After you attacked us even!"

"That was a test."

Shitty test, Mary thought, since we tore them up. Maybe that's why they needed so much help. Because they couldn't defend themselves for shit.

"How many people died for it?" Carmine asked.

"None. Those ships were not under the control of living beings."

Carmine sighed. "Hold on." He turned to Milton. "Mute him."

"You may do so," Sslan said, "but know that the portal is still opening shortly. Regardless of what you talk about without me being able to hear."

"I can't," Milton said, "they came through... I don't even know how. They have control over the comms."

"Oh, yes." Sslan chuckled. It sounded like a dog barking underwater. "There is that."

"Okay then... What do you think?" Carmine asked Alistair. "Should we trust him?"

"Don't see as how we have much of a choice." Alistair shrugged. "We could send a message back to the fleet. Letting them know we're doing it."

"Without an FTL buoy?" Carmine asked.

Alistair said, "Sslan, you need to let us give word to our fleet so they don't send more people."

"You may," Sslan replied. "The appropriate equipment is available and it will send out whatever you wish. Make haste!"

"Milton, you heard him. Hurry." Carmine shook his head. "We'll do it, Sslan. Against our better judgment and if only to get back our people. But this isn't the best way to start an alliance."

"We think it is," Sslan said, "considering how many problems we had that could not be resolved on our own. Friends help one another. That is a doctrine of you humans, is it not? Your history suggests you strongly believe it. You will help us, and we will show our gratitude. Know that it is true. Future friends."

"Yeah, of course." Carmine rolled his eyes. "How long is this trip going to take?"

"For you," Sslan explained, "it will be a short time. However, you will want to ensure that you close all viewports. No screens. Nothing. Beings outside the

Raldor struggle when they look at the portal. It can be... disconcerting. Madness inducing, for your kind. The oddity of it cannot be accepted, explained, or understood."

"This keeps getting better and better," Mary said. "What's next? We'll have to wear blindfolds?"

"That's enough," Carmine said. "Alistair, get the message out to the rest of the ship. Have Engineering do what he said. Make it fast."

Sslan said, "Then I believe our business is concluded. We look forward to visiting with you after you have run our errands. Farewell."

The line dropped.

Mary said, "He laid it on a little thick. And that's not even talking about the weird close all your blinds comment."

"Too thick," Carmine said. "What exactly are we getting ourselves into?"

"What if," Heather replied, "there aren't but a handful of Raldor? Maybe this portal drove them all crazy. Hell, it could be that Sslan's the only one, right? We've always thought they were weird. We might just have the explanation for why. Beyond the fact they're a bunch of jelly tentacle things."

"I guess we'll find out," Carmine said. The light appeared ahead of them, much like the one the three ships came through. "Milton, did you get that message off?"

"I did, sir."

The viewscreen went down. Mary's terminal showed that all windows had been blocked off by exterior shutters. They were ready to proceed into something new… and potentially terrifying. She braced herself for the order. When he gave it, they'd be at the whim of a seemingly insane species.

And thrown to some part of the galaxy they didn't want us getting to on our own.

"Heather," Carmine took a deep breath, "take us in."

Here we go. Mary tensed up as the engines engaged. A thousand kilometers stood between them and the unknown. She had never thought of herself as an explorer, nor did she necessarily want to experience the farthest reaches of space. On the verge of something none of them even heard of, she had to admit she didn't mind the adrenaline rush.

Might not last if the ship can't take it. That thought dampened her spirits. At least it was something different. Best way to turn this frown upside down.

□

Chapter 5

Patrick sat on the bridge while Esher finished his sweep of the fuel center. The place became a mausoleum with a number of dead bodies. All EDF personnel. Scans of each of them might reveal their identities, but it didn't matter. They needed information straight from the computer system.

"You've got connectivity," Esher said, "download at will."

"Thank you." Patrick dragged over the logs from the last week. Trildair's destroyer definitely stopped there. He needed a trajectory for their departure, something he'd be able to trace and follow to the next stop. The fugitive's people didn't seem to know how to keep themselves from discovery.

Not when they left behind so much data. Enough to track them to the first place without any difficulty at all. As he read through the info, he stiffened. A ship docked there sent out a distress call. Shortly after, Trildair showed up. Probably to 'help.' Meaning someone likely became his unwilling guest.

Christ. They're dead.

"You need anything else?" Esher asked. "This place is a little disgusting."

"One last thing," Patrick replied, "check to see if they bothered to refuel before they left."

"Negative. No one's refueled here in months."

"Thanks. Get back aboard." Patrick brought up the buoy information. He gathered the coordinates sent to the device by the destroyer. Once again, he had to marvel at the brazen attitude of his quarry. The man did not care that he left a wake large enough for the worst tracker to follow.

But where exactly is he going that he doesn't care? Something doesn't add up. Or he genuinely is a moron and lacks any sort of self-preservation.

"Hey." Esher sat beside him with a sigh. "Everything's locked down and we're ready to detach when you are."

"I've got coordinates." Patrick turned to him. "What do you think? Why the hell would he let someone follow him?"

"I have two thoughts. One, he doesn't know better and so he's leaving a trail. Or two, he doesn't care because he figures we're all too busy dealing with the Veldon and the Zitha to bother hunting down one guy. Either one is scary in its own way."

"I don't know. I feel like he'd at least try to cover his tracks. Take out the buoy at the very least." Patrick frowned. "We need to check if he followed another beacon after this place. I'm thinking he's gathering some subjects after losing so much at the JTF base. Desperate people can't exactly fight back."

"Creepy," Esher said, "but likely."

"Yeah, I told you this guy's a son of a bitch." Patrick disengaged from the station. He put some distance between them and the structure. "Okay, on to the next place. Looks like they didn't go too far. Just an adjacent system. Likely just to be away from this place in case someone else came looking for fuel."

"He won't be there, right?" Esher asked. "I mean, it's possible that he's been sitting around there for several days, but unlikely."

"I don't expect to find him. But notice that he's gone from the station to an FTL buoy and then another one? He might be afraid to enter empty space. His people may not have the tech savvy to plot a course without the help of a buoy. Which gives us a major advantage. Limits his options."

"Big win for us, honestly." Esher checked the computer. "Two hours to our next destination. Damn, these little ships are fast. I had no idea. I wish we could've had a few of them when I worked in the MPs."

"Yeah, the JTF ships aren't this fast either." Patrick engaged the FTL drive. "We had to modify them ourselves to pull some additional performance out of them. Talk about a hassle. Then if you screwed it up, the techs got all pissy. But they were always too busy to help do it the right way."

"Bureaucracy, huh?"

"Don't I know it." Patrick motioned to the computer. "See if there's anything else interesting in that data. Maybe we can get some names or details about the people caught in the middle of that fiasco back there."

"Who do you think killed all those EDF guys?"

"Trildair, probably." Patrick shrugged. "The security cameras had been shut off a while ago. Which is fishy. Maybe the jackasses running the thing decided to go rogue. I don't know. Hard to say without good data. Even their logs are out of date."

"They might not have turned traitor," Esher pointed out. "They could've just been lazy. Lots of guys get sent there as a punishment."

"I know. But this goes beyond that. Especially now that they're all dead. Anyway, we're on our way. Let's see what we can turn up while we're in transit." Patrick engaged the FTL drive then started sifting through data. It promised to be a long two hours of pouring over some boring data.

He didn't mind.

***

Klaus had no idea how much time had passed. One of the side effects of Colm's experiments made it so such things didn't matter. Pain and suffering became distant echoes in his mind. Only extensive damage, or blood loss could stop him. Not that he didn't feel misery. He'd been conditioned to put it aside.

Trildair's methods involved a combination of isolation and torture. Hours of each. Opening nerves, introducing excruciating agony may have been enough to turn some people to whatever direction the torturer wanted. Klaus put on a proper show, giving them the visual they wanted.

He was only biding his time. They'd slip up eventually. Either believe the conditioning took or lower their guard. Every time they pulled him from the chair, he slumped, forcing them to drag him down the hall. It never felt like the right time to spring on them. If he did it too soon, if he couldn't escape, then they'd certainly kill him.

Colm drove him on. He couldn't die in Trildair's custody. That wasn't going to happen. Anonymous and alone in the middle of nowhere... it wasn't possible. Fate wouldn't allow it. In fact, he began to wonder if this encounter offered a step in the right direction. A chance to get close to his quarry.

If they were rescued, then he might find Colm. The EDF took the scientist with them when they came down for the Korlas person. Which meant he was hiding amongst the fleet somewhere. Just waiting to be killed. This kink, this stop on the path to killing the bastard, only delayed the inevitable.

Cole is likely already turned. Klaus had been thinking about the woman for several days. He knew she was tough, but the process Trildair used would be impossible to shrug off without some kind of defense. Maybe he's already killed her. She may have already broken down. Given up.

After a grueling session on the machine, they left Klaus in the cell for longer than normal. Whenever he came close to passing out, they'd come in to wake him or pump loud noise into the space. Exhausted, starved, and probably dehydrated, he understood how some people might be taken by the process.

Though he suspected they gave them nutrients before the start of the machine. Each time, they got an injection. Which told him they wanted to keep their prisoners alive though they didn't make it pleasant. The men who dragged him around the ship barely seemed alive. They never spoke, never deviated from their course from one place to another.

Had the process stripped them of their personalities completely? All the deprivation must have left them shells of their former selves. Lost beings under the control of a megalomaniac. Though Trildair probably didn't develop the conditioning process. He may have tweaked it, but this took skill.

Colm might have been able to do it. Though he went for a more eloquent approach. The conditioning his subjects experienced involved drugs. Those caused real pain. They altered synapses, removed certain instinctual responses. If Klaus hadn't thought so much about what he lost, he might not have been able to fake the suffering Trildair expected.

Pretending to be in agony proved harder than he anticipated.

It wasn't that he didn't feel the pain. It just didn't impact him the same after Colm's techniques. The suffering was there like a cramp or a knot. Impacted muscles became obvious. He found himself aware of parts of his body that he regularly took for granted. So the trick was to interpret those feelings appropriately.

He needed to put on the right kind of show.

What am I going to do when I escape? Klaus thought about Cole again. If she had been turned or killed, he was stranded on the destroyer. Maybe there's another prisoner. Someone newer without Trildair's baggage firmly in place. They'd be grateful for the save. However, we still need a ship.

Had they dismantled the one he and Cole arrived on? Or would it be there waiting? And could he get it started without her? She hadn't trusted him entirely. Another pilot might know a way. They wouldn't have a lot of time to escape before the guards descended on them. Worse, even if they got out, they might be destroyed.

Trildair will want us dead before he lets us get away. That didn't even take into account they might be traveling faster than light. Which meant they'd be stuck aboard until the destroyer slowed down. Maybe escape really is impossible. They've been saying it and I thought they were using hyperbole.

Some conditioning relied on the truth to turn the victim. Telling a person a fact they didn't want to hear may well break down them down faster than a well fabricated lie. He didn't want to believe. But if they had to rely on rescue, then he might be dead long before anyone had the skill or ability to breach the ship.

They were on a destroyer after all. What did that mean? Klaus didn't know much about military vessels or the JTF. They were cops, that much had been clear, but beyond that, he didn't know how they operated. He couldn't believe Trildair represented their values. The EDF would've shut them down a long time ago.

And the Korlas never seemed like they'd be okay with such things. Their culture seemed to be based on self-righteous indignation. And if they weren't solving the woes of the universe on their terms, they weren't living. He'd heard plenty of stories about how they approached problems.

They didn't have any qualms about killing everyone involved in a dilemma if it resolved the issue. He'd heard about slavers taking over colonies only to be totally annihilated. No trials, no arrests, no offers of amnesty. They would rather slaughter them and have investigators find others than grant a single criminal a chance to carry on.

I guess they don't believe in second chances. Or that people can change. Klaus found himself wondering about that. Has Colm changed since the experiment? The things he's done, maybe so. He's surrounded himself with different people. The EDF no longer tasked him with work. If he's changed...

"No!" Klaus shouted the word. He realized he'd been sitting still for nearly ten hours. His legs had long gone numb. His hands ached. Cold lumps covered his back, knots where he'd been leaning against the wall. When he cried out, the door opened. Two men stepped inside. They grabbed him by the shirt then commenced to beat him again.

The assault didn't register. He ignored it. Dull thumps against his chest, his stomach, and his face. Moving about at that moment seemed impossible. Their attack didn't matter. He'd survive. They always made sure to stop long before he passed out. After all, the constant noise around him, the lights and the buzzing, were meant to keep him awake.

"You have the strength." Colm's voice roused him from his reverie. He turned to the right. The scientist crouched, staring at him with his clinical gaze. Never once had he shown emotion for his subjects. Only cold, calculated interest. "What are you thinking about? Losing hope? Giving up?"

"Shut up," Klaus mouthed the words, letting his breath give them shape. "I have nothing to say to you. Not ever. Nor will I give you the power to talk for me while I'm in here. This is my place to suffer. You didn't concoct it."

"Of course not. It lacks any and all sophistication."

"You are jealous."

Colm chuckled. "Not remotely. In fact, I'm disgusted that this is what they're doing. I thought it would be something far more interesting. A brain parasite. Or some kind of injection. But no. Just standard punishment. Deprivation. They lack imagination if this is their answer to turning you."

"You don't know anything."

"I know plenty," Colm said, "and you do too. They're going to keep at you. After spending so much time attempting to turn you, it's a matter of pride now. And resources."

"Power," Klaus muttered, "and time. Hardly... valuable... resources..."

"Nothing is more valuable than time," Colm replied. "You of all people should know that. Otherwise, you wouldn't be so determined to kill me. Ironic, don't you think? You blame me for wasting years of your life, putting you through a great deal of suffering, ruining you... but the moment you are free to do as you please, you focus on me."

"Vengeance..."

"Obsession, maybe." Colm stood and paced. "You've spent more time hunting me than I spent changing you. But don't you think you owe me a little gratitude? All the things I've done for you warrants some appreciation. Maybe a fond memory or comment. Anything besides what you're doing."

"Gratitude?" Klaus wished he could laugh. "Are you serious?"

"How many of your little adventures would have killed you had it not been for me? My conditioning saved your life. Even now, you're enjoying the benefits."

"Fuck you."

"Oh, vulgarity. You always resorted to it. Don't you find some irony in the fact that instead of arguing with yourself, you've conjured a vision of me? That's not healthy, son. You shouldn't be speaking to a simulacrum of your enemy. Unless the reality is something too unsettling for your mind to embrace."

"Explain."

"Maybe I'm not the enemy," Colm said. "Perhaps you are your worst enemy. Driving you to this state. You've prevented yourself from living. Betrayed potential friends. Stolen. Become a criminal. How are you better than me, again? How do you deserve to judge me? Or even be my executioner?"

"Never thought I was better..." Klaus let his eyes close. "Never cared."

"You must a little or we wouldn't be talking."

"Hallucination. Caused by..."

"Trauma," Colm finished. "I know. You should be able to fight through it. But this isn't a hallucination. It's just you mulling things over in your mind. I happen to be the counterpoint to the conversation. The person asking you the hard questions you want to avoid. Because the truth is you've wasted your life and time hunting me."

"Almost got you."

"And that fueled the fire, didn't it? I was so close you could taste it. Your mouth was watering at the idea of putting me down. And yet, it was snatched away. You believe in fate. Why? Why would that happen if you were destined to kill me? I'd like to know what delusion you've come up with."

"Not... enough suffering... for you."

"Oh, you think I'm suffering? Off on some EDF ship? They didn't imprison me, that's certain. Right now, after Earth, they need every intelligent being to step up and help them. So you're wrong if you think your failure was meant to teach me a lesson. I think you're coming to realize you've made a mistake."

"Won't matter when I'm standing over your bloodied corpse."

"Tsk. You can be single-minded... except when you're not." Colm stopped pacing. He crouched in front of Klaus. "Perhaps you should consider something. If you kill me, what then? Do you die? Are you genuinely only living to slaughter another human being? Or do you have a post vengeance plan?"

"Never have. Don't think I'll start."

Colm nodded. "So if that's the case, then why not just end it now? Give in. Let them win. They can have your body. You'll help them destroy humanity. That includes me. And then you can die happy. Or at least a husk. Whatever they do to you. But wouldn't that be simpler? And it would certainly make sense."

"Go away!" Klaus roared the words. "Get the hell out of my head! God damn it, I have nothing to say to you! Go! Now!"

His outburst brought the guards. They descended on him for another beating. He welcomed it this time. Anything to drive Colm away. Or his thoughts. He had no idea which plagued him or if it was even real. But it didn't matter. The pain kept him focused on the moment.

The future didn't matter.

***

Three more stops. Three empty starships of varying sizes. From a small freighter to a passenger liner, Trildair kidnapped dozens of people as he rampaged through that region of space. But he always left a trail, the buoy consistently giving Patrick and Esher something to follow.

They headed toward the fourth stop, a quiet region with an abandoned EDF colony on the edge of the Zitha border. He may have been after supplies. Often those old settlements contained equipment, sometimes fuel. Scavengers generally couldn't risk such a trip, not when they traveled about on fumes.

"Got the numbers," Esher said. "That passenger ship had twelve people aboard besides the crew of four. The engineer fell ill. The engine broke down. That's what their distress call was all about. They had enough supplies to last them another four days, but I'm not sure who would get there in time."

Patrick nodded. "The others?"

"Couple people here and there. Prospectors, according to the ship manifest and ownership documentation. Bottom line, this Trildair freak took a lot of people. Won't be easy to save them all, boss. Not with this ship."

"If he's in custody," Patrick replied, "then we won't have to save them. They can help us take control of the destroyer and return it to the EDF. That'll be the only way this gets done." *Unless we just assassinate the guy. But even then, no one will contest us taking control of the vessel after he's dead.*

"Still, I do have a recommendation."

Patrick nodded. "Yeah?"

"When we find them, we tag the vessel with a transponder before we take any action. Send a coded message back to the fleet. That'll make it easier for them to track this guy if we fail." Esher paused. "Assuming you've considered the possibility this mission might not succeed."

I've thought about it. Patrick didn't want to voice his concerns. The fact they might not bring Trildair down felt monumentally unfair. The universe couldn't possibly throw such a curve at them. When it came down to it though, Esher was right. We're facing overwhelming odds. Which is my fault.

"Why didn't you requisition a team?" Esher asked. "I agreed to this knowing you didn't because after what Commander Weston said, this person needs to be taken down. Probably should've asked you this before we left. I'm hoping you've thought about this in a rational way and we're not operating on rage."

Patrick sighed. "I have been with the JTF for a while. Long enough to be accustomed to limited backup. We had task forces, teams to take down major targets, but those had to be government sized. Some of my hardest missions involved going undercover with only Eliza as support. And we brought down plenty of targets."

"So you think this is easier?"

"No." Patrick shook his head. "But familiar. This is what I've been trained to do. Not by the JTF, but through repetition. Missions. And while we're not going to build identities and breach the organization from the ground up, we are hitting them at home. It may be more tactical too. In the end, it's all the same. We take down a mark."

"Sure. I like your confidence." Esher leaned forward to check scans. "We're arriving at our destination. One minute."

"If he's there," Patrick said, "get the bend ready. They'll pick up something, but hopefully his people are too braindead to interpret it. I'm pretty sure he isn't watching the scans."

"You're counting on an advantage? Based on the intel from Chelsea Weston?"

Patrick nodded. "Yep. They had some guard wandering the hall there practically dragging his gun. Didn't say anything, didn't deviate, didn't change his speed. If any of the others are like that, then yeah, we've got an advantage."

Thinking about Chelsea made his cheeks burn. I didn't know about her proclivities. All the time I worked with her. We were partners for a long time. I thought for sure she felt the same way. When he talked to her on Sentinel, she made it clear she had eyes for someone else. Then she mentioned who, and he thought he'd been punched in the gut.

Some detective. Patrick kicked himself for that for a while. I should've known. No, really. I should have. It's not like there weren't signs. She played it close to her chest. Gotta give her credit for pulling that off. The revelation about her sexual preference helped him make the decision to go after Trildair alone.

Which he'd never tell Esher. Any other explanation would be invalidated.

"Here we go," Esher said. "You can disengage the FTL drive... now."

"Got it."

The ship groaned. The viewscreen flickered. A vast, empty system opened up in front of them. Patrick's heart dropped... then he saw it. A large vessel some hundred thousand kilometers away. Just sitting there near an asteroid. "Look!" He pointed. "Is that them? Get me a full scan!"

"I'm on it, hold on." Esher waved at him. He nodded after a moment. "That's what we've been tracking. They're here."

"Yes." Patrick slapped the seat. "Get our defenses online, and bend their scans. Make sure there's no power up either." If we came on this asshole just before he leaves again, I'm going to scream. Something told him, they only had one chance. Missing meant Trildair would go somewhere they couldn't follow.

Enemy space or farther than their ship's fuel reserves allowed them to travel. Five more minutes and we'll have a chance to chat. Patrick gripped the flight stick as he increased speed. I'll be sure to make it brief.

***

Trildair left the bridge to check on his experiments. The newest of them had been far more frail than he anticipated. Those he took from a passenger liner had barely a handful of guts between all of them. One died the moment they turned on the machine. Another suffered from a heart attack while the process was described.

Their captain had turned easily enough. Trildair kept him under observation to ensure he wasn't faking. They had a few tests to perform that would reveal any sort of deception. The few that worked out would bolster his numbers, ensuring the destroyer was defended against someone like Klaus getting free.

That led him to his prized possessions. Klaus might have possessed the strongest will of anyone he'd ever tried to turn. The man survived incredible punishment. He weathered beatings without a sound. He never asked questions, didn't bother to engage with his captors. He seemed to be biding his time.

I should kill him. Trildair weighed the benefits many times. The challenge stayed his hand. I want to make it happen. I can beat him. He doesn't have it in him to defy me forever. And when he comes around, I'll have a potent weapon. One that might even replace his precious Nihkal.

That fool should have left rather than gotten himself killed. Trildair hoped the Korla died. If not, he might have given up some serious information about their enterprise. Would it matter? Perhaps to the Uldarn. When I'd have a chance to see them. If they know about it, they might be cross.

Which would likely add one more notch against him. He hated the idea he might fail to achieve his destiny because one of his subordinates failed to die in an orderly fashion. All the drones were equipped with the appropriate measures to ensure they perished on command. Even the exceptional ones.

Though perhaps it doesn't work as well as the Uldarn would like. Trildair raged at the speculation. It won't matter until I find out the hard way. Perhaps watching some of the torture might settle his mind. He needed a distraction. The kind that involved screams. Perhaps Cole is ready for me.

He'd held off on having her physically though it had been hard. He wanted enough of her left to see the disgust in her eyes, the panic, the hatred, the fear. All those terrible emotions contorting her expression while her body willingly gave itself to her filled him with more excitement than the act of sex itself would.

Today's the day. Trildair headed for her cell. I'll have them prepare her. I believe she's on a downtime. But she'd been relatively catatonic for days. Barely moving, hardly speaking. Even her torture didn't result in the same agonized screams as the earliest of those experiences. I should have kept her stable and used her for something else.

Too late, he realized he didn't necessarily need her as a drone. A slave to his whims, on the other hand, seemed far more interesting. Perhaps one of the other prisoners might make up for her. Though he preferred the feistiness. Breaking someone traditionally required willpower. Not the sort of simpering idiots they took from the other vessels.

The ship listed briefly, the artificial gravity struggled with a whine. It corrected itself quickly enough, though Trildair pressed his hand against the wall to be sure they were safe. He hadn't felt something like that before. The exact nature of the problem eluded him. Was it because of a malfunction or did something get too close?

I'd call the bridge but those fools wouldn't likely know. It made him wonder if he should head up there himself. He'd only just left, but if there was a problem, he needed to direct his people. And this is why I miss Nihkal so much. I could've trusted him to resolve any issues like this.

His current brood followed orders to the letter. But they didn't exercise any sort of creativity, no drive to go beyond their commands. That was one of the reasons he wanted Cole and Klaus. He had more of them, but they died in the shuttles fighting that ridiculous EDF ship. I would've loved to get my hands on that.

Trildair waited a good two minutes before letting out a grunt. He turned around, heading back to the bridge. Whatever happened, he needed to get his eyes on it. Loyalty mattered. And he appreciated the fact he didn't have to worry about any of his people rising up against him. But there were times a little personality wouldn't have gone amiss.

The rank and file might have still been pliant. Though the information he had suggested any sense of self might lead to rebellion. Or at least questions. Then I'd have to watch my back. If they recovered their memories sufficiently, thought about how they got into their position, they may seek payback.

No, that's what the superior conditioning was meant to do. Create trustworthy, successful individuals. The hunters were one step below Nihkal. Nihkal had been a step below Trildair, though he still believed himself to be mostly in control of his own destiny. Whatever conditioning he experienced hadn't nearly been so bad as what he inflicted on others.

At least that's how he remembered it.

Guards stood by the door leading to the bridge. Neither of them so much as looked at him as he approached. He wondered how they would respond to an intruder. Would either of them even look up? Or would they stand there waiting to be slaughtered? Like the idiot protecting Chelsea Weston.

The programming is tricky. I have to trust it. I can't start to doubt them now. But he did doubt. And he worried. Because these were the only beings left to protect him. His JTF cover was blown. Those closest to him died. And he was all alone until he returned to the Uldarn. But I must not be empty-handed when I see them.

So long as the strange atmospheric disturbance was nothing more than an anomaly, he could get back to work. Before he ran out of time. And became expendable.

□

Chapter 6

Lyra enjoyed some private time on the bridge. She put her feet up on her console, leaving the scans on the viewscreen. With Zoe operating in the background, she didn't have a whole lot to worry about. If something crazy came up, the AI would provide ample warning. Making it possible for her to relax and read.

The others went to get some downtime. Barty got a clean bill of health from the medics, but he still felt tired enough for some sleep. Keppler helped him out with some kind of sedative. Chelsea and her father had some kind of heart-to-heart talk, probably with him explaining why he didn't bring the Pytheas to save her himself.

Then she'd tell him how she understood. A bunch of stuff Lyra didn't understand, though she had to respect. After what she did with Chelsea, at least. Much as they got along and proved compatible, there were still a few big differences. Mostly in the schmaltzy department about family.

Mary understood Lyra's perspective on their relationship. It kept her from getting too touchy feely about their past. They talked about a few things, cleared the air between them, but beyond hugging it out, they didn't do the whole no, it's me not you dance. Which made things a lot easier to stomach.

Maybe it came from the command structure thing. People taking on the role of officers. They felt the need to ensure everyone felt respected and understood. Partly from training, partly because that's just how they lived their lives. Chelsea talked about acting as the captain of her lacrosse team.

Or whatever rank system they had in that field. Lyra couldn't recall. But she knew Gareth held a similar title when he played sports too. Anything to pit one team against another. Those people turned into officers. Mary wanted to know why Lyra never pursued a job as a military officer.

It probably came down to the fact she didn't like team sports.

"Hey." Eliza's voice startled Lyra enough that she nearly fell out of her chair. "Oof. Sorry about that. I didn't mean to—"

"Don't worry about it," Lyra said. "I was in my own world. What's up? I thought you'd be sleeping or something."

"Couldn't." Eliza flopped in the pilot's chair. She'd been certified to take the helm on the Pytheas just before they left. Her license for the JTF counted, making her a good backup for Chelsea. "Just... been thinking. Too much probably. Are you nervous about where we're going? What we're doing?"

"Nah." Lyra shrugged. "After the other nonsense we've been through, this doesn't seem any crazier. If you talk to any of the others, they'd call it important. So there's that part of it too. We can enjoy a purpose." She smirked. "You don't look amused. Are you a true believer? Cause if so, I'll stop making fun."

"Not necessarily," Eliza said, "but I guess I understand where they're coming from. This is better than tracking down that Trildair guy with Patrick. I'm not sure if I would've been able to get behind that entirely. I probably would've wasted a lot of time trying to talk him out of doing it."

"You wouldn't have had any luck?"

Eliza scoffed. "Hell no. I knew the look on his face. He made up his mind and he intended to hit that place hard. Regardless of what it might cost him. Which I guess is why he didn't want me to go with him."

"He's planning on killing Trildair," Lyra said, "right?"

"Yep."

"Not a bad idea. Considering how busy everyone is right now. Who knows how long he'd sit around in a prison?"

"That's not the way we do things."

Lyra chuckled. "Believe me. I know."

"Yeah, I read your file. The EDF exonerated you for all your crimes. They've even talked to the Korlas to ensure they don't hold it against you. I guess you've stepped up for them… us, huh?"

"I guess so. After stealing the Pytheas to save Chelsea, I thought they'd feed me to the Korlas piece by piece."

"Why'd you do it?" Eliza asked. "Risk yourself like that."

"Didn't have a choice," Lyra replied. "She's a friend." A hell of a lot more than that, but I don't know this girl enough to confide in her. I'm not sure how Chelsea feels about the situation yet. "I'd do it for any of my crew members. That's how we do it out here. And yes, before you ask. Even the pirates."

"I wasn't going to," Eliza said. "But it's an interesting point."

"How did you and Patrick end up there?" Lyra frowned. "I heard you weren't even assigned to that station."

"He heard about Chelsea," Eliza replied. "Then we were off."

Lyra bit the inside of her lip. "Did they have a thing or something?"

"They were partners when they started at the JTF. Both of them hot out of the EDF." Eliza shook her head. "Part of why he coddled me, I'm sure, since I don't have the experience she did. I never thought much about it before, but it makes sense now. He respected a fellow soldier."

"Ah." Lyra nodded. "So they weren't like... an item, were they?"

"That part I'm not sure of. Just that they worked closely together. Thing I don't get is how they ended up in two different fields. She ended up hunting down pirates, mostly alone, while Patrick did undercover work. Looking into narcotics and weapon sales. I provided background support."

"Must've had some kind of falling out?" Lyra offered. "No, then he wouldn't have rushed to see what happened."

"I don't know. Maybe he thought he owed her. He's got a serious sense of duty. I like him. He's always been good to work with. But sometimes, he can be a real pain in the ass. Enough to be frustrating. Like this whole Trildair thing. There's no freakin' reason to go down this path."

"That's not necessarily true. He's got a serious sense of duty, and that guy was a real monster. I saw the dead expressions of those people onboard. I killed one of them. It was horrible. And maybe Patrick... I guess he knows that right now, there are people out there who aren't going to find much help from the authorities."

"Because of the fighting." Eliza nodded. "That makes sense. Horrible, but it makes sense."

"Definitely. And who knows where he plans to take his victims? Back to where we're going? Somewhere worse? Or does he want to infiltrate more organizations? It's hard to say. But wherever they might end up, at least with Patrick on the guy's ass, any victim might still stand a chance of recovery."

"You want him to be noble?"

Lyra chuckled. "I'm not that woman. I'm learning to care about what we're doing. You know, piracy isn't the most positive thing in the universe."

"Why did you get into it? You don't seem like a bad person. What would've compelled you to… break the law?"

"I hate authority," Lyra said, "and I didn't like being told what to do. That's the super short version, but it sums it up perfectly."

"You were EDF before, right?"

Lyra nodded.

"And your sister, she's with the EDF. How could you leave her behind for this? Wouldn't your decision have had an impact on her?"

"No. Lucky for Mary. Not that she needed it. She could've risen above anything I did. Besides, we had no contact for five months prior to my discharge. She never visited me when I spent time in jail. Never talked to me while I was off doing illegal stuff. So for all intents and purposes, I gotta say… she did the right thing."

"But she's family."

Lyra lifted a brow. "You got family members you worry about? I'm guessing not."

"No... I was an only child. My mom was single. She passed before I finished school."

"Family is always more important to people who have little to none." Lyra chuckled. "Which means I should feel the same as you, I guess. Well, I'm a terrible person trying not to be. I'll be the first to admit I've got a long way to go."

"I guess I'm lucky in a way," Eliza said. "I didn't lose anyone close to me on Earth. When I met people on Sentinel, and I saw how it impacted them... I felt guilty for being relieved. That I didn't experience what they did. The way they looked when they talked about it, and how they suffered... maybe I'm a terrible person too."

"Nah." Lyra waved her hand. "Survivor's guilt doesn't count. You should've talked to one of the shrinks. I think it would've helped."

"Did you?"

"I... don't really like talking to professionals. That was another strike against me when I was in the military. You don't have a choice but to visit them once in a while. And what was worse, I got in enough trouble that I had extra sessions to get through. All of that contributed to my attitude."

"Why'd you join the military? You must've known it wasn't suitable."

"We didn't have a lot of choice. I didn't have any prospects. Both of us needed to pick some government service so I went with the military. Mary followed. She ended up loving it and I..." Lyra shrugged. "Ended up a wanted criminal pursued by your organization until Chelsea finally caught up with me."

"Quite a path." Eliza sighed. "What do we do when we get to where we're going?"

"Recon mission. If this was any other ship, I'd say we hop in, grab some scans, and get the hell out. But since it's the Pytheas, and we've got terrible luck when it comes to things being 'routine,' I'm sure we'll all have to do something. You're all about support, right? Computers, piloting, etc.?"

"Yep."

"You'll get along with Zed. I'm glad we've got someone who can do a little shift work. Give people a chance to relax. The question is whether or not we'll have to go to the surface somewhere. I'm guessing we'll need to perform an investigation. At the very least, get a look at a structure or city."

"I hope not. Last time I landed ended up being the worst night of my life."

"When I got jettisoned from the station..." Lyra shivered. "Yeah, I know what you mean."

"Actually," Eliza said, "yours is worse. Hey, I'm sorry for barging in here like this. Just dawned on me you might've been enjoying some downtime. I should've asked."

"No big deal. I'm glad to have a chance to chat. I thought we'd have more time when we were sitting around Sentinel. Turns out everyone found a way to stay some kind of busy." Lyra glanced at the screen again. They were getting close to crossing the border. Once they did, they'd be dropping out of FTL some thirty minutes later. "Getting close."

"Wow. Have you ever entered Veldon space before?"

"Nope." Lyra sent a message to the others, letting them know how close they were. "It's easier to be a criminal when you look like the people you're stealing from. Hijacking Veldon stuff, even their merchant class vessels, can be tricky. They have a lot of firepower on those, and the civilians are still way bigger than us."

"I haven't seen one in person before."

"We ran into them at the embassy near the border," Lyra said, "gotta be honest, it had been my first time seeing them hostile. I'd gone to places where they'd been taken prisoner. Which was no small feat. I heard they'll usually fight to the death. I never did find out how the people caught one."

"Yeah, I'm glad we don't police the Veldon."

"Maybe," Lyra said, "it might come to that someday. What if the Veldon fell prey to the Uldarn the same as the Zitha? Then their forces were forced to run out to fight. They attack Earth, which we construe as revenge for the war. This buys them time to use their new force to track down the scientists."

"So what do you think we'll find? A resistance?"

"Nothing's impossible." Lyra shrugged. "And if we do, then we might just have another ally. Would be weird. And hopefully people can get over what happened. They should, considering they were likely manipulated in a major way." She paused. "Like what Trildair almost did to Chelsea."

"I hadn't considered the possibility of finding benevolent Veldon." Eliza hummed before turning to Lyra again. "Would make this trip a lot easier, wouldn't it? If we didn't have to fight or struggle with them? Just... make friends. Show them that we're trying to fend off the Uldarn too... save the universe."

"Now you've got some ambition." Lyra grinned. "I like it. And think about this. How grateful will the universe be when we save it, hmm? Can we expect some decent compensation? Maybe a nice retirement package on one of the older Korlas planets? The ones that are basically resorts with endless resources."

"I've never even seen one of those."

"Oh, they're to die for. Seriously. There was one I visited before I met Barty. Just after I left the military before I turned to a life of... well, crime. And I blew most of the savings I had there. It was absolutely amazing." Lyra winced. "Until the end when there was a brawl... and a shootout... and a lot of yelling. But that's not the point of the story."

"Just that it was nice until you screwed it up?" Eliza chuckled. "Is that it?"

"Yeah, that's also the story of my life in a nutshell, so well done."

Gareth stepped onto the bridge. "Hello, ladies. Thanks for the message. So what've we got? Another half hour?"

"About that," Lyra said. "We're close. We'll pass their outer defenses, but according to Zed and Zoe, we won't trip them. Not until we leave FTL."

Eliza tilted her head. "Shouldn't they pick up FTL travel still?"

Gareth replied, "We have ways around that with the Pytheas." He took a seat. "Let's check all systems. Make sure we're a hundred percent. I don't want any surprises when we get there." He tapped the comm. "Zed, report to the bridge. Barty, I need you in Engineering. Bring Ithila with you."

So much for relaxing. Lyra started the diagnostic application. Time to be serious. She looked forward to seeing Veldon space in person. Not many of her peers on either side of the law could say that. Won't be the bragging rights it might've been a year ago. But it will be fascinating.

If they made it back alive to talk about it.

***

Barty popped his armor on, standing up straight as it covered his body. The helmet stayed off, which was a new addition to his personal routine. Another tap would bring it online. He also added sensors to ensure if something unexpected happened, the armor would protect the wearer by overriding the preference.

"Nicely done," Ithila said. "I appreciate your consistent attempt to improve the product."

"Yeah, well…" Barty shrugged. "We're done with everything else so might as well keep busy." He'd been introspective after the medical bay. Between saving Eliza and nearly dying himself, he wasn't sure which created the most anxiety. If she had died and he survived, he knew it would've been worse.

"I downloaded all the KIS data concerning the Veldon border. It's unsurprisingly thin. Our people haven't properly gathered data in months. I had hoped we would go in with something. I hate being blind here. That said, beyond their attack on the colony that resulted in the destruction of your embassy, they have been relatively quiet."

"Beside sweeping our planets?" Barty asked.

Ithila cleared his throat. "Yes."

"It's okay. I get what you meant. I'm a little raw still about what happened on the surface."

"I'm sorry I left you," Ithila said. "I thought you would've had a clear shot to the landing zone."

"If you had stayed then you might be dead. Or all of us could be. I think you did the right thing."

"I appreciate that." Ithila approached. "So we're good?" He extended his hand. "I've been concerned."

"You visited me in the medical bay." Barty shook his hand. "Relax about it, brother. We've been through enough together to know you didn't do something on purpose. Besides, everything we're doing is risky these days. The ambassador and Bryce both..." He sighed. "Anyway, I'm sorry about getting mopey. Just sayin', it's all good."

"Thank you." Ithila jabbed his thumb over his shoulder. "Do you want to be on the bridge when we arrive?"

"Nah, I think I'll stay back here in case they need me to do something." Barty approached one of the monitors. "Besides, I can patch in from here. Watch the situation unfold. You can hang out here too. In case I need help. Unless you think you'll do better on the bridge."

"Can I ask you something? About your past."

Barty nodded.

"You were a criminal. But you're not now. And I don't expect you'll be going back. Is that true?"

"Nah, I'm back in the EDF. They expunged my record. I'm a hundred percent onboard with them."

"Understood." Ithila frowned. "But what about Lyra? When this is over, if she leaves the organization, what will you do?"

"Lyra saved my life," Barty said. "And I've done the same for her. She's a friend. I like her. But we've had this talk. Sort of. If she doesn't stay with the EDF, then we're going to part ways. I'm really hoping she makes the right call though. I've got confidence since she's so close to Chelsea."

"Do you think she might return to a life of crime?"

"Maybe. If she and Chelsea have a falling out, I could see it. But then there's Lyra's sister too. Mary has some influence. Why do you ask?"

"Because you're both excellent assets," Ithila said, "and I have spoken to my superiors about something."

"Uh oh."

Ithila chuckled. "It's not bad. We are extending the reach of the KIS. We are admitting humans into the ranks. Not anyone, of course. But you and Lyra are both admitted. If you would like to be. I would take Chelsea and the Commander as well, if they are interested. Perhaps even Zed."

"The whole crew, huh?"

"You know each other. Work well. I think it is important to keep teams together when they can deliver."

Barty asked, "What's the KIS like to work for?"

"We have a lot of room to do the right thing. A general objective is presented. Then we go about making it happen. That's why I like the idea of working with the two of you. It should not cause Lyra any sort of bristling since I know she isn't one for taking orders. Not much anyway."

"No, you're right about that." Barty loved the idea. If he went back to the EDF after the conflict, he probably wouldn't be assigned anything too important. Not with his rank and past. They may have expunged the record, but enough people were in the know to limit his options. The KIS would be a fresh start. "I like the idea."

"Good. What will it take for you to accept?"

Barty narrowed his eyes. "Is my involvement contingent on Lyra?"

"Absolutely not. I merely told you about her because you're friends. Close, if I may say. I understand about the life debts you both share. Seems like you'd have the opportunity to pay some of them off. And of course, accrue some more. Our business is not light. We get into enough trouble to require violence."

"You have an interesting way of saying it."

"May I be frank?" Ithila asked.

"Go for it."

Ithila pursed his lips. "We intend to requisition the Pytheas. I would like to keep Commander Weston on as the custodian and leader. But we want to use this vessel for some of our operations. It is suited. Until we can build more. As of right now, I'm not sure anyone has the precise understanding of how to do so."

"Probably not. I think the EDF is pretty excited about having this too."

"Indeed." Ithila smiled. "But my people are persuasive. And right now, your command structure enjoys our assistance. We can negotiate many things. But this is payment for the overall service. Not to sound mercenary, but we've got a lot of space to cover. This vessel moves quickly."

"Cool. Way above my pay grade though. I won't talk about that part to anyone."

"You may, if you wish," Ithila replied. "It doesn't matter. That said, if you would like to present the idea to Lyra, I would appreciate it. I'm not sure how to approach her yet. Or talk to her about important things. She... represents many human traits I'm not entirely comfortable with when it comes to conversation."

"Like what?"

"Forceful. Direct. A little harsh. Our women can be those things, but they do so in a different manner."

Barty laughed. "I'll just bet. Yes, I'll talk to her about it. Maybe Chelsea too. Though I'm thinking you could just address the whole ship at some point if you wanted. Talk to them all about it. See what happens."

"I hadn't considered it. But I will. Thank you."

"No problem." Barty stretched. "But you know the next question, right?"

"No..." Ithila frowned. "What is it?"

"Payment, man. What's the compensation like?"

"Fair and more than generous. We also have salvage rights to many of our discoveries. I've done quite well for myself as a result. I don't have a lot of time to spend anything either, so it's all put away. Waiting to be used when I decide to stop working in this line of business. Which I think we all need to consider."

"Someday," Barty replied. "I'm a hundred percent in. This sounds way better than anything else I've ever done. Working for the spy agency. Gotta say, it beats piracy. And guard duty by a damn long shot." He shook Ithila's hand. "Thank you for bringing it up. You made my shift."

"I'm glad." Ithila gestured to the monitor. "It appears we've got some activity. Are we about to leave FTL?"

"Yep." Barty set the screen to mirror the bridge visual. It flickered while waiting for them to emerge. When it finally came on, empty space appeared. Distant stars seemed to flicker against a black backdrop. "I'm both disappointed and relieved. I half thought we'd appear in the middle of a Veldon fleet."

"And you're disappointed we didn't?" Ithila asked. "Are we in the right place?"

"Lyra's damn good at navigation. If this is where she set the course, then we made it." Barty leaned against the wall. "Zed should be up there running scans in a moment." He turned to Ithila. "If this is what we have to look forward to, maybe you'd be more comfortable on the bridge after all."

"Nah." Ithila waved his hand. "There's no point. Might as well remain on hand. Just in case."

Barty nodded then returned his attention to the screen. He doubted much would happen. Not for a while. The Pytheas needed to explore the system. Scan the area. Find out where the Veldon went. Or maybe they aimed for an adjacent territory so they could slip in quietly.

Whatever the case, he doubted they'd need him for a while.

***

Chelsea relieved Eliza for the helm position. The young lady moved over to one of the other terminals to provide backup for Zed. As they dropped out of FTL, the screen came on revealing a whole lot of nothing. That had been unexpected. Even aiming for quite a bit of distance between them and the Veldon, they should've seen something.

"Full scan coming shortly," Zed said. "There's a habitable planet in the fourth position around the star. Looks like it was an outpost. Ten settlements. No life signs yet." He clicked his tongue. "That doesn't make any sense. The colonies we lost to the Veldon still had people on them. What happened here?"

"Bombardment," Eliza said. "Looks like orbital strikes from multiple battlecruisers at least based on the devastation. Or one that had plenty of time to hit them for the better part of two hours." She turned to them. "Plenty of debris in orbit as well. I think some of it might have come from a space station."

"First up," Gareth said, "send word back to the fleet with our exact position. Give them the coordinates of that world and include your initial scan data."

"I'm on it," Zed replied. "Shouldn't be long."

"Good." Gareth stepped over to Chelsea. "Set a course for that planet. I want a closer look." He pointed at Lyra. "Put us on ready defense. Weapons, shields. Make sure we're ready to go in case this is a trap."

Why would it be? Chelsea wondered. It's not like anyone knows we're coming. There's no way they anticipated some random ship from the EDF would show up waiting to be attacked. Couple that with the state of the place. The amount of damage and devastation suggested nothing survived.

"Zed," Gareth asked, "how's the environment? Can anything live down there?"

"Well..." Zed sighed. "Some patches are pretty rough. Radiation levels are high over a couple of the settlements. Signs suggest power stations exploded, causing most of the damage. It'll impact the whole planet soon. If anything's alive down there, it can't be doing well. The computer estimates it's got about a week before the atmosphere's toast."

Chelsea asked, "And that's a Veldon colony down there?"

"This," Gareth said, "is where we conducted negotiations during the war. Our people came to this system. No one went to the planet's surface though. Everything took place out here in open space. They had a space station out here as well."

"Wait," Lyra replied, "you made it seem like we were going somewhere we'd never been before. That we blew past the border. Why didn't we meet closer?"

"This is where they felt the most comfortable," Gareth explained, "don't forget, they basically lost the war. Our government didn't want to obliterate them. Everyone hoped we might form an alliance with them. Start on a proper foot. Instead, we ended up with a cessation of hostilities agreement."

Chelsea added, "We found ourselves at an impasse with them fast. Despite the fact they lost, they still had a lot of pride."

"Of course," Lyra snorted. "If any of those diplomats are alive today, I bet they're kicking themselves for giving up. Or feel like idiots for holding back the military. Imagine how different it all would've been if we hadn't stopped."

"It wouldn't," Chelsea said. "The Uldarn would've found someone else. Maybe the Korlas."

"Excuse me," Zoe replied, "it seems to me that the Uldarn picked the Veldon because they were a culture in distress. Same with the faction of the Zitha they abused. Perhaps they've been waiting for this opportunity for a long time. Watching from the shadows until the right time to come out."

The ship drew nearer to the planet. A red grid fell over the planet with flashing blue dots appearing at various points. Zed pointed out that they represented higher life signs. Some Veldon. The others, he hesitated to say until he double checked the data. As he hovered over his terminal, Zoe spoke up.

"They are human."

"What?" Gareth asked. "How? What do you mean?"

"Yeah," Lyra added, "how would they even get there?"

"Something to ask them," Zoe replied. "There are five humans in one of the settlements and eight Veldon in the same vicinity. Grand total number of Veldon lives over the surface of the entire planet equals less than forty. Based on facilities and the size of the towns that are now mostly lost, I estimate over ten thousand of them lived here before."

"Whoa..." Eliza finally spoke up. "What happened here to kill so many of them? Who could have done it?"

"The Uldarn," Gareth said, "or even other Veldon. Same as the Zitha. Why this place?" He tapped his chair. "Possibly because they had more contact with other cultures, even though we didn't visit the planet. We talked to them. Offered resources. Who knows? It's all speculation until we get those humans out of there."

Lyra asked, "Do we know they want to leave?"

"What?" Chelsea scoffed, "of course they do! That planet's dead! If they don't get out of there, they'll all die."

Lyra shrugged. "We have no idea. They might have come willingly."

"We'll find out." Gareth stood. "Zed, attempt to contact them."

"Scans show tech," Zed replied, "but they don't have anything to receive our communications."

"I say we put down," Lyra said. "Let's have a look. Maybe we'll find evidence of those vibration weapons. Either they'll be using them or we might find some lying around."

"Seconded," Chelsea added. "Regardless of what we find, we have to get the humans out of there." Though I'd like to know what they're doing here. Were they abducted? Or are they traitors? Both seemed highly probable. After the JTF situation, she didn't put anything past her own kind.

"Alright," Gareth said. "Take us down." He tapped the comm on his chair. "Keppler, take a look at the atmospheric reports. You might need to help some people who suffered from radiation poisoning. Or something worse. Get acquainted with the problem before we bring them to you."

"Great," Keppler grumbled, "can't wait."

Gareth stood. "Barty, Ithila, you're with me. The rest of you will stay in reserve. Let us check it out before we commit anything else to the situation."

Chelsea spun in her chair. "Begging your pardon… but wouldn't it be better if you stayed here? I can lead the ground team."

"I…"

"Remember," Chelsea interrupted, "you're in command. We kinda need you running the plays, right?"

Lyra snorted. "More sports nonsense. I love it."

"Alright, Chelsea." Gareth waved at her to follow him into the hallway. "Eliza, take over the helm. Take us in to the south side of the settlement. Prepare for landing."

Once they were in the hall, Chelsea started to speak. He waved her quiet.

"Better that you ask for a private talk," Gareth said, "than throw that out in the middle of the bridge."

"This isn't exactly a normal EDF ship, Dad. We've been through a lot together. I'm not sure we need to be—"

"Disciplined?" Gareth asked. "Courteous?"

"Come on, really? You weren't that bent out of shape, were you?"

"It's not about that just... make sure we talk about this kind of thing in private." Gareth scowled into her eyes. "Maybe I didn't want you to go after what happened with the JTF. Having you safe on the ship—"

"Stop it. I'm not here to be safe. Anyway, after what happened to you at the JTF station... I started to worry too."

"Fair point." Gareth clapped her on the shoulder. "Cheeky ass. Let's get this done. Head down to cargo and prepare to disembark."

"Got it." Chelsea gave him a half-hearted salute. "Thought you might like a little more disrespect."

"Go." Gareth walked away. "Just get."

Chelsea ran into Barty and Ithila along the way. She gave them a quick briefing before they arrived in the cargo bay. She kicked on the armor then grabbed a rifle. Their equipment provided environmental protection, even against concentrated radiation. At least for a good hour or two.

Those humans are going to be screwed, Chelsea thought. I don't know how they've survived as long as they have. She hoped they had some answers. If the Veldon maintained any presence in their territory, they'd probably be along soon. It seemed doubtful though, unless they were the ones who bombarded their own colony.

Wouldn’t be a huge surprise.

□

Chapter 7

Kensington went over Gareth's reports again. He skimmed them before, mostly gathering the larger details. With Sentinel seemingly under control, he turned his attention to addressing his backlog. Which meant going over nearly a hundred log entries from various departments.

No wonder Gaston was exhausted all the time.

The casualty report came up. Gareth posted the various people he worked with who died between Earth and meeting up with the EDF. Sergeant Bryce Dryer died in the line of duty. He was listed as an embassy bodyguard who joined Gareth after they were captured by criminals at a compromised fuel depot.

Ambassador Nila Chance was also listed. She died at the fuel depot while attempting to gather data which proved invaluable to the EDF efforts. He'd never met her before, though it turned out she had plenty of contacts in the intelligence division. Enough to explain how she acquired the information.

Gareth listed the known criminals they fought as well. Two of them escaped and their names combined with the ambassador's made Harold freeze. He stared at the screen for a good five minutes, unable to move. A chill washed over him. The man's name was Alfred Toombs.

His accomplice was known only as Ethyl.

They were responsible for Nila Chance dying. The destruction of a JTF ship as well as the fuel depot. They attempted to murder Gareth and his team before fleeing the area with sensitive data. Which they turned into verifiable and convincing identifications. That of Alfred Chance and Ethyl Crane.

God damn it.

"Why?" Harold said aloud. "Why kill the ambassador then assume her identity? Why help us?" He couldn't deny the fact that Alfred managed to get them two major allies with his efforts, one of which should have been impossible. What compelled him to have a change of heart? Why?

"Sir?" Reggie came in.

"I have to tell you something," Harold replied. He pointed at the screen. "You won't believe this."

"There's a problem on Sentinel?"

Of course there is. Harold sighed. "What is it?"

"Some kind of violence broke out. Civilians attacking our people. It's crazy."

"Are they containing it?" Harold asked. "Are the Zitha getting stirred up?"

"Comms are down to the surface," Reggie explained. "But I've spoken with Ghrenda. They aren't going to take action against our people. They're letting us pacify the situation. So far, it's going okay. But I think we should send additional forces down immediately."

"What gave it away?"

"A building exploded," Reggie said. "And one of our tech guys caught on to the weapons fire while he was doing a routine scan. So… there's that."

"Send people," Harold replied, "however many you feel is necessary. I'll let Bracknel know." He ran his hand through his hair. "Then hurry back. Because we've got another issue outside of what's happening down there." Potentially worse, maybe. I don't know. I'm not sure what to think.

Reggie hustled out of the room. Harold sent a quick message to Bracknel, letting him know to keep his shuttle in orbit or to fall in with Ghrenda's ship. There was no reason for them to head down right away without each other. Once the violence was placated, they could commence with their conversation.

Harold planned to be late to the affair. The start of the meeting promised to be a formality. Each side offering up praise to the other cultures. He hated that kind of thing, which made it easier to be thankful for Bracknel. Regardless of how people felt about him, he'd been in politics long enough to be a proficient ass kisser.

Understood, Bracknel wrote him, I'll trust that you're doing everything in your power to help. When you can, you should come down early now. That way, we can give you the credit for what you've done. Humbly, of course. So the Zitha don't feel like they should have stepped up. Maybe get yourself ready sooner.

"Son of a bitch. That's what I get." Harold grunted as he stood. His dress uniform had been pressed and prepared, white on top of black trousers. He pulled it on and started the process while waiting for Reggie. I hope they can get down there in enough time to make a difference.

He finished buttoning himself up when Reggie burst in again.

"Good timing," Harold said. "Is everything in order?"

"Yes, sir. They're on their way."

"Excellent. How many did you decide to send?"

"There's a balancing act," Reggie replied, "because if we sent too many, it would look like we didn't have confidence in our troops. Too few, and they couldn't get the job done. I elected to send thirty."

"You think that's enough?"

"It looks like we're doing okay down there. Thirty more will provide reasonable security boosts. I think we'll be fine."

"Okay, I'll leave that to you." Harold sat at his desk. He spun the monitor around for Reggie. "Read that information."

Reggie's eyes twitched as he absorbed the data. His brows lifted. He met Harold's gaze. "Are you kidding me?"

Harold shook his head. "What the hell am I supposed to do with that?"

"I… have no idea. The information tracked. We made sure of it. We triple-checked them both."

"The guy's good. And a murderer." Harold leaned back in his seat. "I'd like you to look into Alfred Toombs. We have access to the JTF and Korla databases. Find out everything you can. Then send it to the Patton. They should know. I'm sure you can guess where I'm going with this information."

"You don't think he stole the ship, do you?" Reggie asked. "Why now? After getting the Likari and the Zitha on our side. That doesn't make any sense!"

"I don't know, but they've been out of contact for a damn week. I want the information. We need to know what we're dealing with."

"Understood." Reggie shook his head. "Damn that guy. I'm stunned, sir. Seriously."

"It's not on you. If your tech people didn't catch him, then he's good. We'll figure out how he did it and shore things up. In the meantime, make sure you warn them." Harold gestured. "In fact, use my terminal. We don't have time to waste." He paced away, standing in front of the window.

Everything looked peaceful out there. Ships bunched together to perform various tasks. Cataloging resources found on Sentinel or performing repairs. Civilian ships and military, Zitha, Korla, and Likari all together. If not for the Raldor, the Veldon and the random violence on the surface, Harold might have believed they found peace.

Whoever is responsible for the attack on the surface needs to be dealt with harshly. Harold dreaded a real crime. He had no desire to sentence someone to execution. We won't have a choice when we catch this person. Another Aevers, I suppose. Unless he happened to set something in motion before his death.

Harold had only met him briefly. He seemed like a reasonable man back then. A solid officer, in fact. Of course, they were enemies with the Zitha then. Fighting them masked prejudice, turned it into patriotism. Gaston talked about the trouble with peace. They trained to kill then expected everyone to switch off the hatred necessary to be good at it.

"Message sent," Reggie said. "I'm not sure how long it'll take to get to them. Or for them to respond. I checked the coordinates. Meeting up with the Raldor required our people to go pretty far."

Harold nodded. "Keep me informed. When you hear from them, let me know right away." He gestured for the door. "I'm expected to head down to the surface earlier than I anticipated." He paused. "You'll be in charge while I'm gone, Reggie. I'll send out a message to let everyone know."

"Whoa, what?"

"While I'm gone," Harold said. "I trust you."

"I'm... not exactly..."

"Don't lose confidence now." Harold clapped him on the shoulder. "You've got this. Besides, the real trouble's on the surface. With the reinforcements you sent, that'll be resolved soon enough. Then we're back to the business of dealing with the real aggressors. And finishing our investigation."

Reggie walked with him as they started toward the hangar. "Whoever started all this internal nonsense..." He lowered his voice. "They're responsible for Gaston. Don't you think?"

"I don't doubt it. Though I'm hesitant to make that guess without evidence. Maybe when we find the mastermind behind the attack, we'll finally have some answers." Though I'm not counting on it. Whoever put this in motion isn't on the surface. They're safely tucked away on one of those peaceful ships out there.

Watching the carnage. Waiting for the next time.

"We have to stop them," Reggie said. "If I have to set up a real task force from all the different cultures, I'll make it happen. I'm tired of having to worry about internal problems when we've got a real threat on the outside."

"Start putting it together," Harold replied. "Get them working as soon as possible. When the dust settles and we've got prisoners, they'll need to get down there to interrogate them. Find out everything they can. Any investigation will have to be nimble. Who knows who might be down there to cover things up?"

"Understood." Reggie motioned behind him. "I'm heading back to the bridge to make that happen. Good luck with your work on the surface."

"Thanks." Harold bit his tongue to hold back some snark. I should be helping him coordinate our people to find the perpetrators down there. Instead, he'd be sitting on a shuttle, potentially outside any sort of communication range. Maybe even a target if the mastermind behind the attack found access to the weapons on a larger ship.

That was a level of conspiracy he didn't feel comfortable indulging. Even paranoia had its limits.

***

Rivo left behind the tranquil scene, into one of rubble and dead bodies. He recognized some of the corpses. They were unarmed, people caught up in the crossfire with the rebellious assholes causing trouble. One of the faces made him stop. He dropped down beside the woman, touching the side of her neck.

Though the way her eyes stared into the sky, he knew she'd been gone for a while. A large stone had crushed her pelvis, pinning her to the pavement. He hoped she'd died quickly. Lingering there with all the gunfire going off would've been a terrifying way to go. Bleeding out... unable to move...

Rivo closed her eyes before standing again. He couldn't remember the woman's name. She went around to the different worksites, providing food for those who couldn't leave for whatever reason. There was no way she'd been amongst the attackers. She was truly an innocent.

The carnage littered amongst the street ahead told plenty of horrible stories, lives snuffed out and left to rot in the sun. Rivo proceeded, drawing his weapon as he walked. The next half hour would likely see a lot more dead. Victims of some ideology he didn't understand. Nor had he heard anything about it.

Not a mutter, nor a whisper. Rivo couldn't remember anyone lingering in small groups to discuss their plans. No one told him about any meetings or gatherings that seemed suspicious. He couldn't fathom how the attack even started without some coordination. But maybe that wasn't the point of the affair.

They might be a distraction. The thought probably occurred to all the military people as well. If so, then they must be working on a plan to counter the next phase of the assault. Whatever that turns out to be.

Something extreme, probably. Hell, they already brought down a building. Why not the whole settlement?

"Freeze!" The voice made Rivo jump. It came from behind him and to the left. "Put the gun down!"

"You're giving people a chance to surrender?" Rivo asked. "Who are you?"

"Wait, what? Rivo?" A man approached, one of the civilians. He looked familiar. "You shouldn't be out here, man. This isn't something you want any part of. Believe me."

"Why? Who put you on this path? What the hell's your name again, anyway?"

"Chancy," he replied. "Don't you remember? I worked with you and Trivak on the comm tower for the starport when we first got here."

"Oh... shit." Rivo nodded. "Chancy, what's going on?"

"Revolution, brother!"

Rivo blinked. "Uh... what?"

"You heard me, man! Revolution! We're throwing off the chains."

"Which chains are they?" Rivo asked. "Specifically."

"They're driving us to give in to those oppressors. The raiders. Wait. Aren't you in on this? Hell, I would've thought you were the one that organized this!"

"Uh… why would you imagine that? I've been working my ass off. Way too hard to be telling you jackasses to start some kind of crazy ass coup. Shit, you know that a bunch of us died pulling this caper? Someone cut the comms, but that won't help. The military will figure it out and send overwhelming numbers down here. And then—"

Chancy's head burst.

Chunks of meat splashed Rivo in the face, stinging his eyes. He fell on the pavement, a rock digging into his lower back. Footsteps came running toward him, metallic clattering on the stone. He squinted in their direction. They were blurs, two men in full body armor. The security forces.

"Freeze!" They both aimed their weapons at him.

"Whoa!" Rivo shouted. "I'm good! I'm with you!"

"Looks like one of these pricks. Just shoot him."

"Hey!" Rivo waved his hands. "C'mon! I'm good! That other guy was out here causing trouble, not me. Can we please take a step back? Calm the hell down?"

"Contact!" The soldiers opened fire.

Rivo tensed, screaming as flashes lit up the street a few feet above his head. A firefight broke out. More cries of pain filled the air. A body fell over his legs, someone heavy. He kicked at them, shuffling away before a pair of hands dragged him to his feet. He swayed, struggling to maintain his balance.

"Hey!" a woman cried out. "Rivo?"

"Yes..." Rivo wiped blood from his eyes. "Who the hell are you?"

"It's Nelly. You know... I'm the workers' clerk?"

She's the lady assigning people to manual labor. Sending them all over the settlement. I can't believe this woman's part of the damn revolution. Rivo peered at her, blinking until his vision cleared.

Filth covered her pale face, chunks of mud clung to her hair. She carried a rifle, holding it in front of her with the barrel aimed off to the left. Three other people milled about, forming a perimeter. Nelly grabbed his arm when he swayed again. Her grip stabilized him though he doubted it would last.

"You okay?"

Rivo shook his head. "No, those sons of bitches were about to kill me."

"They're all over the place," Nelly said, "we've been trying to link up with others. Make a real stand in the square before we hit the ambassador's tower." She smirked. "They won't be able to stop us all if we form up, right?"

"I..." Rivo bit his tongue. Don't be an idiot. There are four of them. "You're right. Yes. If you... if we get together, and face the enemy, then we can definitely make a mark. After all, this plan seems to be going well. I didn't know when we were forming it, but now... yeah, I'm glad we tried after all."

"You..." Nelly laughed. "Of course it was you. I thought Trivak wouldn't let you pull off anything like this, but I'm glad I was wrong. Of course you'd be the one to lead us through this. What did the Zitha do to you?"

"We don't have time for specifics, but everyone's been impacted by them in one way or another." Rivo gestured over his shoulder. "Before we get to the fighting, we need to get to the comm tower."

"Why?" One of the others asked. "We already took it offline."

"Yeah, we're going to blow it up." Rivo nodded emphatically. "Just annihilate the shit out of it. That way, no one's bringing it back online. Save ourselves a bunch of trouble, you know what I'm saying? Plus, it'll make a statement. I told the others we should've done that from the onset. So now, I'm in the field, we'll do it."

"Whatever you say." Nelly picked up one of the security rifles. "Here you go, sir. Let's make this happen."

"Yeah." Rivo took the weapon. "You're on point, Nelly." He watched her head off. God, what am I going to do when we get there? I can't kill all four of these people alone. Nor did he want to try. He'd worked with all of them. They were fellow workers, people he hung around all the time.

Now they've made themselves the enemy. Damn you, guys. You know what the military is going to do to you? Rivo fell into step with them, marching at a brisk pace. At least I'm moving in the right direction. I've got plenty of time to come up with a reasonable plan. The comm unit he brought with him had broken in his fall.

Can't call for backup. Can't tell Trivak what's happening. If I don't find a way to secure the comms, I'll end up dead. The worst part was he had no idea which side to worry about. Security forces look at my clothes and figure I'm with the bad guys. At least the civilians think I'm with them.

If he could communicate with all the civilians, convince them to stand down, then he might end the fighting in a relatively peaceful manner. But those enjoying the thought of a revolution might not stop for anything. He'd have to take the chance. Not that he had any choice of what to do next.

I'm committed. Whatever that means.

***

Marsha fell through a window into a burned-out storefront. Someone started using firebombs on personal property, which escalated from a small uprising to a full-on riot. Civilians caught up in the mania started trashing things as if they'd become possessed by the violence. Never mind the fact they made everything worse for themselves.

All these resources trashed. Supplies they could've used to live comfortably down here... they're burning it for no reason.

These thoughts went through her head seconds before she hit the floor, sliding several feet through the ashes of some product or other. Her attacker came in after her. A young man, tall and covered in grit. He jumped at her. She rose her foot, catching him in the abdomen before hurling him over her head.

As he went sailing into a busted up shelf, he took it all with him. Marsha crawled to her knee then drew her sidearm. She fired twice after him, but he'd managed to scamper away.

Damn it. Where the hell are you? Scuffled footsteps off to the left caught her attention. She spun, firing once. The blow caught his leg, making him tumble to the ground. He'd been charging her before the hit.

"Don't move!" Marsha shouted. "Just stay down!"

"Go to hell..." He spat on the ground, attempting to crawl toward her. "You can't... repress us... can't make us..."

"What?" Marsha asked. "Do what? What is it you think we're forcing you to do? Other than survive."

"The Zitha..."

"Are here to help! They're in the same position as we are! How have we not been clear about that? You guys have seen them hanging out around their forest minding their own business. So what? You thought coming out here and killing people would be a good idea? Burning your own businesses? Blowing up buildings? How does this help?"

"We have... to make... a statement."

"That you're worse than the Zitha raiders?" Marsha asked. "Congratulations. You've succeeded." She rolled him onto his stomach to secure his hands. Shadows fell over her. Instinct screamed at her. She listened, throwing herself backward onto the ground.

A barrage of weapon fire scorched her prisoner, igniting his clothes. Marsha blasted the forms just outside, putting three of them down in short order. A fourth dashed off. She stumbled after them, leaving the building. The person remained armed... they were far enough away that she didn't trust them to stop.

I can't let them cause more trouble. Marsha shot them, putting the person down. God damn it.

Comms went crazy. Other parts of the vicinity fell under heavy attack. Marsha still hadn't found William. Long-range communications still remained spotty as well. But more ships seemed to be flying around overhead. Maybe one of those has some reinforcements. We could definitely use the help.

Marsha followed the HUD on her helmet as she once again set out toward William's beacon. She had a good block together. The quickest way to get there involved an alley. She didn't necessarily look forward to it. Those proved rather narrow, just big enough for two or three people to pass through side by side.

At least I'll see them coming, I guess.

Gunfire echoed from various directions, most of them distant. Explosions occasionally punctuated the high-pitched chirps of the energy weapons, either from grenades or volatile parts of different structures. Marsha crossed an open field, breaking into a jog. She looked around at rising smoke and floating dust.

How can the alliance recover from this? A riot in the middle of Sentinel. Civilians going crazy in the only well guarded human city right now. There's no sense of self-preservation. No forward thinking. Despite all the work we've done to inform them of what's happening and what we're doing.

Who compelled them to commit all these atrocities? What voice held more authority than those these civilians supposedly trusted?

We saved them all from certain death. And they do this?

Marsha rarely felt disdain for the people she protected. Plenty of soldiers openly sneered at civilians, as if they'd never been in their shoes. That had never seemed particularly fair. But that was before Earth fell and so many colonies were turned to dust. Now, they seemed more like savages.

Don't. Marsha shook her head. These are people driven wild by mob mentality. I've been dealing with plenty of individuals that aren't crazy. I can't start hating them now. Which required some effort. Particularly since these rioters forced their hand. They'd become armed somehow, probably breaking into an armory.

We have so much to do even after this violence is quelled.

Work she dreaded.

The alley loomed ahead. Marsha didn't hesitate, plunging in without slowing down. Her heart pounded in her ears, which in turn made the sound of her comm glaring. She didn't have time to turn it down nor could she shut it off. Those bits she caught indicated her people organized well. They were repelling the forces.

Though it didn't seem like a certainty. Holding back the tide of armed civilians became more difficult as their numbers seemed to increase. Marsha wondered if some of them joined in after the fact, having had nothing to do with the initial rush. Fear of missing out came into play. Perhaps a concern they might be on the wrong end of the winning team.

What do they think they'll gain? The military fleets could just leave them here, let them starve.

Glass shattered just to her left. Marsha slid to a halt, spinning on her heel while swinging her weapon in a wide arc. Someone tried to come out through the window. They took the blow to the face, shattering their nose. When they fell, their foot got caught and as they fell, their leg snapped like someone stomping a twig.

A second figure came at her from the flank. Marsha jabbed the butt of her rifle into their gut. They bent at the waist with a huff. She kneed them in the face then started moving again, jogging down the alley.

Two shots burst from another window up ahead and to her left. Marsha shifted to the opposite side of the alley, laying into the opening. A high-pitched scream made her wince. A younger woman, probably someone no older than fifteen. They didn't shoot again, so she kept going.

Three figures appeared at the mouth of the alley, as if they intended to block her passage. She hip fired, sweeping them with fully automatic fire. One danced, another bent at the waist and the last was tossed backward. All three died in moments. She only had another twenty yards to go.

A shot from behind nearly seared off her foot. Marsha blind fired backward, evading to the left. Another couple blasts struck the ground around her. They weren't the best shots, but with the narrow space, they didn't need much luck to take her down. What surprised her was the perseverance.

The fact they continued pursuing her, finding reinforcements to press the advantage constantly.

Marsha glanced. Five people seemed to be chasing her. The fact they decided to run might have saved her life. Up ahead, the mouth of the alley loomed. She had another twenty seconds when more forms blocked her way. God damn it! But they weren't civilians. They wore armor.

"Get down," the voice spoke calmly in her ear. "Now, please."

Marsha threw herself to the ground half a second before the newcomers opened fire. They ripped through the ranks of the civilians, cutting them to pieces. They kept at it for a good twenty seconds before finally letting up. As they did, they advanced, forming a perimeter before offering her a hand up.

"Thanks." Marsha got to her feet. "That was close."

"I'm Lieutenant Marrik," he said, "we came down to help. We have this section secure and are about to make a final push to the embassy building. Are you injured?"

"No, I'm fine," Marsha replied. "Did you see a downed man? William Nesmith?"

"We haven't been talking about the wounded, ma'am. Sorry." He jabbed his thumb behind him. "You're welcome to head out that way, of course. They've got the street so you should have a straight shot to wherever you want to go. I'd offer an escort, but we're down here to ensure the enemy is nullified."

"No problem." Marsha paced by. "Thank you again! I appreciate the save."

"Good luck. We'll see you soon!"

Reinforcements. Marsha let out a sigh of relief. I have to thank whoever took it upon themselves to jump in. She hoped it would be enough to restore order to the city. They didn't have a long time to go before things might have gotten totally out of hand. It already has. That's why I needed someone to save my ass.

At least they were taking back control. One street at a time.

***

William awoke to the sound of screams and gunfire. Flickers made him wince, turning a bad headache worse as he tried to ascertain what was happening. People shouted, some of it in his ear, others muffled as they cried out near enough for him to hear through his helmet. Wherever he was, no one bothered to take off his gear.

That's something. I wonder if it's good.

"Down!" A woman's shrill scream made him hiss from pain. The sharpness of the voice in his helmet made his skull rattle. "Protect the prisoners! Do not let those pieces of shit get in here!"

Are the civilians shooting downed people now? The situation came back to William, including why he was there. A riot broke out in the city. We had to get involved immediately. And I nearly died. The realization sobered him, helped him fight through the cobwebs of just waking up.

"I need a report," William croaked. "What's going on? How many are there? How long have I been out?"

"We don't know," the same woman said, "pretty much on all fronts. We're doing our best to protect people like you, but if you can talk, you can probably shoot. So hop up and aim your weapon before they charge in here again!"

"I... think I was shot. And rocks hit me... I'm... one of the buildings..."

"Sir," the woman appeared in front of him. He could barely see her blue eyes through both their darkened visors. "I understand you've been through some shit. I'm sorry for it. But if you can, we need your help right now. There are four passages they can come through and we've got two people. One more would not go amiss."

"I'm on it." William bobbed his head. He took a knee, swaying as he aimed at one of the open passageways. A dozen bodies piled up around him, some in armor, others dead civilians. He couldn't believe the number. Too many to easily count at the moment. "This is absolute madness."

"You're telling me."

"What's your name?" William asked.

"I'm Locke. My partner's Eaves. He's not talking right now on account of being hit in the neck earlier."

"And he's still fighting?"

Locke chuckled. "Like I said, we don't got too much choice. But a couple shuttles put down nearby. Pretty sure they were loaded up with reinforcements. We might just come out of this alive yet. Maybe even win. Though what does victory look like when you gotta shoot a bunch of your own?"

Not pretty, William thought. Recovery might take a long time, if it was even possible. How many families lost people they cared about? How many of them were torn apart by this idiotic riot? He couldn't imagine. Nor did he want to consider the damage control they'd be working for the next several days.

Unless the ambassadors die. William frowned. That would end it all quick enough.

The rioters didn't seem to care about what it meant to attack the Zitha alliance. Luckily, none of them had any contact with the Likari. William figured they might've put an end to the violence real fast. He couldn't believe they had the peace of mind not to jump in. He figured human leadership would've been all over it regardless of the perpetrators.

Shadows danced on the wall. The HUD caught up a moment later. Three people moving down the way. Not security personnel. Scans showed they were armed.

"Possible contact!" William shouted. His own voice boomed through the mic. Damn it, take a deep breath!

"Same!" Locke called. "Keep your corners! Don't let them through or we're done!"

Civilians burst through, opening fire wildly. They didn't aim, they just sprayed in all directions as they tried to breach the courtyard. William blasted them as they entered, putting all three down at once. He redirected his fire to the other entrance, tearing another group apart to support Eaves.

Something seemed different about these. They didn't shout, they didn't scream, they barely made noise when they died. Each of them dropped as if they'd been automatons shut off by the weapon fire. And they streamed through continuously, dozens of them rushing the area.

William's weapon turned hot as he cut down more than he could count. Eaves went down from a shot to the head. Locke shifted position, moving to stand beside William. They backed together into a corner, shooting down the final rush of crazed attackers. Scans showed only one person still coming, one in armor this time.

"You okay?" William asked. The wall around them was covered with black scorch marks. He took at least two hits to the shoulder, one to the leg. Armor prevented the worst of the damage, but he ached worse than before. As he slumped against the wall, he turned his attention to Locke. "Hey! Talk to me."

"I'm..." Locke leaned forward, using her rifle to hold herself up. "Christ... They got me in the gut. Seared part of my helmet. I think... I think I'll be okay..."

"William!" Marsha's voice broke through the comm chatter. "Are you in that courtyard? What's going on in there? Can I come through without being shot?"

"Please do," William said. He checked the scans of the other wounded. None of them made it. The rioters got them all. Almost as if they had intended to kill the injured. "We're... the only ones who made it." He tapped Locke. "Please don't shoot the person coming from the right. They're on our side."

"Couldn't... if I wanted..." Locke groaned as she slumped backward, slamming against the wall. "Ouch. That... really... hurt..."

"You'll be fine." William hoped he hadn't lied about that.

Marsha emerged from the tunnel. She slid to a halt near a pile of several bodies. "What the hell?" She looked around. "How? Where'd all these people come from? Surely, the entire colony didn't turn against us."

"I don't... don't think they are originally... from here..." William struggled to explain. "They acted... weird."

"Okay." Marsha came over to join him. "Reinforcements from orbit came down. We're taking back the area." She looked at Locke. "You okay?"

"No..." Locke shook her head.

"I'll get the medics to look at you both." Marsha returned her attention to William. "Do you feel up to making it to the embassy building? I'm having people rally there for what I expect will be the conclusion to this nonsense."

"I'm not sure..."

"I'd rather do it with you than without you," Marsha said, "but I understand. Looks like you've been shot a couple times." She paused. "Scans show you're mostly bruised. I'm sure you're in pain. I'll just..."

"No." William touched her hand. "I'll make it." He gestured to Locke. "Just make sure she's safe. I don't want to leave her here alone if we're going to rush off to a rally point." I'm a damn idiot. This is not a good idea. Unless they finished off the worst of the enemy force, he couldn't imagine another firefight.

Marsha made a call, diverting some of the security forces to their position. She moved amongst the dead, checking them out. William wanted to join her, but he needed the chance to sit still. Every part of him seemed to ache. His head throbbed. The medics would give him something for it.

Until then, he sat there and suffered.

"I'm sorry about Eaves," he said. "That guy... he put up a fight."

"And all the others," Locke replied. "You're lucky you woke up, I guess. You'd be dead too. I can't believe we weren't able to defend them."

Me either. William closed his eyes. I'm sorry. I'll find out who did this to you. All of you. They're going to pay for it. The last wave, the huge number of those people charging in to kill the wounded hadn't been regular colonists. They were dressed like civilians but didn't act… alive.

That sounds insane. It was the best he could come up with. Like robots. I wonder what the medical reports will say about them. Or if we'll ever understand precisely what we encountered here.

Half a dozen security forces entered the clearing. One of them made a direct line to Locke and William. They interfaced with their armor, giving them each an injection. William's arm felt cool as it rushed through him, chasing away the pain and the throbbing. He felt almost good enough to follow Marsha.

I have to fight through this.

The medic gestured to Locke, making it clear they needed to move her to their base of operations. Two guys helped her. She looked back at William, offering a nod. He returned the gesture.

We only had a brief contact, but I feel like I've known her forever. William hoped he might catch up with her again after everything ended. Two people stayed behind to defend a bunch of wounded. Sacrificing one of their lives. I have to thank her in person. I owe her big time.

But just then, he had somewhere to be.

Marsha helped him up. "Make the last push?"

William nodded. "Let's go."

□

Chapter 8

Franklin slept through their rendezvous with the EDF Patton. When he woke up, he'd been taken off the ship and put under the care of the chief medical officer aboard the battleship. After eight hours of unconsciousness and an hour of recovery time, he found himself in a briefing room.

Ethyl, Sean, Tesh, and Alfred sat with him. There were four rows of five chairs, each bolted to the floor. A window looked out over deep space. The main screen in the room was embedded into the wall with a podium off to the side. All the controls for the area occupied the bottom, a massive touch screen.

Captain Carmine learned the details of the mission Sslan insisted they undertake. The Raldor ambassador took incredible glee ordering them around. He probably knew the EDF wouldn't continue to do his errands for long so whatever he asked them to do would be the end of it.

"Anyone know what's up?" Franklin asked. "Any clue what we're doing specifically?"

Alfred replied, "Only that we're nearly in position. Whatever that means."

"Fantastic." Franklin sighed. I can't believe we're still catering to that squid bastard.

Bjorn seemed to be sitting beside him, away from the others. He crossed his legs at the ankles. "You gotta do what the orders tell ya, brother. That's the way it's always been. And when the squids are calling the shots, then you jump when they slither. Or is it undulate? I never knew the difference."

One involves motion and snakes. The other is probably right. I have no idea.

"Lucky I can hear you," Bjorn said. "But I get it. The others might think you're crazy. Though newsflash. You are. After that charge on the station? Damn. I don't think I've got it in me to be so nuts."

You pushed me to do it!

"You didn't have to. I'm dead, dumbass. If you don't wanna be, then you should probably ignore the person you're imagining sitting here."

Captain Carmine entered the room. "Hello, everyone. Sorry about the tardiness. I'm going to dive right in." He brought the screen online, showing a topographical map of a complex nestled in a hillside. "This is what we're here for. A complex on a remote world in Raldor space."

Franklin grumbled, "Perfect. Another raid."

"Pretty much," Carmine said, "but I understand why they didn't turn you loose on this one alone. I'm afraid they insist you take part in the attack, which is somewhat disconcerting. You should all know I fought against that as much as I could. You've all dealt with the Raldor enough to know it's not simple."

"Not remotely," Alfred replied. "What do they want us to do? Why are we attacking that place? And who are we fighting?"

"I'm getting to that." Carmine changed the view to the front of the structure. A sheer wall was met by a natural staircase leading to it. "You'll see here that this is the preferred approach if you were invited. They also have a landing pad in the back up high. It's protected by a variety of high powered turrets."

"What do they have in there?" Franklin asked. He gestured to the walls. "That makes it look like a prison of some kind."

"That's precisely right. We're looking at a well guarded facility containing a variety of beings that attacked the Raldor in some capacity or other. Then failed horribly and found themselves locked up. I'm told there are Korlas, Zitha, humans... even some Veldon. They kept them here."

"For what?" Tesh asked. "Why bother when they could just as easily kill them and not worry about an escape?"

Carmine sighed. "Experiments." That brought a gasp from Tesh. "Yes, I know. It's all kinds of illegal. But that's not the problem right now. The Raldor have lost control of the facility. The inmates have taken over.

They're holding the Raldor scientists hostage. This poses a threat to our efforts in a number of ways."

Sean snorted. "I can't wait to hear this. Why should we care if a bunch of torture victims take hostages? How's this our problem?"

"We free the scientists," Carmine said, "then the Raldor join the alliance. We have a powerful ally against the Veldon. If we don't..."

"Yes?" Franklin prompted.

"Then we go home. No harm no foul, I guess. But the Raldor will not help against the Veldon and we're out in the cold. All your efforts to this point will have been a waste of time. I'd rather avoid that. What about you?"

Alfred stood. "Absolutely. We've come out here for a reason. We're going to win them over one way or another. It has to happen. Besides, how bad can this prison be? Maybe when we're done, we can release the prisoners. Let them go back to their cultures and escape this place."

"Probably not," Carmine replied. "Because they... are not exactly acting sane. We'll get to that. Our approach is to attack from two sides. I've mobilized a strike force to hit the left and forward position. While they create a distraction, Franklin will lead a team to slip through the enemy defenses and penetrate the hold."

"Just like that?" Franklin asked. "What do you want us to do? Take up teleportation? We can't get through that rocky business. There's no way. And even if we do, we'll find ourselves facing off against a hundred guys. I'm scrappy. Sean and Tesh are good. But those odds are too much for us."

Carmine replied, "We'll draw the enemy away from their position. A shuttle will sweep through to open you a passage. They'll sweep through the whole area to make it seem like we're just carpet bombing them. That should give you everything you need to get inside, find the scientists, and get out."

"So the objective," Tesh said, "is to rescue the scientists? We're letting the enemy keep the facility?"

Carmine shook his head. "No, but your objective is to get them to safety while the strike force takes the prison back from the inmates."

Ethyl raised her hand. "Just to get this straight, we're going to kill a bunch of prisoners who were tortured by the Raldor. Top it off, we're going to save the freaks doing the damage to them in the first place. Is that the gist of this? Because if so, I'm not sure how you can justify working with them."

"Look." Carmine sighed. "I don't need to tell you all what we're up against out there. I've spoke with Sslan as has Ambassador Chance. If we want to change the way they behave, we have to be in a position where they'll listen. We've jumped through a lot of hoops so far. This is the final one."

"Supposedly," Ethyl muttered.

"They're going to join the alliance," Carmine pressed. "And in order to do that, we help them. And while yes, I find it deplorable that they tortured and experimented on prisoners, their captives attacked the Raldor first. Their crimes range from murder to piracy. The Zitha sentence people like that to death."

"Preferable," Ethyl replied, "when the alternative is to become a fuckin' lab rat."

"Alright," Franklin stepped in, "look, this is the cost of doing business with the Raldor. Someone thinks that's acceptable, we're not in a position to argue. We do it, get out, move on. What sort of armaments are we looking at? Are the prisoners going to be wearing armor? And how long have they had to dig in?"

"They've held the facility for twenty days," Carmine said. "They have rudimentary armor and decent weapons. This is because the Raldor use..." He weighed his words for a long moment. "A workforce, let's call it that, to protect themselves. That equipment fits humanoids and so—"

"Wait." Ethyl interrupted. "Are you telling me that these freaks have people working for them that guard their shit? You've gotta be kidding. That's insane! Why would they do it? What's the incentive? Don't tell me. They don't get experimented on, right? They can be autonomous?"

"Some come from lost colonies," Carmine explained, "others came to the Raldor with offers. I don't know the particulars. I can tell you that they're all dead. There are no friendlies on the surface beside the scientists."

Tesh said, "Is that because the security forces turned on the Raldor too?"

Carmine frowned. "Why would you say that?"

"Uh..." Tesh shrugged. "Doesn't it make sense? If they found out what the Raldor were doing, wouldn't you turn on them? I mean, most of us aren't cool with the idea that our own people are being tortured for no reason. What kind of experiments were they running anyway? What did they want to know?"

"The Raldor," Alfred said, "are obsessed with the notion of ensuring they can survive in other environments. This planet doesn't qualify so they have to live within the laboratory compound. Which is what has kept them safe for the most part. The prisoners couldn't breach the area nor could they survive it if they tried."

"Really?" Franklin sighed. He rubbed his forehead. "So how the hell do we get them out of there if we can't even go in?"

"When you arrive," Carmine replied, "you'll make contact. They have pods which they'll occupy. They can operate them and follow you through a passage here." He showed them on the map. It was a passage at the back of the facility. "When you reach the end, your ship will be waiting. Your Likari will pilot it."

So Deina's still involved. Franklin wondered. Seems simple enough. If we don't have to fight so many people. "I have one more question then I think we'll be good to go. How can we be certain the Raldor will keep their word? I'm done jumping when they go boom. This has to be the last thing they push on us."

"I agree," Ethyl said. "Hell, I don't think we need them as it is. They should kiss our asses as we head for home."

Carmine replied, "That's not your call to make. And we have assurances. Ambassador Chance agrees with them."

"Uh huh." Ethyl laughed. "Whatever. I'll shoot anyone you point at, I guess. But mark my words, y'all. When the people back home find out about what these creatures have done, and they will, you think it'll be easy to maintain an alliance? You think it'll be something humans or Zitha want? You'd better have a plan."

"We do," Alfred said. "Just trust us. Get the job done, and we'll be good to go."

"Whoa." Ethyl pointed at him. "You tellin' me you ain't comin'?"

Carmine replied, "The ambassador will remain aboard the Patton to provide support from the bridge. Between him and our tactical officer, you should have everything you need. Air support, the strike team, resources... we are overkill for this mission, ladies and gentlemen. We just have to get it done."

Ethyl fell silent, but she nodded.

Great. I guess we're ready. Franklin stood. "We'll gear up and head out, sir." He waved at the others. "Come on." Tesh and Sean joined him immediately.

"I'll catch up," Ethyl said, "gotta talk to my charge, if you don't mind." She turned to Carmine. "In private, sir."

"Of course." Carmine nodded. "Don't take too long. We're starting this operation within the hour. Strike team's ready to go. When you're ready, we'll launch." He shook Franklin's hand. "Good luck, Lieutenant. I have every confidence you'll make this happen. We're counting on all of you to do your part."

Yeah, I understand why Ethyl's not pleased. Franklin felt grateful he wasn't in Alfred's shoes. She's going to light that bastard up. And he didn't blame her. He thought the mission sounded like bullshit too. Carmine's determination to go along with it surprised him, though they hadn't had much time to talk since the Patton arrived.

I'm flattered they believed Sslan and came to help us. Though it just stranded them in the middle of nowhere too. They were all at the mercy of the Raldor. If Sslan wanted to give them more 'assignments,' there wasn't much they could do about it. Comply or remain their prisoners. Like those poor experiments.

The others talked about defying them, as if they had an option. Sslan painted it like he might let them go.

Why would he? Franklin agreed to his ridiculous demands before because he didn't have a choice. Alfred's assurances meant jack shit. As did finishing the mission to retake the prison.

"Look on the bright side," Bjorn said, "we're doing something. And moving forward is better than sitting still. Even if you don't like where you're going."

That's bullshit and you know it.

"Could've made you feel better, if you didn't think about it too much."

You just summed up our differences. I spent time thinking and you never did.

"Which of us is happier?"

I don't want to think about that. Franklin honestly didn't know the answer.

***

"You kidding me?" Ethyl asked. She leaned back in her chair. "You've gotta be. Because there's no way you think this is okay."

"Calm down," Alfred rasped, "c'mon, I told you—"

"Stop. Did your Captain Carmine love the idea of you volunteering me to do this? I got no reason to go down there. None. I don't give a shit about some Raldor assholes. I kinda hope they burn."

"Well, I'm sure you'll find a way to get through the work without too much effort."

"Work, huh? That's what you call going down there to fight people who escaped torment and torture? You want me to kill a bunch of people who," Ethyl leaned forward to whisper, "could have been you or me? I should kill you right now. Break your goddamn neck for all this."

"What would that accomplish?"

"You'd be dead."

Alfred huffed. "Then what? You know they wouldn't let you go, right? I'm an ambassador, remember? One that brought the Zitha and the Likari to the table. I forged alliances no one ever thought possible. You're just a bodyguard. A sour one at that. So don't think they'd hail you as a hero."

"Maybe I could tell them who you really are then." Ethyl shrugged. "You think about that?"

"Why are you so resistant to just going down and doing some dirty work? You've done it before."

"Because, you oblivious sack of shit, I nearly died the last time I went out there! And that was just as unnecessary!"

"I'm tired of having these conversations." Alfred stood. "So either you go or I'll have you put in the brig. There are no two ways about it. And I'd like to add that if you decide to get all high and mighty again, I'll just have you arrested. These conversations are over." He started toward the door.

Ethyl dashed forward. She grabbed him by the collar then spun him around. He barely got off a gasp before she shoved him against the wall, pressing her forearm to his throat. "You're cute. Talking the kind of shit you just did. Acting like you're some hot shit EDF man now. But I've got news for you."

"Let... me... go..."

"I know where you come from. I got all your dirty secrets. And yeah, you can put me in the brig. You can have them schedule me to be shot. But it won't happen before I expose you. They won't give a shit about all your accomplishments when they find out how you became Ambassador Chance."

"You... wouldn't..."

"Why? From inside a cell, I got no reason to keep your secrets." Ethyl tilted her head. "This is the deal. I'm going down there. I'll help Tesh, because I like her. When it's over, and we go home, I'm leaving. You make it happen. If you don't, I'll kill you. If I can't, I'll expose you. Either way, you'll be done. Do we have an accord?"

Alfred glared at her.

Ethyl shoved her arm harder into his throat. "I asked you a question. If I have to repeat it, I guess you're sayin' no."

"Fine! Okay! Okay! Just let me go!"

Ethyl stepped back. "I'm holding you to it. Don't fuck me over. I will do it. Make no mistake about my conviction. This is not what I signed up for. And maybe I have been repeating myself. I would've hoped you'd listen by now. But I guess we weren't the friends I thought."

"We were," Alfred said, "you should've gotten onboard."

"Why? So I could be like you? A pretender? Waiting to be discovered?" Ethyl shook her head. "I'm fine with who I am. I thought you were too. I wish I would've known different. But I guess I had to learn the hard way." She opened the door. "Guess I'd better catch up with my 'team' before they gotta leave without me."

"I'm not sorry," Alfred said, "if you're curious."

"Why would you be? You got what you wanted. Adoration. A position you don't deserve. And I thought you wanted to steal something." Ethyl laughed. "I'm a damn fool. Oh well. Least I'll die next to some genuine people. Tesh and them are at least honest. You... I doubt you know yourself at this point."

Ethyl left him there, marching down the hall. She half expected shoot her from behind. It wouldn't have been a surprise. He might've been saving his own life. She had every intention of follow up on her promise to him. If he tried to hold her, she would do everything in her power to end him.

Considering how Franklin felt about Alfred, Ethyl figured she had an ally in taking him down if necessary. But as long as she could go free, she'd let him have his illusion. Even if he deserved to be blown away.

***

Tesh leaned against a boulder as she waited for the strike force to start up the action. Ethyl, Sean, and Franklin stacked behind her. She insisted on taking point, leading the way to the breach once it happened. After what happened on her last mission, she felt like she had something to prove.

If only to herself.

The others kept quiet, listening to the chatter as their allies approached. Deina dropped them off a ways out, requiring them to hike to their destination. Though she honestly didn't see the point. Unless the prisoners had no access to technology, they would've seen the ship on scans. They knew a battleship took orbit.

Their silence confused her. Why not reach out? Make contact with them to see if they might be friendly. Clearly, the Patton was not a Raldor ship. Had she been in the prison, she would've been looking for every opportunity to get out of there. Even if it involved another cell with a moral culture.

Tesh agreed with Ethyl about them. She wanted their superiors to question the benefits of allying with the Raldor. One problem stuck in the back of her mind, something she didn't want to bring up for fear of playing devil's advocate. Maybe the EDF or the JTF or the Korlas did the same thing to the Raldor.

Or even each other.

"Get ready," Franklin said, "the ships are incoming. Air strike in less than sixty seconds."

Ethyl patted Tesh's shoulder. "I'm right behind you."

Still not sure why she came. Tesh sensed her aggravation when they boarded the ship. Whatever she said to Alfred hadn't gone well. The falling out must've been epic. Enough that she wouldn't have been surprised if Ethyl found a way to avoid the mission entirely. Bodyguard work wasn't infantry work after all.

"Twenty seconds," Franklin announced. The ship engines roared overhead, growing louder as they approached. The strike team started blasting away, shooting at the tops of the walls. They were the distraction, the people luring out the fight. Once the air strike hit, all units would converge.

And the real fighting would begin.

Ethyl should be happy that at least we're a rescue unit, Tesh thought, and not the front line hitters. Those men and women knew how to throw down. Against a bunch of poorly equipped former prisoners, it should've been an easy win. Tesh would've liked to know how many people they faced.

But it probably didn't matter. Carmine committed more than fifty soldiers to the fight. Half of them went at the flank. The others would drop in once they held the courtyard. Then they'd sweep the whole building, taking it back. All the while, Franklin's team got the scientists to safety.

They were tasked with getting the scientists out in the event that the prisoners planted bombs. The safe room couldn't survive a big detonation. Sslan made it clear he didn't trust the soldiers not to do something crazy in the structure either, which contradicted his desire to save the place for later.

Maybe they are insane.

The vessels swooped in, laying down heavy fire across the outer wall. Each impact rattled the ground, making the stone beside Tesh vibrate. She flinched from the blasts, which seemed to go on forever. When it finally ended, she felt disoriented. Her head spun from the sudden silence.

Which didn't last.

The strike force opened fire while charging. Their attacks flickered in the distance, splashing through the breached walls. Enemy forces returned fire, green beams streaking from the prison.

"Go!" Franklin shouted, "this is our opportunity! Make it happen!"

Tesh cursed under her breath before shoving off the wall. She stayed low while running from her position, making for the nearest breach. This took them up a slight incline through loose dirt. Every step took some effort, slowing them down enough to make her heart thump in her chest.

She felt convinced that any moment might be their last, that one of the enemy would spot them and pick them off from the safety of cover. Though as she peered at their destination, she saw a few chunks of body along with piles of dark debris. Most of the wall had been obliterated.

Movement caught her eye. The prisoners hustled to meet the strike force. Carmine's plan worked. No one so much as looked in Tesh's direction as she reached the first chunks of stone lying around the area. As she slipped closer, she crouched beside a piece of the wall to get a look at the courtyard.

A dozen men wearing pieces of armor crouched to throw shots at the armored troops coming their way. They didn't stand a chance. She waved at Franklin to join her, then directed his attention to those prisoners.

"Do you think we should finish them off?"

"No," Franklin gestured toward the main structure. "We've got a window over there. We'll take it. You've all got the navs on your HUDs. Follow them to the scientists. We do our part, and get the hell out. I'll take the lead." He hustled away.

Tesh grunted as she followed him. She hadn't even left the cover when Franklin took a shot to the back. The blow knocked him to the ground. One of the prisoners burst from a hole in the ground, covered in dirt and debris. He stumbled as he made his way toward the lieutenant, screaming incoherently.

"Son of a bitch!" Sean shouted while tearing into the man. He got him three times before the body fell, the scorched face melted beyond any chance of recognition. "Check him!"

Ethyl got to Franklin first. She dragged him back to cover. "You okay?" She asked.

"Yeah," Franklin muttered, "think so. How the hell did he avoid scans?"

"Something in the soil," Sean said, "and he was lucky as hell. You sure you can go on, boss? We've got this."

"HUD says it was a concussion hit. I'll be fine. Just need to catch my breath."

"I'll take point," Sean replied. "Ethyl, Tesh, watch my back. Franklin, you hold up the rear and keep moving. I'll breach the second I get to the building. Go!" He sprinted, making it across the yard without taking a shot this time. Ethyl kept up with him, keeping guard while he went through the window.

Tesh hung back for Franklin. He wasn't moving nearly as fast as their companions. By the time they joined the others, Sean was already in the room. Ethyl followed. Tesh guarded the area. Franklin coughed a couple times, leaning against the wall. The conflict raged some two hundred yards away, making it hard to focus on him.

"You sure you're okay?" Tesh asked. "That cough…"

"Get through the window," Franklin interrupted. "Hurry."

Tesh scowled, hesitating to comply. He tilted his head. She crawled through the window.

The others cleared the room, standing on the opposite side by an open portal leading out into a hallway. Tesh stacked on Ethyl. "What's up?"

"Follow me," Sean said. "Moving in three… two…"

"Wait!" Tesh interrupted. "What about Franklin?"

"Go," Franklin ordered, "I'll catch up to you. Just move."

I don't like it.

Sean finished his countdown, sliding out into the hall. Ethyl followed with Tesh taking up the rear. She aimed behind them, walking backward as they advanced down the hall. Franklin hadn't even made it into the building yet. Maybe he's hanging back for a good reason. He might be linking up with the strike force.

The stone hallway didn't seem like a place the Raldor would normally live. It clearly had been made with humanoids involved. Old masonry made up the walls, bricks layered on top of one another to form an arch above their heads. There were no lights illuminating the area. Tesh's HUD turned it gray, showing it stretch off over a hundred yards.

"Contact," Sean whispered before pulling the trigger. The flash from his weapon looked like a white blob, the sound echoed through the corridor. A body slumped to the ground. "Two more on the left. Ethyl, they're yours."

"Got it." Ethyl shifted to the side, laying down a quick burst of shots. The targets didn't even fire their weapons before they fell to the ground dead.

Sean cut hard to the right through a passage Tesh hadn't seen. Her waypoint navigator didn't come up, as if it hadn't been transferred properly. I have to keep up with him then. The new passage was smaller, big enough for them to go single file. It reminded her of servant's quarters in an old castle she toured as a child.

Blips appeared behind them, gray dots indicating the computer had no idea how to categorize them. Which meant they were the convicts. Any soldier with armor would have come up green. They were moving in their direction. She turned, waiting for the first of them to make it to the smaller hallway.

They had a curve coming up, but they wouldn't get there in time. The first of the convicts came through the passage. Tesh blasted him in the chest. He stumbled back into his companions who shoved him aside. The second the wounded one cleared the area, she fired again, putting a second one down.

She bumped into the wall, then shuffled to the side to use the bend as cover. The third of her targets leaned in to get a look. Tesh fired, searing off the top of his skull.

"Move!" Sean shouted, "we're almost in position. Don't lag behind!"

"I was watching our backs," Tesh muttered. She turned, hustling to catch up with them. She joined them in what looked like a medical bay. Tables with straps for hands and feet lined up in groups of three. Twelve of them occupied the room in all. Blood soaked them and the floor, giving the metal a rusty look.

A flickering light overhead gave the area a horror vibe, something out of a terrible stream. Tesh lowered her weapon, turning in place. If this is what the Raldor did to them… but wait a minute.

"Something's wrong," Tesh said.

"Yeah," Sean replied. "Those sick bastards."

Tesh shook her head. "Not just that. The Raldor couldn't have performed this kind of torture themselves. They must've…" She paused. "They had some of the convicts do it. People were acting as their hands in here. That's the only explanation for what we're seeing, right? Because they can't survive out of their capsules on this planet."

"Jesus," Ethyl said, "you're right. But how? Did they have collaborators? Or did they talk them into doing their bidding in exchange to not be on the slab? No wonder they wanted all the convicts dead. Some of them might be able to give us answers to these questions and it wouldn't look good for the squids."

"Not our problem now," Sean replied. "We have to get to our new 'allies.' He gestured across the room. "That door leads to the safe room. Look at it. There are scratch marks. Scorches too. The convicts tried to get in. Probably desperate to kill those sons of bitches. And yet... they stayed safe."

"How did they eat?" Tesh asked. "The prisoners. What did they do?"

"Probably had enough supplies to last a while." Sean shrugged. "Doesn't matter." He approached the door. "Yo! Raldor scientists! I'm Sergeant Sean Bertrand with the EDF. Sslan sent us to get you out of here in case the convicts had bombs. We need to move if you want to live through this!"

They didn't reply.

Ethyl said, "Maybe they didn't hear you."

"Uh uh." Sean hammered the door with his fist. "I'm sure they're monitoring us right now. Come on! Open the damn door! Unless you want to get crushed to death in the event of a serious disaster! Let's move!"

"How do we know," a distorted voice boomed over the speakers, "you are not with the scum?"

Tesh said, "Because we had to kill a bunch of them to get here! Don't you guys have scans? Our ship is in orbit! We're here to help you!"

They didn't reply for nearly thirty seconds. When they did, all of them spoke together in a strange, out of key harmony. "We will open the door. Our pods do not move swiftly. We assume you wish to go out the back. We can lead the way. You must keep us safe. Do not allow the pods to become damaged."

"Yeah, yeah," Sean said, "just hurry up."

Ethyl moved to the door, aiming her weapon around the corner. Tesh waited for the Raldor. Things moved faster and easier than she anticipated. Something felt wrong though. The fact Franklin stayed behind made her nervous. And they hadn't heard from the strike force. They should've made short work of the convicts.

Tesh tapped the comm to reach out to Franklin... or the ship. The connection appeared to be jammed. "Uh... guys?" She nudged Sean. "You got comms?"

"Just to you two," Sean replied, "must be interference in this place."

"I don't know..." Tesh shook her head. "Something feels wrong."

An explosion made her jump. Ethyl yelped, hopping backward as she scampered away from debris closing up the passage. There didn't appear to be another way out, though the Raldor implied the way to the back of the building was somewhere nearby. And they had yet to open the door.

"What the hell is going on?" Sean asked. "Hey!" He slapped the door. "You pricks coming out or what? We need to move!"

"We will come out," the voices spoke in unison again. "In good time."

Another explosion went off. The lights turned on brightly overhead. They burned, even through the armor. Tesh shied away from it but there was nowhere to go. The floor lit up as well, so intense her helmet went full black. She was blind... her comms stopped working... muscles felt leaden.

"Sean!" Tesh shouted. "Ethyl!"

Neither replied. Tesh felt light... and tired. She fell.

***

Mary stared at the comms. The ships did their part, tearing through the defenses of the prison. Afterward, they maintained a flight pattern around the area to provide support as needed. The strike force made good progress into the courtyard. Franklin's party breached the area.

Everything appeared to be going according to plan.

Then comms dropped. Only for a moment, but long enough to startle her. When they returned, she received a message from Franklin. He let her know he'd been shot and the others made their way into the prison proper. They should have already caught up with the scientists but he hadn't heard from them yet.

"Captain," Mary turned in her seat, "word from the surface. Lieutenant Hale states his people have entered the building. They should be at the location of the scientists now. He hasn't heard from them."

Carmine asked, "Does that mean comms are down?"

"Give me a second." Mary turned back to her console. "Lieutenant? Are you saying your comms are down?"

"Not exactly..." Franklin coughed. "I mean, they could be. I... don't know."

"How badly are you injured?"

"HUD shows that I should be fine, but I'm not so sure about it."

"I'll divert forces in your direction. Please stand by." Mary sent out a general alert, directing a squad to Franklin's position. Prepare for triage and first aid. She checked the comms. Her message got through though she wasn't sure how. The interference had increased considerably. "Something weird's going on down there, sir."

"Confirmed," Milton added. "I've got some dramatic energy spikes."

Carmine sighed. "Get Sslan on the line. Where's that ambassador?"

"He was just here," Heather said. "I thought..."

"God damn it." Carmine grumbled. "Someone find Chance and get him back up here immediately. Mary, figure out those comms. I want our people back on the line as soon as possible. Heather, increase orbit to maximum distance. Just inside comm range. And Milton, I want a full scan of the prison right away. I think—"

Before he could finish the sentence, power dropped. Consoles fell offline, plunging them into darkness. Dead silence fell over the bridge though a whine broke it a moment later as the emergency lights kicked on. Mary stiffened, turning to look at the captain. She'd never seen anything like that.

"What just happened?" Milton asked.

Carmine said, "Funny you should ask since I was about to put the question to you. Heather? Mary? Do either of you have anything at all?"

"Negative, sir," Heather replied. "Helm is completely down."

"Comms too," Mary said.

"Must have been..." Milton shook his head. "I don't know. An EMP? But it would've had to come from inside the ship!"

Alistair stood. "I'll head down to Engineering. Check in to find out what happened and see if I can help."

"Talk to security," Carmine said. "Be sure they're on personal comms to coordinate around the ship. Get people into hazard suits as soon as possible." He motioned to the others. "That goes for us too. Everyone in suits until further notice. If life support went down too, we're on borrowed time."

Wow. Mary dropped down below her console to access the emergency hatch. She engaged the manual lever, reefing on it three times before the thing opened. She pulled the kit out, drawing out her suit. This is going to be no big deal. We'll have things back up and running in no time.

"What's the biggest concern?" Milton asked. "What should we be focusing on?"

"Helm," Carmine replied. "Without it, we'll burn up in the atmosphere. Or crash into the surface… in which case, we'll wish we burned up."

"I hadn't thought of that…" Milton's voice trembled. "How… wait… that should… from our distance, we'd… that'll be in less than an hour!"

"Which is why Alistair's on his way to Engineering." Carmine finished putting on his suit. "Coordinate with the different departments. Power is our number one priority. Mary, I want you to reach out to the shuttles. They might be able to tractor us away from the surface. But not if we don't get ahold of them soon."

"I'm on it, sir." Mary switched on her personal comm. She tried to reach out, but the HUD in her suit showed she didn't have enough signal. "I need to get down to the observation deck. I might be able to rig something with the generator there if it has any energy left at all. Do you mind?"

"Do what you have to," Carmine replied, "and make it fast. Everything we do from here out has the potential to save our lives or end them. Work efficiently, folks. This is the kind of disaster you've trained for. Make it count."

Ah, pressure. Mary headed for the ladder to leave the bridge. If this happened up here, I wonder what's going on down there. With the strike force and Franklin's team. Or if they're already dead. If the Patton survived the strange power failure, they might just find out. Providing it's even possible.

This might all come down to luck. In which case, we're in a lot of trouble.

□

Chapter 9

Harold tapped his foot as they made another lazy circle around the settlement. He found it impossible to believe his people had yet to quell the attack on the surface. What were they doing? Maybe Reggie should have committed more than thirty additional forces to the problem.

His comm buzzed several times before he acknowledged it. He'd been staring out the window, lost in his thoughts. Ghrenda's name appeared on the screen. I'm sure this will be a fantastic conversation. He established the connection.

"Greetings, Captain," Ghrenda said. "I see that you're flying circles with us. Not exactly the best thing to do with our time, is it?"

"No, it certainly isn't."

"Do you know why the action below is happening?"

"Some kind of riot," Harold said, "we're trying to quell it." Preferably without killing the civilians though I'm not going to say that to him. Partially because he'd wonder why and also, I can't guarantee I'm right. Our people might be fighting for their lives. "We sent down some reinforcements."

"Comms are spotty," Ghrenda replied. "We're willing to send our people in as a special task force if you feel that it would benefit your team. I'm not sure that it will, of course. When pulses rush, it may lead to something we do not want. Not to suggest our two people might want to shoot one another but—"

"No, I understand what you mean," Harold said. "We need to keep any potential volatility out of the equation."

"We agreed to have this meeting in the settlement because we were under the impression the civilians were safe. I'm somewhat concerned to discover they are so adamant against our alliance. What do you suppose is the cause?"

"A rabble-rouser," Harold replied. "Someone that either worked with Aevers or maybe even the person who pushed him to the activity. We'll find who they are and take care of them. Mobs as they are can be swayed by a powerful voice. Someone charismatic. This is something we have to work out."

"Do you have any suspicions?"

Harold shook his head. "I don't want to hazard a guess either. Whoever it is seems to want chaos though. They must know we can't face the threats we're looking at without each other." He sighed. "What are your thoughts? I'm sure you've been sitting around thinking about it too."

"I'm afraid it might be one of my own people," Ghrenda said. "If I'm to be honest, I could see some hard-liner pretending to be human somehow. Or even convincing one to start this mess. Even before I arrived at the station to take over security, they may have caused this trouble. So of course, I'm going through every possibility."

"Don't go too crazy about it," Harold replied. "When we start anticipating an unknown enemy, we can make anyone fit the role. It's important to ensure we're focused on the evidence. You know... I've got an idea. I wanted a group to investigate this when it's over. Maybe we should combine forces on that."

"Bringing them together," Ghrenda said. "Yes. I like that very much. The sooner we start working together in that capacity the better. I'll put together a list of potential candidates. On another note, I'm worrying about William Nesmith and Marsha Silva. They were helping coordinate the security efforts down there."

"I haven't heard from either of them. I believe local comms are on down there though. If we got closer, we might patch through the interference."

"Or," Ghrenda replied, "we might land on the rooftop pad. Make our way into the embassy chambers where we can take command of the situation. See if our presence might not instill some confidence in your soldiers and slow the civilians down. What do you think?

I know our advisors are against it, but you and I are military people."

I like the idea, Harold thought. But if the two of us do end up dying because some asshole makes it through the door with a bomb, our cultures will be in bad shape. But was that true? Maybe on the Zitha side. Bracknel could take over the EDF easily enough. He wanted to anyway.

"Let's do it," Harold said, "before we head down, I'll have an additional force brought to provide security for the building. You should probably do the same."

"Understood. See you there, Captain." Ghrenda dropped off the line.

Harold connected with Reggie. "I'm heading down to the embassy now. Send an additional twenty security personnel to supplement our forces there. We'll try to establish comms with orbit as soon as possible. Also, hold off on the investigative team. I want to create a partnership with the Zitha."

"Understood, sir," Reggie said. "I have some other news as well. The Patton... we didn't get through to them. A long-range scan shows they aren't where we thought they'd be. I've got someone sweeping the surrounding areas. The ones with buoys to send information back and forth."

"Are you saying they probably didn't get the message about the 'ambassador'?"

"It's unlikely, sir."

Great. Well... he did his part with two cultures. If he's doing the same with the Raldor, then it might not matter too much.

"Understood. Thanks for the update. I'm focusing on our current problems right now. Talk soon." Harold killed the connection. Where'd you go, Carmine? You're not the kind to go off on a tangent. He should've sent word back. Unless it got intercepted or garbled. We can't afford to lose them.

He wanted to send someone else to check in with them. That would have to wait. Maybe until after the fight with the Veldon. Too many things remained in the air. The best he could do was take them one at a time. Starting with the insurrection on Sentinel One. Everything else occupied the back burner.

***

Rivo marched down the street with a purpose. He wanted to show he knew what he was doing, that he had the situation under control. Nelly matched his pace, staying right by him the whole way. He wished he could question her about the situation, find out how she got involved or why she thought it was okay.

Pretending to be part of it made him anxious. If they found out, they'd kill him. He had no doubt about it. Why hadn't they asked him some questions? Like why they were mobilized to such violence? Yes, they had the

Zitha to blame, but that couldn't be the whole story. And if it was, he didn't have a lot of faith in his own species.

If I got over it, anyone could. The thought made him feel like an ass. Unfair. Seriously, unfair.

Another ship started down toward the surface. Rivo caught the engine flare out of the corner of his eye. He turned to look, stopping to watch. The others did the same. It was moving fast with two more following. They're going for a full-on retaliation now, I bet. That'll put an end to this shit.

"Damn," Nelly muttered, "you know what that means."

No, I have no clue.

"I took a hit to the head," Rivo replied. "Direct me."

"That way." Nelly gestured to the right. "We rendezvous at the depot."

Depot. Son of a bitch. More weapons?

"Right!" Rivo nodded. He started walking that way. "Arm ourselves. Get better weapons. Link up. Mount a real offensive. Push through the lines and—"

"Explosives," Nelly said.

"Excuse me?"

"Are you okay?"

Rivo shook his head. "No, I'm pretty far from it, actually. But it's coming back. Let's just get there as quickly as possible." He rubbed his head to help sell his story. There has to be a way to warn everyone. I need to find a way. Whatever it takes. Did they have enough explosives to destroy the embassy?

"Too bad the Zitha representative won't be there," Rivo said. "Figure we could tear it up then, huh?"

"Plenty are there. This union won't last."

"I had a thought," Rivo replied. "While I was lying there. Last thought before death. What do we do about the Veldon? When we succeed, when we prove that we don't need the Zitha, how are we going to contend with the bigger threat? The one that's driven us to a random planet we've basically pre-fab colonized in a week?"

"There's a way," Nelly said. "And those we leave behind will find it."

Shit. That answered the most pressing question. They're ready to die. Just going to commit suicide to blow that building up and take as many people with them. All to end the alliance with the Zitha. Wow. And they thought I spun up these maniacs. I'm flattered they believe I could organize this much chaos.

I guess.

"You know that?" Rivo asked. "Like for certain? Because let me tell you, when I was about to die, I started thinking that maybe not."

"What're you saying?" Nelly grabbed his arm. They stopped. The other three took up a position around them. None of them said a word. They didn't even really look at him. "What do you think we should do then if not what we're rallying for? Because to me, it sounds like you're having doubts."

"Why? Because I don't want to run over and die without a moment to think about it? Do you? Are you that eager to be killed? For a cause you can't possibly understand? Be serious with me. When you agreed to all this violence and carnage, did you really look in the mirror and say yep, today's the day, I guess!'? Because I don't think so."

"The Zitha killed..." Nelly shook her head. "No, slaughtered countless humans! And other species too! They've been at the heart of problems for generations and now we're supposed to just make nice with them? I don't think so!"

"Genocide is the answer?" Rivo asked. "That's what you're saying. We should've wiped them out completely. Killed every single one of them. Because if you're not suggesting wholesale murder of all of them, children and the elder or injured, then you're not making any sense."

Nelly glared at him.

"Just tell me straight. You're totally fine with the senseless murder of children. That's the only way you end a culture. Utterly destroy it. Burn the shit to the ground. All the people. Every. Single. One. Tell me you're okay with that, and we'll march for those explosives right now. I'll lead the damn way."

"But you don't sound convinced. And you were the one to start this."

"Minds change," Rivo said. "Yours could too. But if you genuinely feel like I just said, then I don't want to live on this world or with any of you. I'd rather die. I'd rather bring the whole thing to the ground, honestly because we're doomed. Then, maybe the Veldon had the right idea to attack us."

"What're you suggesting?"

"That fate stepped in. Decided we were done. The Uldarn, or whatever they are, might just be the catalyst for the universe saying we're too intolerant to live anymore. I admit, I've been a piece of shit about things. I've talked about other cultures in a way that was far from pretty. But I was wrong. And this is too."

"You're still willing to go over there?"

"If you answer the question wrong, then yes." Rivo nodded. "I'll make it happen." Just a lot sooner than you think. He didn't want to die, but he had to stop these people at any cost. Even if that meant blowing up another building and taking them all with him. "So answer me. Will the death of every single Zitha satisfy you? Is that what should happen?"

"Yes." Nelly waved her hand at the others. They fell into formation behind her immediately. "So let's go. Show me that you're really ready to die for what you say. Prove to me that you're ready to die for your cause.

This is your opportunity. The Zitha alliance will end and humanity will prosper."

God damn it. Rivo's shoulders slumped. I can't believe I have to find a way to destroy all that shit. This is going to be a real shit show. He picked up the pace, catching up with her. Maybe someone will find us first. Chances were slim. At least until they had the explosives. Most of the security forces would rally in front of the embassy building.

They aren't expecting this kind of final stand.

***

William felt a little better after his visit with the medic, enough to make the trek to the embassy building. Marsha stayed close, her hand hovering near his arm as if he might stumble at any moment. He understood her concern. After what he'd gone through, he expected to be much worse off.

They only had to walk four blocks to get to their destination. The territory had been claimed by security forces, so they didn't necessarily have to worry about anyone gunning for them. Not until they arrived at their destination. If they encountered more of the freaks that charged the wounded area, he figured they had a real fight ahead of them.

"Nesmith?" Ghrenda's voice poured through some heavy static. William paused to increase the gain and apply some filters. "Can you hear me?"

"Barely," William replied. "Are you aboard one of those shuttles coming down?"

"I am. Captain Kensington is as well. We're going to take charge in the embassy building. We'll provide some support. A number of additional troops are on their way to protect the building as well. I'm assuming that's where these rioters intend to hit. They don't like us much, I suppose."

"History," William said. "They're living in the past."

"Not all of them, surely. I'm guessing at least half of the people starting this are in the mood for violence. Trying to take back something they lost when the Veldon hit them. Regardless, we'll have time to discuss that later. My people are staying inside the building. We will not kill any humans unless they come inside and specifically target us."

"What about the Likari?" William asked. "Or the Korlas?"

"The Korlas are present in orbit," Ghrenda replied, "but they do not have anyone on the surface. No one important anyway. The Likari... who knows? They're likely busy remaining esoteric and strange. I don't think they're going to get involved though so it's up to us. Which suits me fine."

"Understood. We're a block out."

"When this is over," Ghrenda said, "I want you to have involvement in a task force to discover who was behind this. You and one of mine should do the trick. Show everyone we can work together. But before you protest, I should say I'm about to land and can't hear your complaint. Talk to you later."

The connection dropped.

"Ghrenda?" Marsha asked.

William nodded.

"They're coming down, aren't they?"

"Yep."

"Great." Marsha kicked a rock. "We can't guarantee that these maniacs don't have a plan for this. That they might do something insane like... I don't know. Crash a freighter into it. They have access to heavy machinery and God knows what else. I wouldn't put anything past them at this point."

"Well... let's hope they become reasonable." They won't. William saw the blank looks on the faces of those he killed. They didn't even care that they'd been shot. They charged recklessly, without a second thought. It made his skin crawl. There are more of them. We're probably not going to be able to stop them all.

"How many do you think there are?" Marsha asked. "We have a census but I feel like we've neutralized half the damn colony."

"Someone brought them in," William replied. "How, I don't know. It's not like there aren't dozens of ships monitoring this planet. Unless one of them helped somehow. We have received a lot of deliveries. It's more than possible something slipped through. You don't think they brought people though… do you?"

Marsha shrugged. "Probably, yes. In fact, it seems likely."

"Then masked their presence," William said, "with a bunch of the people down here. Wow. That's… horrifying."

"Threw a bunch of lives away to hide the fact they brought plenty more. So they're either sure this is going to work or they don't care what we find out from the bodies. This is about chaos or obliteration."

"What's the difference in the end? If we were plunged into a fight with the Zitha or even thrown apart, it wouldn't matter. We're done. Anyone with half a brain knows this. And yet here we are. Fighting our own." William slapped his leg. "Again. Sons of bitches. I can't wait to look the person in the eye who started this."

"If we're lucky enough to find out who that is. I'm not even sure there's a plan to uncover them."

"There is. I've been asked to be part of it."

Marsha shook her head. "Of course you have."

"What's wrong?"

"Just that I'd like it if you didn't have to be involved in something else. We're busy here and… I don't know. It feels like that would be dangerous. Someone orchestrated this with incredible care. They knew what they were doing. And now..." Marsha shrugged. "They've pulled this off twice."

"Improbably, yeah. But the first time failed."

"This will too," Marsha said.

Maybe.

The stairs to the embassy building loomed ahead. Security forces put down mobile cover at the base, the middle and the top. They stationed several people at each, all aiming their weapons in different directions. A mobile turret sat in the center with a shield around it. They were prepared for a frontal assault.

What about something from the air? William hoped the various ships flying around might cover those. When Captain Kensington and Ghrenda arrived, they'd likely work on the comms. Once those were up and running smoothly again, the civilians wouldn't stand a chance. No armor, limited numbers, and no comms meant they faced a death sentence.

This is a win-win for the person who wanted to cause trouble. If we survive, we kill half our workforce. And if they win, then the leaders of two cultures might be dead. William reached the stairs. It felt safe, somehow despite the fact he knew better. This place might be tough, but it's not impervious to heavy attack.

Marsha took control of the situation, talking to the soldiers about weak points. While she did, William paced the area, looking at the buildings some five hundred yards away. A lot of windows looked out on their position. Plenty of places to put someone with a rifle. Enough of them might be a real problem.

Half of these weren't even occupied yet. No one moved into the buildings. They were prepared for commerce, business, and social services. Now half of them had been damaged enough they required extensive repair before anyone could go inside, let alone find them habitable. Such a waste of resources.

Movement caught his eye from the right. William leaned, squinting to get a look. His scanner didn't pick anything up. The HUD picked up security personnel moving into position. It directed his attention to the sky to look at the incoming shuttles. But it seemed to ignore the motion on the other side of the open square.

He adjusted the computer, narrowing the field to the specific area. A group gathered there. They were armed, but remained in position.

"Marsha," William said, "look." He directed her attention. "Do we have people over there? My scans aren't picking up defensive tech."

"No." Marsha joined him. "Everyone's here." She directed the turret in that direction. "We'll reach out to them. Give those people a chance to surrender. If they do, then..."

The crowd rushed, opening fire as they did. William jerked to the left then ducked, dragging Marsha with him. They hustled over to one of the metal plates offering cover just as the turret unleashed on them.

Cannons let out a cry loud enough to make William's helmet cut down on the noise. He gritted his teeth then risked a peek to see what was happening. Pieces of the civilians ripped clean from their bodies, seared off by the weapon emplacement. Eight of them died in seconds. Another three followed.

A second group charged from the opposite flank. The turret couldn't turn in that direction fast enough, but security forces laid into them. Those in the front went down first, tripping those in the back. These seemed more in control than the ones William faced earlier, as if they knew what they were doing.

Shuttles swept over the area. The side panels opened, allowing additional security forces to cut into the rear of the attackers. Blasted from two sides, the crowd dwindled to little more than groans and corpses in a few moments. The respite felt brief. William doubted those people threw their lives away for nothing.

They were prompted. And we're about to deal with something real.

"What is wrong with them?" Marsha asked. "Did these people act like the ones you saw?"

William shook his head. "No. These people shouted."

"Excuse me?"

"The ones that charged us in the courtyard," William said, "I don't remember them making any noise. They just... came at us. And died without a groan. It was eerie. So no. The people we just saw weren't like that at all."

A mass of people gathered near the building at the far end of the plaza. They didn't advance, in fact they began milling about inside the structure. His scanner struggled to count them all the way they swarmed about one another. Like insects preparing for battle. The thought gave him a chill.

"There they are," Marsha said. "That's... a lot of people."

"And when they charge..." William shrugged. "I don't even know what we're going to do about it."

"Put them down," Marsha replied. "And keep this building safe. Along with everyone in it."

Shuttles landed on the roof.

Comms crackled to life. Captain Kensington addressed people. "We have brought considerable reinforcements and we'll offer air support. If those rioters charge, we can finish them before they get halfway across the courtyard. I am attempting to communicate with them to come up with a peaceful resolution. Standby. Do not fire until I give the order."

Marsha set the comm to one way so only William could hear her. "No one wants to shoot them."

"They'll make it so we don't have a choice," William replied. "I guarantee it. After what I saw, all of those people we're looking at will be dead in the next half hour. Or they'll somehow succeed. Enough bodies thrown at a problem might be enough to get through."

"I don't get it," Marsha said. "Why are they doing this? If they won't be around to enjoy their success, what's the point?"

"We'll find out who benefits later." William put his hand on her shoulder. He gave her a squeeze. "Right now, we have to focus on keeping this building secure and surviving the encounter. We do those two things, everything else falls into place." Half a dozen security forces came out of the door, filling the ranks on the stairs.

"At least we've got numbers." Marsha looked back at the others. "That's a lot of firepower on our side of things."

Air support too, William thought. Though that's going to cause a stir amongst the survivors. We'll have so much diplomacy to get through before this is over. He drew a deep breath, preparing himself for the next few minutes. Looks a lot worse than the fight on the Zitha station… and I thought that had been the worst day of my life.

***

Rivo stumbled as Nelly shoved him along the street. She'd disarmed him shortly before. Supposedly, they were close to the depot though he had no way of knowing. Nothing around him looked familiar. Not with all the dead bodies, blackened walls, and other carnage. The debris in the streets alone looked like more than twenty hours of work for a team of ten.

Even with heavy equipment.

That didn't cover the downed buildings or policing the corpses. Rivo generally kept his people away from taking care of bodies. He hated the idea someone might have to round them all up. Where would they even go? Incineration? A couple people had died during the first week of their work on Sentinel, so they started a graveyard.

I don't think morale would do well if we suddenly had enough bodies to populate the whole damn thing.

"Move!" Nelly shoved him again.

"What are you doing?" Rivo glared at her. "Why are you in such a hurry to die?"

"Because we're in the middle of a time crunch. And I won't let you dally. Buying time won't help you. Just move!"

"I am moving, god damn it!"

"There!" Nelly pointed to two people standing out front of a building. "That's where it all is."

What does she plan to do? Strap it to people? Force them to make a mad dash for the structure? It won't work! Rivo saw how they intended to protect the embassy building if necessary. The soldiers thought about such a problem. He thought they were being paranoid before. I won't question them again.

The two people standing guard didn't look at them. Neither even twitched as they entered the building. When they crossed the threshold, Rivo felt his heart drop. There were at least fifty people milling about the open space, setting crates beside one another. A different person opened them.

Only one guy seemed to be talking. He directed the others, giving them orders as they went about their mindless work.

"Wellik!" Nelly shouted. "Hey!"

"Oh thank God!" Wellik hurried over and hugged her. Rivo thought he recognized him, but he couldn't place from where. The man couldn't have been much older than thirty. He wore a full beard, his dusty brown hair curled around his head. "I thought you might not make it here in time."

They seem like they genuinely care about each other. So why are they this eager to die?

"We made it." Nelly pointed at Rivo. "Look who I found."

"Rivo Dess." Wellik clapped Rivo on the shoulder. "I thought you'd be sitting back guiding the troops, not down here amongst us all. What a privilege to meet you in person before the final push. Come to lead us directly.

This must be important if you're willing to put it all on the line for us."

"Not entirely," Nelly said. "He may be having some doubts."

"About the cause?" Wellik tilted his head. "I don't understand."

Rivo replied, "Don't worry about it. Doesn't matter. Those crates. They have the explosives?"

"They do." Wellik nodded. "And just through those doors... the plaza of the embassy building. We can obliterate it with what we've got."

"Yeah?" Rivo snorted. "Christ, kid. Are you an idiot? What're you going to do? Run it over there? They've got a turret up by now. Probably plenty of cover to shoot at anyone leaving this building. You don't even have armor. What do you think will happen to those explosives when an energy blast hits them?"

"Oh..." Wellik looked even more confused. "He doesn't even know the plan, Nelly. Are you sure he's in on it? That he started it?"

"I thought he must have," Nelly replied, "but maybe he's with them."

"Are you people insane?" Rivo shook his head. "I'm with humanity. I care about people and making sure we prosper! No, I didn't plan your ridiculous raid! But if this is what we've come to, then I don't even know what to say. You're all..."

"Attention," a voice boomed over the city, projected by a number of speakers positioned around the embassy plaza. "This is Captain Harold Kensington. Whatever grievance you have, this is not the way to air it. We need to have a conversation. I invite the leader of your organization to do so via communicator."

Nelly scoffed. "Here it is. The lying bastard!"

Like she ever heard from him before.

"We do not wish to hurt you," Kensington continued. "The fact of the matter is, we don't even know what this is about. Please place your demands so we can see about addressing them. I stand ready to take a call from your leader. Unfortunately, I do have to warn you about charging this building."

Wellik said, "They'll kill us all. I'm sure he knows we're aware."

Rivo grabbed Wellik, yanking him around to face him. "Maybe you should listen and not throw these lives away!" He pointed at the others. "What's wrong with them anyway? They haven't so much as tilted their heads to listen to what he's got to say! What's going on with you guys?"

"The EDF," Wellik replied, "doesn't control me."

"If you charge," Kensington said, "then we will have no choice but to use lethal force. Please do not make us do that. We are willing and able to work with you. This doesn't have to turn into a bloodbath. I await your call and connection. The time for fighting is over. Now, we need to talk. Your move."

Nelly moved over to one of the crates. "Our move indeed. Get them geared up."

"What is the plan?" Rivo asked. "He just said if you charge, he'll use lethal force! I already told you what will happen if those bombs take an energy blast. You going to make a scene? Show them what you're made of? Protest by dying? Come on! Think! One of the two of you can still do that even if these poor bastards can't."

Wellik joined Nelly. "You think they won't kill us still, Rivo? That we're not going to be executed for all this? Our cause requires us to make a sacrifice. And it will be grand. You see, you're right. The frontal assault will cause them to kill these people. But they can't focus on every side. Not the way they've set up on those stairs."

"And so," Nelly continued, "when we get out there, the amount of ordnance we bring will be more than enough to turn the entire plaza into a crater. And the embassy building will fall with it. We've thought this through. We've got experts, too. They know how to destroy things. Perhaps even better than the military."

I can stop this one, Rivo thought. Make this place explode. Show the others what's going on. He considered the next few moments. If I make a mistake, they'll just kill me. I won't do anyone any good. But these other people don't seem to be paying any attention at all. Nor do they appear to be a threat.

Rivo had worked around explosives before. The sort these people used at least. He'd watched plenty of demolition teams take out rock formations and other obstacles so they might build an outpost or create living space for people. They could be impressive though they tended to only use the exact amount required for the job.

Some didn't even go for detonation, opting for energy weapons instead. They had more control over the reaction. Lower cost colonies went the old fashioned way. Bombs tended to be cheaper than fancy weapons. Those places relied on projectile weapons for self-defense against the wildlife in the area.

These thoughts distracted him from what he had to do.

Wellik and Nelly both had their backs to him. Rivo rushed forward, grabbing Nelly by the hair. He dragged her backward, yanking her pistol from its holster. As he expected, the people around them didn't even respond. They just kept working with the explosives, putting it on themselves.

"What're you doing?" Wellik went for his weapon. Rivo shot him in the chest. The blow knocked him over the explosives. He let out a cry.

Nelly threw an elbow, nailing him in the sternum. Rivo let her go, kicking her in the backs of the knees as he did. She went down, reaching for her weapon. He fired, narrowly missing. Fortunately, it hit the floor. He dove on top of her, using his weight to pin her to the floor.

Maybe I'm close enough. Rivo wrestled with her until she ended up on her stomach, pressed to the floor. He tapped his comm. "William! Marsha! Anyone! They're coming at you with explosives! All sides! You have to be quick! You have to—"

"Get him off of me!" Nelly shouted. She started bucking, making it difficult to keep her down. "Hurry!"

Rivo punched her in the back of the head. The blow stopped her from thrashing around. He thought it bought him a moment until the people around him grabbed him from behind, dragging him away from Nelly. He threw a kick as they lifted, the toe of his boot catching her just below the floating rib.

He thrashed about, trying desperately to free himself. Half the people in the room wore the explosive vests. They were ready to charge out there and when they did, they'd likely herald the coming of all the rest of the freaks. His captors gripped his biceps, though he maintained control of his stolen pistol.

I know what to do. The thought of it burned almost as much as what would happen in the next few moments. This is the only way. If my message didn't go through to the others… if they didn't hear me, then I have no choice but to at least prevent a quarter of these nut jobs from getting out there.

Struggling didn't help. Those holding him maintained an iron grip. He might as well have tried to break handcuffs. Every time he jerked to the left or right, they didn't so much as move with him. They were as unbending as metal. It didn't make sense. They weren't robots. But whatever happened to them gave them an unnatural strength.

They have no sense of self-preservation either. Whoever made them like this is sick. Or completely insane. How would one turn a living being into this sort of fleshy machine? And do so with enough to warrant an army? They had invaded Sentinel One. A large enough group to threaten every life on the colony.

I hope Trivak makes it out of this. Rivo resigned himself to what had to happen. The next few minutes would determine whether or not he managed to give his people a fighting chance. Or if he'd end up dead while so many humans threw themselves into oblivion for some madman's suicidal cause.

Nelly stood, nursing her side. She glared at him then spit blood on the floor. "I should've killed you out on the street," she rasped the words. "Wellik! Are you alive?"

He didn't respond.

"Yeah, he's done, lady." Rivo tilted his head. "And so are you. This little attack isn't going to work."

"It already has." Nelly advanced on him. She reached for his gun.

Rivo kicked her in the groin. She doubled over, stumbling back as he lifted his weapon. Fuck. Sorry, Trivak. I hope this wakes them all up out there.

"Don't!" Nelly shouted. "You can't!"

"I wish that was true." Rivo pulled the trigger. His blast struck one of the explosive crates. The reaction was instantaneous and abrupt. A white light burst from it. Searing heat filled the room.

Nelly screamed. A deep boom cut her short. The others stood placidly, dying in utter silence. They hadn't been alive for a while. Rivo thought about it in his final moment, as the ground shook and the walls around him collapsed. He felt the heat though his mind refused to accept reality.

He was gone before the ceiling collapsed.

***

"Did you hear that?" William asked. "Marsha, was that Rivo?"

"Yeah." Marsha hurried over to join him. They stood at the base of the stairs. She pointed across the plaza. "What's going on over there?"

"Those are the people Kensington addressed." William tapped his comm. "Rivo, come in. Can you hear me? I didn't copy your last message, over." He waited a moment. "Nothing."

"Interference, maybe," Marsha said. "Let me play that back. I can clean it up." She turned away, focusing on the computer controls on her left arm.

William continued to stare, watching the people mill about the building. He doubted they had any intention of listening to the captain's demand. If they wanted to talk, they would have already reached out. Their demands, whatever they were, needed a punctuation mark. Something no one could deny.

What they didn't understand was the fact they would lose all of their credibility and any sort of leverage by killing faction leaders. More likely they'd be hunted down like dogs. Just before the cultures started tearing each other apart in a second front style war. Something that would've ended civilization as they knew it.

At least for us.

"He's saying they're coming at us from all sides." Marsha hummed, turning in place. "They'd have to cross the plaza. But they'd be coming upon sheer walls on all sides but the front. Where the stairs are. He mentioned explosives too. They can't possibly have enough to do any real damage."

"Have you seen what the civilians use to clear debris? Obstacles to building?" William shook his head. "They probably have way more than they need. Providing they can get close enough to set them off.

You'd better warn the commanders. I'll reposition the troops to get better coverage."

They both turned away when a resounding boom rattled the ground. Concussive force struck them from behind, throwing them to the ground. William rolled on his back in time to watch flames hurl some two hundred yards into the air. Scattered debris from the building rained down into the plaza.

Other structures went down around that one. The concussive force annihilated three buildings and compromised several more. He scrambled to his feet as his HUD showed movement from the other three sides. All but the front where they had the mainstay of their defense.

Including the turret.

"Move!" William shouted, "take them out! Fire at will! I need eight people in the back immediately! Air support!" His voice was drowned out by comm chatter and the roar of ships overhead. Dozens of people came spilling out of the streets, maybe a hundred on the eastern side.

Like the ones that attacked the wounded, these made no sounds whatsoever. Scans showed they all wore high explosive packs. Each one might've been enough to take down a wall or obliterate a tall boulder. Any ten of them might be plenty to put a dent in the embassy building.

William opened fire. Explosions all around him made him wince as the other soldiers laid into the approaching forces. Every pop of a vest took out at least one more though the people spread out enough to ensure they didn't lose enough to matter. At first, it seemed like they wouldn't even make it twenty yards.

At fifty, William wondered if they'd survive.

Shuttles swept over the scene, scorching the ground as they went. Every pass took ten or more. Pieces of dirt and cement flew in the air, colored by misty gore. The once tranquil area, a wide open space for people to congregate and meet. The idea had been to provide them a peaceful place to work together.

Craters split the garden boxes. Paths were pulverized to glassy sheets. Bits of clothing and corpses marred the grass and still standing trees. The suicide bombers continued their approach, bursting like confetti every time they took a shot. Scans showed they only need to get five through on any side to cause considerable damage.

Enough to take it down? That seemed unlikely.

"Where are all these people coming from?" Marsha shouted. "How did they get them here? This is more than all the colonists we brought!"

William kept shooting. He didn't reply, just fired as fast as he could. Five of the security forces pressed forward on the left. They got out in the field, blasting away in an effort to push the enemy line back. As they opened fire, a group of the civilians changed course to fall upon them.

They all exploded together, annihilating the soldiers in a great flash. Their armor didn't protect them, nor did they have a chance to flee. The crater left behind was telling as well. Though William wondered exactly how they intended to destroy the building when the foundation was a sheer surface.

Then a couple got close enough to detonate. They didn't. Instead, they began running toward the front of the building. Only three at first. As they burst from multiple shots, they left behind darkened stains on the wall. A crack here and there, but nothing too dangerous or threatening.

If it hadn't exploded... Was Rivo with them? Did he cause that detonation? William shouted into the comm, "Close the doors! Barricade it! Make sure they do not get inside!" That was the plan. Break through the line, spread the security forces thin, get a few people in to cause as much damage as possible.

As one neared the foot of the stairs, he took three shots from the turret. His explosion knocked down one of the defensive barriers, ripping it from the stairs. William hadn't realized someone anchored them down. Chunks of mortar came up with the metal plate and it still flipped in the air as if it had been flung by a catapult.

"We can't stop them," Marsha said. She pressed against him. "There are more than three hundred out there still! They're making a charge. Even the shuttles can't... not when they're all spread out." She turned to William. "They're going to get through. We can't stop that."

"I..." William couldn't argue. He looked around, saw the masses vaulting over craters, dying in droves, but Marsha was right. Eventually, they'd get through. And when they did, it would be over. Though he'd probably be dead long before he had the chance to watch the building go down.

Fighting to the end felt futile. Particularly when even the shuttles couldn't finish them all off. He steeled himself. The nearest group made it within a hundred yards.

"Greetings," Ghrenda's voice burst over the loudspeakers. "Living bombs are a despicable way to get your point across. It hasn't worked for any culture before. Fortunately, we have a way to deal with it. We only needed a moment to discover your method of detonation. And—"

A high-pitched noise followed, loud enough to make William's helmet cut off all sound from the outside. He watched as the bodies exploded without being shot. Silence made it surreal. Dozens of people, hundreds... all died in short order. Their bodies left behind black stains, which promised to be the only evidence they ever existed at all.

Rivo… William tried him on the comm. Chatter died down. The security forces didn't have anything to say. They watched the horror unfold until the final corpse vanished in a flash. No one moved more than to look around. William didn't see any cheers or elation. No hugs or high fives.

I'm not surprised. Watching so many people go in short order… it sickened him. Even as he thanked God they didn't get close enough to kill him or Marsha. Though they were damn close. A sport field. That's all. No distance at all and we would've ended up like those other soldiers. How many of us died in this?

Rivo did not respond.

"He's not going to," Marsha said. "Not if he was in that building." She pointed. "And if he had been, we won't find him."

"I can't… I can't pretend… I mean, I need to see for myself. I have to find him. I have to…"

"Calm down." Marsha put her hand on his shoulder. "We have a lot to do. And that's just one thing." She motioned around her. "We lost nearly two dozen people in that push."

"How? Why'd anyone go down there!"

Marsha shook her head. "A few sacrificed themselves. Preventing larger groups from getting closer. You didn't see the clusters? The suicide bombers closing in on soldiers who dared to go out there? They took them out and anyone else nearby. We're ridiculously lucky they didn't make it to the stairs."

"Yeah, I get it." William slumped onto the stairs. His injuries started to bother him again. A throbbing pain hit his temples, making him nauseous. "Jesus Christ. What the hell did we do here today?"

"Watched a lot of people die," Marsha said, "and given our cultures a chance to recover. But we have to act fast. Find out why this happened, discover who was responsible. When we do that, we can heal. Until then... we're just as busy as we were before. Maybe more so at this point."

"She's right," Ghrenda said. He stood behind them. "We have to come to terms with this quickly, William. And clean this mess up fast."

"You hit the frequency on their detonators," William replied. "How'd you figure it out? That shouldn't have been possible..."

Ghrenda sat beside him. "They used remote detonators anyway. Someone out there wanted to blow them up when they wanted. When Riut figured it out, I had him detonate them all. Before they could reach the embassy building. Fortunately, there were no others active in buildings or we might've taken down more structures."

"I should've thought of that." William looked down. "I was so busy..."

"Don't," Marsha interrupted. "You were hurt. We were fighting our own. And it was to the death so..."

"She's right," Ghrenda continued. "I can't have you beating yourself up anyway. The two of you need to work with my people to find the culprits responsible for this tragedy. As quickly as you can." He stood. "I'd say you should start later, though. We're going to have our meeting inside."

"Still?" William swept his hand over the plaza. "With all of that out there?"

"Just proves how much we need solidarity," Ghrenda said. "We'll have people start cleaning right away. The two of you need to leave the planet for now. Get back to your ship, take orbit, get some rest. See your medical officer. When you're done, after our meeting, I expect you both to be investigating."

"Yes, sir." William nodded. He watched Ghrenda leave before pulling off his helmet. "Funny. I thought that guy would be a total maniac. Like... raider to the core. Not someone we could ever do business with."

"And now?" Marsha asked. She pulled her helmet off as well then scratched her head. "What's your thought?"

"He might find himself in charge of this new alliance. He's a better choice than Bracknel." William sighed. "But I'm with him. We should get that medical aid. Or I should at least. I can go back to the ship if you want to stay here."

Marsha directed his attention to Captain Kensington. "I think they've got someone in charge here. We should go. Like he said, we have a lot to do after all this. We can't be exhausted and beat up either. This has to happen the right way. No cutting corners or twisting facts."

"I'm with you." William pushed himself up. Marsha steadied him. They stared away from the plaza. "Okay. I can't believe all that just happened. I can't believe..."

"Don't think about it," Marsha replied. "It'll occupy all our thoughts soon enough. Hey, you and I made it. And I think that warrants something."

"What's that?"

"I love you, William. Feels a little soon to say it. But considering all we've been through, and what's happening... I'm not holding it back for the sake of social convention. I love you. And that was worth fighting for today."

"I love you too." William held her hand. "And yes, if there was any reason to save this place today, it was this feeling right here." Along with saving what was left of humanity. Keeping this alliance alive. Giving ourselves a fighting chance to get through this. All of it matters. And if they had their way, they'd keep it alive.

In whatever capacity society required.

□

Chapter 10

Eliza breached atmosphere, bringing the ship in for a landing. She'd gone through plenty of simulation time with the Pytheas, but didn't have any practical experience. When they encountered heavy turbulence, she had to fight back a rush of panic. All the surface destruction wreaked havoc on the weather patterns.

"Steady her out," Gareth said. He spoke in a calm tone, which surprised her. Considering the violence of their descent. "Take your time with the maneuvering thrusters."

"It's the predictability," Eliza replied. She ground her sweat slick palms on her pants. "We're going through wind in total chaos. I think we'll have to push through it with a lot of bumps. Sorry about that."

"She is correct," Zoe added. "I'd like to also point out this ship can handle the pressure we're under. Many would not be able to do so. Which would explain why there are people on the surface still. I doubt anyone could rescue them. Certainly not the traditional Veldon ships met during the war."

Which is probably the only one that had a vested interest in keeping people alive. Eliza guessed anyone alive below had been in defiance of the Uldarn. The old military machinery didn't have what it took to push them back. We're looking at the remnants of a society. One we easily believed they had it in them to destroy our culture.

The screen showed nothing but dark, swirling clouds. Scans let her know she still had plenty of altitude. But breaching cloud coverage would be nice to get a sense of the settlement. How bad off were they? Did they have any shelter at all? Or would they find a bunch of people barely alive, scarred and scorched from the radiation?

Readings indicated they passed through the sort of contamination consistent with old style nuclear weapons. Only more than humanity ever had back on Earth. Before the armistice, before all the various societies merged, the human race maintained the capacity to annihilate themselves many times over.

Space travel calmed some of the animosity down. It gave them a purpose beyond posturing and threatening to kill each other. What had the Veldon done? The briefing on the attack on Earth indicated they hadn't obliterated Earth with radiation. So why here? Why ruin the colony?

More questions. Too many, in fact.

"Time to land," Gareth said, "what've you got?"

"Uh…" Eliza hesitated. "Six minutes, sir. I'm taking it slow so we don't take any damage from this front."

"That's okay. They've waited this long." Gareth cleared his throat. "Lyra, how are the shields?"

"Holding," Lyra replied. "We're fine. We could probably take it a lot faster if you wanted. I'll keep an eye on the defenses. Let you know if we need to slow down. Those people we're about to meet might be happy to see us. But they're definitely in need of some immediate support."

Zed added, "They've needed help since this attack happened. Zoe and I are getting a good grasp on how long the planet's been like this. At least a month."

"A month!" Gareth scoffed. "Those people survived down there for a month?"

Zoe said, "It wasn't that bad several weeks ago. It's progressive, remember. The planet will die eventually. There may have been survivors in the other settlements too."

The ship broke through the clouds. The settlement sprawled out over a dozen miles. The outskirts remained mostly intact while a blackened crater was all that remained of the central area. Scans showed the life signs at the far eastern side, amongst some of the few remaining buildings that appeared structurally sound.

A lazy energy beam rose from the surface then blurred as it went straight for the Pytheas. It struck the bow before Eliza could respond. The blow wasn't hard enough to be felt over the constant battering of turbulence. They'd be out of the worst of the weather soon enough. An attack complicated matters.

"Direct hit," Lyra said, "shields held at ninety-five percent. But those things are pretty powerful. Not the vibration tech we've come to see from the Veldon either. Definitely their old gear. I didn't know they hit that hard." She turned to Gareth. "How did you guys contend with it before our enhanced defenses?"

"We tried not to get hit," Gareth replied. "Eliza, do what you can to evade any other assaults. Who the hell is shooting at us? And why?"

"Automated turrets," Zoe said. "They are not controlled by the inhabitants. In fact, a few of the Veldon seem to be attempting to shut them down. I suspect they will have a difficult time as the area has been secured with defensive barriers and shields. Along with some more automated defenses."

"Of course," Zed snorted. "The one thing that survives in this place is a bunch of weaponry. How am I not surprised?"

"Attempt to jam it," Gareth ordered. "See if you can't cut the AI off from control. Eliza, we can risk some more speed. Get us on the ground ASAP."

"Yes, sir." Eliza dipped the nose then fired the rear thrusters, increasing speed. She tapped the maneuvering thrusters to shove them toward starboard. The motion hurled them much further than she anticipated, but it worked out. Another attack rose from the surface, this time a volley of shots.

All of them missed.

"Great job," Lyra said, "keep that up, and we'll be below their attack pattern in a minute. Uh... forty-five seconds to be precise." She cursed. "And it looks like they want us to earn it because here comes some more."

Eliza didn't see anything. She assumed Lyra picked up an energy surge. She hit the bottom maneuvering thrusters then veered them to port. Of the six blasts coming their way, only three caught them near the rear thrusters. This gave them a rumble seconds before they left the turbulence.

She leveled out, taking them back toward the survivors. They'd be landing in twenty seconds though she felt like they were going way too fast.

A text message appeared on her terminal. I'll help. Relax. Forward thrusters fired so their nose went up. They dropped swiftly before coming in for a hot landing. More weapon fire disappeared into the sky. The towers could no longer target them. They'd made it into position though Eliza's heart raced.

I can't believe we did it!

"Great work." Gareth stood. "Zed, let Chelsea and the others know they are clear to begin their exploration. Lyra, I want you to watch the scanner like a hawk. You see any danger, you call it out immediately.

Eliza, don't let your guard down. We may have to launch at a moment's notice."

And leave the others? Eliza bit her tongue rather than asked the question. She figured the commander knew his business. He didn't have to answer to her. But I can't imagine leaving our people on this planet. Not even for a few minutes. Their armor would protect them from the environment for a while, but eventually, it would break down.

Likely within ten hours. Maybe less if they got into a firefight. Damage could break down the integrity of the defenses. I'm glad I'm not out there. And the fact Patrick went off on his own... he'd probably have joined Chelsea to explore the area. Make contact with the Veldon. I wonder what kind of risk he's in right now.

"We are secure," Eliza said. "But we're ready. Give the word, and I can get us out of here."

"Chelsea and the others are disembarking," Zed added. "But I don't like those defenses. They're really trying to crank down to get a shot at us. Weird."

Lyra waved her hand at the screen. "Probably malfunctioning. Had there not been people around them, I would've happily blown them to shit."

"Keep an eye," Gareth said. "Bring up a tactical comm, Zed. I want to have constant contact with the away team."

"No clue how to do that..." Zed mumbled.

Zoe said, "I've got it. The comm is online."

Hurry, guys, Eliza thought. This planet's done with living creatures. I think it would like to violently die on its own terms. After surviving their last mission, she felt sensitive about seismic activity and the concept of a world trying to shrug off offenders. They started a forest fire and obliterated large sections of a mountain.

Leaving behind ruins not unlike these. Only with less civilization based contaminants. Well, if the people could answer some questions, it would be worth the visit. Though staying any longer than they had to put them in serious jeopardy.

***

Chelsea led the way down the ramp. The Pytheas kicked up dust, cutting visibility to less than thirty feet. Her visor shifted to thermal. A few blobs appeared on the right side of the nearest building. All of them seemed to be surrounding the defensive turret. None of the survivors approached.

"This way," Chelsea said. She headed to the left, away from the Veldon members. She wanted to make contact with the humans first. Scans indicated they needed to clear a quarter mile to get to their location. Through at least three buildings and a down a stretch of road.

A heavy wind buffeted her from the left. She leaned into it as she hustled along, keeping her rifle aimed dead ahead. An orange glow caught her attention from dead ahead, emitted through a ground floor window. Flames struggled against the wind but when it slowed, they came right back.

Scan suggested the burning came from some kind of volatile leak. Some older colonies used natural gas for power. Considering what this place represented, with any sort of diplomatic envoys coming to visit, she would've thought they'd use the most up-to-date equipment.

Instead, the last remaining settlement turned out to be like some of the earliest human colonies. Even Mars.

"Scans are picking up weapons," Ithila said, "both a stockpile and on those Veldon."

"Eyes up then," Chelsea replied. "They seem busy, so let's give them the benefit of the doubt. They could be trying to take that thing offline. I'm guessing they'd like to get off this planet if at all possible."

"Meaning," Barty added, "they won't be too discerning about trying to steal the ship. So we need to be cautious. We didn't go over rules of engagement."

"If they shoot at us," Chelsea said, "we return fire. But we're here for answers so try not to start by killing people."

"Technically," Ithila replied, "they are Veldon. And they tend to shoot first. Just... as a point of reference."

They reached the first building with the fire roaring inside. Chelsea glanced in the window. Charred bodies rested on the floor, while others were fused to the wall. It appeared an appliance had exploded, incinerating those within the room, probably killing them instantly. Which might have been a mercy given the state of the area.

"Keep moving." Chelsea directed them to the back. "Barty, take point." She jogged backward after Ithila took the middle. She watched the scans of the Veldon some three hundred yards away. They had yet to move in their direction, but they just have known about the away team.

Though maybe without technology, they had no idea. Why not go to the ship? They likely know that if we take off, the turret will start shooting again. And since they can't be sure we'd survive a full-on blast, taking it offline is a top priority. All a guess, but it makes sense in this situation.

Chelsea caught up to Barty. He'd stopped at the corner. When she looked around, the wall of the structure had collapsed outward. More bodies scattered about the area. Definitely Veldon, though few of them were whole. At least a couple had been blown to bits with the largest sections settling into holes or crushed by debris.

"Wow," Barty said. "This is carnage. You guys think this is what Earth looked like?"

"Probably in some parts," Chelsea replied. "We have to keep moving. Get to the other side of this place where the humans are. Give those Veldon a chance to do whatever they're doing."

A horrible thought occurred to her. What if they're trying to make the turret shoot the Pytheas? Take it off its axis. God, that would be ridiculous. They'd be totally suicidal at that point. She prayed they wanted to make friends, to find a peaceful way to leave the place before they all died by poison.

Chelsea took the lead this time, moving through the debris. She had to slow it down to make it without tripping. The remains still smoked, as if the explosion happened recently. That didn't make a lot of sense. More likely, something from the sky made it happen. Rain from earlier in the day perhaps.

They cleared the treacherous part of the field, moving into a crater. The ground crunched under her feet, shards of glass and molten filth. As she started up the incline after the lowest point, she glanced away from the settlement toward the horizon. A green-brown haze cut down visibility to less than a hundred yards.

But there was nothing out there. Just an endless wasteland pockmarked by craters from the orbital bombardment. Which meant the Veldon didn't execute a precision attack against their own settlement. They laid down heavy fire, unconcerned with the impact beyond ensuring the structures went down eventually.

Or maybe they targeted people trying to flee the carnage. Chelsea imagined a precession of civilians rushing into the vast openness only to be cut down by heavy fire. Their deaths would have been immediate, but the terror between leaving the buildings and dying... the thought made her sick to her stomach.

"You okay?" Barty asked. He stood beside her. "You stopped."

"Thinking." Chelsea pushed on. "About what happened here."

"Nothing good," Barty said. "Atrocities."

He's putting it mildly.

The next building remained standing though fire scorched the interior. Why it stayed aloft, she couldn't guess. But it seemed like a harsh wind might bring the whole thing down. They gave it a wide berth, hustling to clear the place before moving on. Their destination wasn't too much further ahead.

Scans showed the humans remained together in a structure. Drawing closer presented more details. They found a way to hide underground. Twenty feet in fact. It didn't appear to be a bunker, but maybe a reinforced basement did the trick. How, she had no idea. Battlecruiser weaponry should've collapsed the building above them.

Meaning they'd be dead regardless. It would just take longer as they starved or suffocated.

Chelsea slowed as she came upon the first organic remains scattered across the area. She counted a dozen torsos before giving up. Those were human. As she drew closer, there were Veldon bodies as well. Probably a hundred in all, though it would be difficult to tell since none of them were whole.

"A building stood here," Ithila said, "that's what happened to these people. A direct hit to the structure likely caused whatever power system to explode. They were all too close to it."

"Maybe," Barty said, "but they'd be crushed by rubble, wouldn't they?"

Ithila said, "The new Veldon weapons vibrate. They may have turned the walls to dust. But the reactor..." He shrugged. "I don't know. I could be wrong. There's debris from other structures. This is an atrocity though. A real one."

"Keep moving," Chelsea said. "Comm check. Pytheas, do you have us on scans still?"

"Affirmative," Zed replied. "You're getting close to the humans. Those Veldon are still tinkering with the big turret. Not sure what they're up to. The power's online for it."

"Let me know if they come our way."

The next building held the people they wanted to see. Chelsea directed the others to fan out as she headed for the front of the structure. Ithila went toward the back. Barty remained in position to cover them both.

His vantage gave him a clear line of sight to the ends of each, though if they needed him, he'd have to make a dash.

An opening spread out in front of the building, a plaza or courtyard. It had become a wasteland, pocked with craters and dust. Chelsea didn't see any more bodies, just wreckage including a couple vehicles that had been annihilated. How the hell did the turret survive all this then?

The emplacement sat a good two hundred yards away, looming over the city like a gargoyle. It didn't do much to protect them against the assault, which must have frustrated the colonists. Everything else fell around the one thing meant to hold off such attacks and it remained unscathed.

Chelsea glanced around the corner. The front doors seemed to have hinges. They were intact and closed. She approached. Her HUD showed movement inside. Taking aim, she waited a tick. Bursting in on the people might cause trouble. Sometimes saviors were difficult to differentiate from invaders.

"I've lost you," Barty said. "Chelsea, you've left my field of view."

"It's okay," Chelsea replied. "Join me at the front. Ithila, hustle to get to the other side. I think we're about to have a welcoming committee."

"Is that a good thing?" Ithila asked. "And I'm on my way."

I hope it is. Chelsea didn't know how to answer the question. Scans didn't show weapons, though she may not have been able to pick up anything too primitive. If they came charging out with clubs and frying pans, then she'd be in a bad way. Then there's the Veldon behind us.

"Watch out!" A voice shouted from inside, just before the door burst open. Several people huddled in the shadows, but one stumbled out. He wore a tattered EDF uniform, his hair askew. Filth caked his face and hands, blood stained his tunic. "Are you… you people are with the…"

Chelsea nodded, but she didn't lower her weapon. "We're EDF. Who the hell are you?"

"Lieutenant Sylas Gimbal." He offered a quick salute.

"I'm Lieutenant Commander Chelsea Weston. We came out here to find out what happened to the Veldon. What they were up to. Have you heard about the attack on Earth? Do you know they invaded?"

"Yes." Sylas nodded. "My team and I took refuge here."

"What were you doing?" Barty asked. "What the hell's going on?"

"We worked for Nila Chance, an ambassador on the border. Our intelligence office put us under her command to gather information about the Veldon, just in case they were on the verge of attacking. We sent back what we could but our ship was destroyed. Shot down on this planet."

"So what happened next?" Chelsea lowered her weapon. She climbed the stairs. "What about the Veldon that are monkeying with the turret? Are they hostile?"

"No!" Sylas shook his head emphatically. "In fact, they're on our side. They've been hiding us here. That's…" He bowed his head. "That's why this colony was attacked. The Uldarn-backed Veldon annihilated this place. Every settlement. Blew them straight to hell, poisoned the atmosphere until this place here became the last place to hide."

"Jesus," Barty muttered. "So you guys were running around behind lines with the Veldon to gather intel? That seems insane. How long were you operating like that?"

"Six months," Sylas said. "And it worked out great. Our ship employed some state of the art tech. The ability to bend scans. We could park near a natural satellite, tap into comms, and listen for days. But… let me tell you guys something, if you have a ship, I'd rather we talk about this from the safety of orbit… or even on the way out of Veldon space."

"What about your saviors?" Ithila asked. "The Veldon that protected you."

"They…" Sylas shrugged. "They've talked about staying no matter what. They're sixth generation. Lived here their whole lives."

"Are there other Veldon that are friendly?" Chelsea asked. "The original fleet maybe?"

"I don't know… I don't think so." Sylas shrugged. "Regardless, we don't have hazard gear, Lieutenant Commander. Can we please move?"

"Right." Chelsea gestured to Barty. "Gather them up. Lead them toward the Pytheas." She turned to Ithila. "I don't know about you, but I'd like to talk to those Veldon. Find out why they want to sacrifice themselves rather than come with us."

"They would surely be assets," Ithila said, "if they know anything. I'm with you. We can talk to them together."

"Great." Chelsea nodded. "Okay, Barty. You know what to do. We'll see you soon."

"Be careful," Sylas called, "they're reasonable, but don't be hostile. You know how this culture can be. Even the friendly ones are a little twitchy."

I can't ask him to come with us. He's exposed. He needs medical attention. Chelsea nodded. "We'll keep it in mind. See you back at the ship." She turned away, heading toward the turret, plunging into the dust. Out in the open, they likely appeared as little more than silhouettes. Dangerous ones with full armor.

Please don't shoot us on sight. I'd prefer a peaceful talk. But they were Veldon… and walking up on them carried risk.

***

Gareth leaned forward, staring at the tactical map of the area. There were so few people alive on the surface, it was easy to track their people. But the situation felt wrong. Something about it screamed in the back of his mind. It wasn't the environment or the humans but those Veldon. They hadn't even tried to make contact yet.

That's fishy, but they're busy. Maybe they don't care. What more can we do to them? There's nothing left to take. Or destroy for that matter.

"They've made contact," Zed said. "Barty's bringing the humans back right now."

Gareth tapped the comm down to the medical bay. "Keppler, we've got incoming people requiring medical aid. Be on the ready."

"What's wrong with them?" Keppler asked.

"They've been exposed to God knows what." Gareth shrugged. "I have no idea. Plan for a full check."

"Whatever." Keppler killed the line.

"That guy," Lyra said. "He only cares about that experiment."

"Not true," Zed replied. "He's just gruff when things don't involve the serum. Zoe gathered some more information about that turret. They're juicing up the power levels. Giving it a boost. I guess when it didn't take us down, they figured they needed more help. Are they insane?"

"Desperate," Zoe said. "Broken. Afraid. They aren't thinking clearly."

"Nope." Lyra leaned back in her seat, hands behind her head. "Because even prison would be better than suffocating when the air turns so foul nothing could live down here. But they'd rather shoot at it."

Gareth didn't necessarily agree. "Zed, get me a system scan. Make sure we're still alone."

Lyra turned in her chair. "You don't honestly think anything's coming back this way, do you? I mean, look at this place. It's beyond trashed. Who would even want to come back? The Veldon beat the hell out of their own people. Pretty sure they don't have anything else to do but—"

"Uh..." Zed interrupted. "I've got contacts."

Lyra cleared her throat. "I... take all that nonsense back."

"Thanks," Gareth said. "I appreciate it. How long before they get here, Zed?"

"Twenty minutes. Maybe half an hour at most."

Damn it. Gareth reached out to Chelsea. "We've got ships incoming. It would be good if you came back right away."

"We're about to make contact with the Veldon," Chelsea said. "Which will complete the mission, don't you think?"

I don't care about the mission. Get your ass back to the ship! Gareth bit his lip. Calm down. That's not the answer.

"You need to hurry," Gareth replied. "I can't guarantee we can take them. We might have to run."

"We won't be long. Besides, you didn't plan to leave the Veldon if they turned out to be friendly, did you?"

I kinda did, yes.

"Of course not," Gareth said. "Just... hurry." He looked at Zed. "How long before Barty gets back?"

"They're nearly here. Three minutes."

If Chelsea had come back with them, we'd be on our way out of here.

Eliza raised her hand. "I've got the incoming ships on scan now. They are definitely the Veldon. Six of them, all battlecruiser designation."

"Newer ships," Zoe said, "so certainly not friendly by any stretch."

Gareth tapped his foot. Options bounced around in his head. Attacking seemed like a reasonable idea. They might not expect the sudden explosion of activity. On the other hand, they were behind enemy lines. It could warrant a conversation. Perhaps these Veldon happened to be reasonable.

"Hail them." Gareth leaned forward. "Let them know we're rescuing these people. Make it fast."

"Yes, sir."

"You don't think," Lyra started. "You know... never mind. I don't have my fingers on the pulse of this situation at all."

"Prep weapons," Gareth ordered. "Shields after we get everyone onboard. Eliza, when I give the word, I want you to take off and race for orbit. We'll need to clear it fast. Last thing we want is to fight down here." That turbulence alone bothered him. He didn't want to be fighting them while bouncing around.

Particularly as they lazily drifted around the planet while targeting them.

"People are aboard," Keppler said, "and I'll be starting the process of checking them over. Please don't bounce us around too much, huh?"

"No promises," Gareth replied. "Send Barty up here."

"I can't," Keppler said, "he dashed out and said he needed to get back to Chelsea."

Of course he did. "Zed, tell him to return to the ship before he gets too far away." I don't want to have to pick them up while the enemy can take shots at us. That will not go well. He took a deep breath, trying to relax. He started to feel flustered, which struck him as odd. The situation was mostly under control.

So why am I struggling here? Gareth felt some of the frustration settle, though it didn't go away entirely. It hovered, just in the back of his head, making him anxious. Probably because Chelsea's still out there.

Whatever happens, I have to get her back to the ship. I can't risk her a second time. Why'd I let her talk me out of going?

The enemy ships approached. Would they attack or talk? The Pytheas had the firepower to take one or two of them on. Six seemed like a stretch. The kind Gareth preferred not to test. One way or another, they'd get out of the system. But Chelsea and the others needed to get back to the ship.

***

Chelsea slowed down as she approached the Veldon. They had their backs to her. Their weapons were stowed so she lowered hers, aiming at the ground. One finally turned to look at her. She'd only seen a few of them out of their armor. None of these had any protection on at all other than some loose fitting garments.

Each of the Veldon stood more than seven feet tall. Thick fur covered their bodies, particularly their faces. Only dark eyes and black lips stuck out from the fluff. Their stubby hands ended in claws, though they tended to keep those relatively short. The one made eye contact with her before stepping closer.

"Hi." Chelsea held up her free hand. "We came to help the humans and thought you might want to talk.

Maybe even get out of here before it's too late. I hope you can understand me?"

The Veldon made a grunt noise, followed by a low growl. The speaker in Chelsea's helmet translated.

"Greetings, human. I am Laiva. You are EDF."

Chelsea nodded. "Chelsea Weston. What're you doing?"

"Preparing the turret for the attack." Laiva tilted their head as she snarled her words. Chelsea had no idea what gender they were. "Our not-kin have returned. Likely due to your ship. We will need to stop them if we hope to save those of us who are still on this planet. Before they are killed."

"How many are here?" Chelsea asked. "I thought it was only you guys and the humans."

"We have some of our young," Laiva said. "They are in the bunker. It is safe for now. But it will not be if they land."

"Look, there's not a lot of time."

Ithila stepped forward. "You should get them and return with us to the Pytheas. Our vessel has enough room to take you away. We can escape them."

"We cannot." Laiva waved their hands about, as if they were conducting a symphony. "The ships are already here. Departing would be a mistake. With six of them coming close, they can take you down. Our scans prove that out. So we must keep them busy. Which is what the turret will do."

Chelsea shook her head. "Begging your pardon, but it didn't even nudge our defenses, guys. Come on. Please, you should come with us. Right now. I'm sure—"

"If you wish to help," Laiva interrupted, "then you will prepare for the landing. They are on their way. The landing will take place just on the outskirts of our settlement. And the bunker must be protected. You have superior weapons and armor to us. It will make short work of the enemy."

"One second." Chelsea stepped away. "My dad's not going to like this, Ithila. He wanted us to leave."

"If they have young ones," Ithila said, "then leaving would be irresponsible. Cruel even. They would all die."

"We don't exactly have the numbers to push a real attack force back." Chelsea turned to Laiva. "Why are they doing this? What happened? These are your people, aren't they? What does not-kin mean?"

"There has been civil war," Laiva said. "And we were thrust into the middle of it. Those who could not fight, died. Those who tried to defend, failed. The majority of our military was destroyed before we even knew we'd been attacked. All because we nursed the Uldarn. Because we supported them."

"I don't know what that means," Chelsea replied. "What do you mean nursed? They were injured? How many are there? Where are they?"

"You have many questions," Laiva said. "And I will answer them all if you help us. But we must save our young. Get them away from this place. After the not-kin have been repelled. My people, such as they are, will assist you. We wish to see an end to this conflict as well. Which is why we helped your intelligence operatives."

Barty jogged up. "Hey guys! Gareth's kinda pissed. I ditched as soon as Sylas and the others got back to the ship. What're we doing? I thought you'd be ready to go by now." He looked at the Veldon. "I guess they're friendly?"

"Yeah." Chelsea nodded. "And they have an ask. Something that none of us is going to like, I don't think." She gestured to Laiva. "Show us to the bunker so we can figure out how best to defend it. I need to speak to my commander. Let him know the plan so they can supplement the planetary defenses."

Dad's going to lose his mind. But he couldn't possibly argue against it, could he? There was no way he'd suggest they leave children there. Not when these people have the answers we seek. Would they matter if all of them died fighting off overwhelming odds? No, but that's kind of beside the point.

"What're you doing?" Gareth's voice filled her helmet. "Chelsea, you need to get back here. There are Veldon ships in the area. We need—"

"I can't," Chelsea interrupted. "The Veldon have children here. They're in a... safe room. A bunker."

"So get them and we'll go!"

"The others say there's no time. I don't know what they're talking about but..." She paused as a light caught her attention, three streaks far off in the distance. "The enemy ships have sent down a landing party. That's why they were getting the turret ready. Not for the orbital ships, but the smaller ones."

"I don't care what they're doing, you've got time. You can get back here!"

"We can't," Chelsea said, "but you can buy us time in orbit. Fend those ships off. Lead them away then come back for us. We'll take care of the invaders."

"That's crazy," Gareth replied. "I'm not—"

"Dad. I know the last time I pushed this, I got arrested. But I've got Barty and Ithila with me. Plus a bunch of pissed off Veldon that are parents. I'm pretty sure we've got this. You'll have to trust me. We might find out everything we need to know if we can save them. So I think that's what we have to do."

"Damn it, Chelsea. I swear to God, you really try my patience."

"Always have." Chelsea sighed. "They want to move out. I've got to go."

"Be careful." Gareth dropped off the line.

I'll do my best.

Laiva spoke to the other Veldon in quick sounds the translator didn't pick up. They then waved their arm before heading off. Their conversation seemed to be about the incoming shuttles. Their assessment suggested twenty Veldon ground troops. And they mentioned something about capture.

"What do you mean?" Chelsea asked. "Who do they want? What's the problem? And how do you expect us to fend off twenty fully armored Veldon soldiers?"

"First," Laiva said, "we bring down at least one shuttle with the turret. Then, we kill the rest. We are not wearing armor and we are not afraid. Why are you?"

"Okay... fair question." Probably because they're deadly and have air cover. "So what's two?"

"They want the children," Laiva replied. "And we will do whatever it takes to prevent that. They cannot take them away, young human. We cannot. Now let us move quickly. All of us should be in position before the shooting starts. Come!"

Here we go. Off to what will probably be our last stand. Faith shouldn't have been so hard to come by after what she'd been through. A rescue from a fate worse than death. Surviving a plethora of dangerous situations. Finding her father, alive and well... and young. I should approach defending these people with a spring in my step.

But all luck eventually ran out. When it did, people died. Deep behind enemy territory with starships incoming and limited support. What did I get us into? Salvation or an anonymous death far from home.

***

"Disembark," Gareth ordered. "Take us into orbit. Now."

"Sir?" Lyra turned to him. "What about—"

"They've got a mission," Gareth snapped at her. "Do your job. I don't want to argue with you. Shields up." He secured his safety belt. "Prepare to engage the enemy." The floor vibrated as the maneuvering thrusters kicked in. You'd better know what you're doing, Chelsea. Don't you dare die.

Eliza tilted the nose up then fired the rear thrusters. The Pytheas lurched forward, hurling toward orbit at a rapid pace. Blips appeared on the tactical screen, a number of shuttles approaching the settlement. None of them seemed to acknowledge the human vessel as it ascended.

We don't have time to finish them off. They were too far away and the enemy battlecruisers would be in orbit before they could get into space. Gareth needed to warn them off, push them away from the planet before they had the chance to bombard the surface for a second time.

Zoe said, "The enemy ships are breaking formation. They are still moving for orbit."

Make it harder to stop them. Gareth shook his head. Why? Why do they care so much about killing those people rather than fighting with us? He felt like they might be able to escape if they tried. Except they might have escalated their strike if they saw us evacuating the survivors.

"Maybe," Gareth hummed before continuing, "maybe we didn't attract them at all. These Veldon might be back to finish the job and we just happened to be here."

"Regardless," Lyra said, "I've got the first one targeted. Are we trying to destroy them or is this more of a disable thing?"

"Go for the kill shot," Gareth replied.

"Targeting engines." Lyra paused. "ETA to orbit, two minutes. I'll be able to shoot them thirty seconds after that."

They hit the turbulence again, though this time they plowed right into it. Winds buffeted them from all sides. Shields kept them safe from debris, but they couldn't prevent the motion from the extreme weather. Scans showed they'd be out of it in moments, but while they remained in the flow, it gave the Pytheas a good rattle.

"Incoming!" Lyra shouted. "Evasive!"

"What?" Eliza asked. "I—"

A blast struck them on the starboard side.

"Shields held," Lyra said. "We gotta get away from the planet's surface. Our defenses aren't functioning as well in the storm. All those particulates, the radiation, it's battering them constantly. Putting us at risk."

"We're almost out!" Eliza called. The shaking ended as they breached atmosphere, moving into space. The enemy ships closed. They were on the verge of surrounding the planet. Another few minutes, and they'd be in firing position.

The Pytheas came around, aiming directly at the nearest enemy ship. Lyra announced she was ready to fire. Gareth gave the word.

Cannons discharged, beams ripping through the shields of their target. The hull superheated, causing significant damage. The nudge wasn't quite enough to finish them off though, even as one of their engines flickered out. The others diverted their attention from the planet though, each moving to intercept.

"Is that what we wanted?" Eliza asked. "Because I think we've got a big problem on our hands now."

"Draw them away," Gareth said. "Set course thirty degrees port and fire the afterburners. Lyra, blast them with turrets to remind them we're a threat they don't want flying around here."

"Sounds like a great idea," Lyra muttered, "get six weapon platforms to focus solely on us." She unleashed on them with the turret, popping shots as they moved away from the collective.

"Uh…" Zed held up his hand, "we have a problem, guys."

"What is it now?" Eliza asked.

"Another distortion. More ships incoming."

Gareth tensed up. Maybe they're ours. He knew better. There was no reason for the EDF to come. They've got the coordinates for when we don't report in at some time in the future. When would that be? Long after we're dead so it won't matter. Damn it, if that's more of them… why would they commit a large force to this settlement?

"What's the deal with these Veldon?" Gareth asked out loud. "Why do these Uldarn freaks want them so badly?"

Zoe replied, "When we get them aboard, we can find out."

That's optimistic. Ships winked in on the edge of the system. Well over a dozen. All Veldon. Their engines fired up as they headed toward the planet and the conflict with the lone EDF ship. We're amazing, but this is beyond ridiculous. He had to make a choice. Let them chase him around on the hope he might save the people on the surface.

Or abandon his daughter and flee the system.

The first attack from the enemy ships whizzed by, coming dangerously close. Eliza began evasive maneuvers. Lyra kept shooting. But none of that would matter for long. Not with the ground forces closing on Chelsea's position and eighteen starships coming at them to finish the fight.

Then they'll destroy every life form in this sector. Human and Veldon alike. The Uldarn didn't only have the upper hand, they pretty much won. And if they're willing to do this to their own people, what chance do we have against them? How can the EDF stand up to this kind of callousness?

Maybe they couldn't.

□

Chapter 11

Patrick dropped through the maintenance hatch to the deck below. He stepped to the side, aiming his rifle in both directions before waving at Esher to join him. Once they were together, they hurried to a small alcove to take cover. He needed to assess the area they found themselves in.

"They would've noticed," Esher whispered. Despite having comms, Patrick agreed with him keeping his voice low. It made it easier to listen for anyone approaching. "Don't you think?"

"Probably," Patrick muttered. "There are three things they should have picked up. First, our arrival on scans. Second, when we made contact with their ship. There would've been a shift in gravity to compensate for the added mass of our vessel. And third, when we popped the maintenance hatch."

"Nah, that one I had under control." Esher peered out before continuing. "I got their codes. That seemed like normal operations."

"Very good." Patrick logged into the computer system using his JTF credentials. The fact it worked made him sneer. Son of a bitch is so arrogant he didn't even change the security protocols. Probably never imagined anyone would get this close to him. "I've got the layout of the ship downloading."

"Fantastic. What do we do?"

"I'm torn," Patrick said. "Part of me wants to hit Engineering. Take control of all systems. But then I'm also keen to get straight to the bridge. Find this guy. Put him down immediately. Maybe then we can convince his followers to surrender." If they even listen to anyone but him.

"Tough call. I've run a scan on the ship. We know he's got prisoners. If you account for the number we saw on the other manifests, then he's got a skeleton crew aboard. Barely enough to operate this thing with proper shifts."

"Probably doesn't bother." Patrick sighed. "Okay, I'm putting it to you. Which do you think is a better plan?"

"We could split up," Esher offered, "take both."

"Kind of defeats the purpose of coming together." Patrick hummed. "We could also free some of the prisoners... but that would likely give Trildair another chance to find out we're here. Nope. I think we're going straight for the bridge. Get him first. If he's not there, we can make our way to Engineering."

"You've got the lead." Esher nodded. "I'm right behind you."

Patrick plotted a course to the bridge from their location. They had quite a ways to go, particularly because he wanted to avoid elevators. Blips appeared along the path, armed men he designated as enemies. All the dots turned red. He stepped out of the alcove and started down the hall at a brisk pace with the barrel of his weapon leading the way.

"First contact," Esher muttered, "one hundred yards. Just around the corner."

The dot in question moved in their direction. Patrick held up his hand for Esher to stop at the corner. He paused there, waiting for the person to approach. Few security personnel bothered to wear helmets on duty when they were working on a starship. He expected Trildair's people to do so considering what he was up to.

But when the person didn't pick up the pace nor slow down as they approached, it became clear they didn't bother with such things. Their shadow appeared on the floor. Patrick took a deep breath. The moment the person appeared, he slammed the butt of his rifle against the side of their head.

The man flailed, convulsing as he went down but he didn't even groan. Just dropped like he'd been shut off.

"That was weird," Esher muttered. "Nice hit though."

"I guess." Patrick proceeded, stepping over the body. They bought themselves a little more time by not firing a weapon. Once that happened, an automated alarm would go to security. Even if there weren't people to man it, Trildair had to be monitoring it. If not, then he'd been dramatically overestimated.

Additional blips appeared around them, people coming to that floor. Patrick wondered if a silent alarm went off when he knocked the guy out. He'd heard about trip switches like that before. He kind of doubted they used such things aboard a JTF ship. A normal one at least with plenty of people to work overlapping shifts.

"We'd better hurry," Patrick said, "if we don't get to that ladder before we end up in a firefight, we might not make the bridge."

"Tell you what," Esher replied, "I suggest we redirect to the Engineering deck if people start shooting. Be a lot easier to shut things down. He'll have to surrender."

Patrick clicked his tongue. "Don't think so. Bridge has override control."

"Not the way I intend to do it. We can cut the relays if we're willing to cause some serious damage."

"We'll cross that bridge when we come to it." Patrick picked up the pace, breaking into a sprint. The newcomers were behind them, moving slowly. If they were being tactical, the situation was dire. If not, then they had all the time in the world. But he chose to err on the side of caution.

A lot of lives depended on them, which meant they had a lot riding on remaining unseen. At least until they found Trildair.

Then all bets were off.

***

Two guards dragged Klaus from his cell. It was his turn for the machine. He forced them to carry his whole weight, his feet dragging on the ground as they moved along. It didn't bother them. Neither man seemed to be straining, though even if they were, he doubted he'd know one way or the other.

They made it fifty yards before his captors stopped abruptly. That hadn't happened before. He'd been up and down that area a dozen times at least and they always kept to a strict schedule. He counted the seconds between his cell and the machine, learned the exact distance because of their consistency.

And they just broke it.

What the hell? Klaus felt like he might need to take advantage of it. This is the time. I know it. If I don't take this chance, I might not get another. The one on the left loosened their grip. Another oddity. I don't care. It's a gift. I'll take it.

Yanking himself free, he punched his other captor in the groin. The other one didn't react, even as Klaus yanked a pistol from one holster and put a blast in each of their heads. Their bodies dropped. He saw their expressions half a second before he turned them to molten flesh.

Instead of the placid, blank expressions, they both seemed confused. Totally lost.

What the hell is going on here? It doesn't matter.

They put his clothes in the room with the machine. He knew the exact route to take, jogging along the corridor until he got there. His legs and feet tingled with pins and needles, but he pushed himself anyway. The one thing Colm gave him, the only benefit to the torturous conditioning, was the ability to push through discomfort.

Even at the expense of his health, though he wasn't quite there yet. The moment the man's grip let up on his arm, a surge of energy washed through him. Adrenaline gave him the strength to move, though he didn't know how long he had before he might crash. The goal was to find Cole then get the hell out of there.

And if she was already dead, he needed another pilot.

He came to a halt outside his destination. The door was open. The man who worked the controls bent over the console, tapping away quietly. His one other guard stared at the machine. There was no reason for them to look outside. They expected their own to show up with a prisoner.

Not a man with a gun ready to use it.

Klaus stepped in the room, blasting the man watching the machine. The other one looked up. Their eyes met. Klaus slammed the butt of the pistol against his face, knocking him to the ground. He followed the man down then pummeled him in the head until he stopped twitching.

It took twenty blows to cave the face in. Klaus stood, panting from the effort. He set the gun on the console then went about finding his clothes. I should hunt down Trildair before I leave. That man deserves to die too. He couldn't go without taking that life. Otherwise, I'll be hunting him after I finish with Colm.

But first, he needed Cole. She had to be somewhere on that floor. He'd find her. Just as soon as he was dressed.

***

"Did you hear that?" Patrick paused as he reached the ladder. "Gunfire. On the floor above us. Happens to be near the bridge."

"Who would be shooting?" Esher asked. "I thought everyone onboard was a braindead fish person."

Patrick lifted his brow. "Braindead what?"

"Nothing. Just... you know what I mean! Why are they popping off shots? You think one of the prisoners escaped?"

"Possibly." Patrick started up the ladder. "Let's see if we've got an ally. Might make the rest of this work easier." Or we can end up in a firefight. Whichever. He knew that once things went loud, a timer would start. Trildair would either try to stop them by rallying his people or he might flee the ship.

If he got away, finding him again might be impossible. But if he rallied, Patrick felt certain they'd be overwhelmed. With someone else pulling the trigger, he wasn't sure if the timer started.

Best to operate as if we're on borrowed time. Patrick hurried. And be happy we've got some spare time at the end.

***

Trildair jumped when he heard the weapon fire. It seemed distant, though that didn't stop his heart from pounding. Adrenaline made him shake. He hurried from his position to check the internal scans. He still wasn't sure what made the gravity shift. Though he'd only just dug into the technical aspects of the device.

An alarm went out that he missed. One of the drones fell unconscious. Others went to check on them. Then there was gunfire near the machine. He knew who was responsible for it. Klaus had to be it. None of the other captives had the willpower or the physical endurance to take so much punishment and still manage to inflict violence.

That son of a bitch has to be killed. Trildair regretted it, but he couldn't risk that sort of drive translating through the conditioning. He brought the camera up for the room. It didn't work. The screen showed offline. He's a cunning animal, that one. I'll have to double the guards to ensure he doesn't make another idiotic attempt on the bridge.

He sent out a signal for five soldiers to return to the bridge immediately. Then he remembered to pick them. Every single crew member aboard would've come running had he forgotten. As convenient as it was control the people around him, there were downsides. Many of which became easy to forget in an emergency.

When they get here, I can focus on Klaus. Until then, he had his two security forces aim at the door just before he locked it down. Anyone comes in, they'll be dead before they have a chance to look around. That made him feel safer. Though he wouldn't feel entirely comfortable until Klaus had been found.

And put in a bag.

***

Klaus tapped into the rooms nearest the machine. One contained two dead people, likely expired due to Trildair's deprivation. In the next, a woman reclined on the floor in her own vomit. She bled from various points on her arms where she seemed to have chewed herself, possibly from starvation.

He hadn't considered what the experiments would do to regular people. Not to the horrifying extent of broken bodies rotting in rooms after dying mostly alone. Though the fact he found one where the people had been together struck him as odd. Perhaps that place had become a storage closet for corpses.

Why not jettison them? Probably for the horror aspect. Showing them to some of the people had to be shocking. Colm didn't bother with this stuff. His methods tended to be scientific. The goal of those experiments involved the betterment of people, even if he didn't have a lick of concern for the comfort or well-being of his subjects.

They'd at least have their own minds at the end. If it had worked out properly, they would've been better. Technically, Klaus was a success. Colm should have been better to us. Talked more. Had some bedside manner. Instead, he was cold about it. Taking notes while we suffered.

Not unlike Trildair in that way. Though this man seemed to enjoy the torture. Colm just didn't care.

Each space Klaus checked displayed another brutalized prisoner. Some dead, others mutilated, and a couple merely catatonic. Probably ready for whatever programming Trildair planned. Why did he wait? What was the plan? How did his process work overall? These questions might interest the authorities someday.

I'm not bothering to gather that shit. They can do it themselves if they catch up to him.

Klaus reached the last door in that hallway. Footsteps from around the corner gave him pause. They walked slowly, so more of the brainwashed guards. He held his weapon high, watching the shadows until the last second. When they rounded the corner, he opened fire, blasting the first one in the head.

The second turned to him with surprising speed, much more they had displayed before. There was nothing lethargic about this guard. Rather it appeared to have the same reflexes as a normal person. Enough that Klaus had to lunge forward to knock their weapon away before they shot him.

As the rifle went off, the blast ricocheted off the floor. Klaus pressed his pistol against the man's ribs, pulling the trigger three times. The body stiffened, but the person stared into his eyes, unfeeling. Without so much as a flinch.

The guard shoved Klaus back and started to lift the rifle again.

Klaus dropped backward to the floor, shooting again. This time, he got the guy in the gut then the throat. One of the two put them down. If they can take that kind of punishment, I need to ensure I'm going for the face from now on. He crawled to his feet then opened the door.

Cole leaned against the wall opposite. She stared into space, but took a deep breath.

"Hey!" Klaus hurried over to crouch in front of her. He touched her chin, lifting her head so he could look in her eyes. "Come on, it's me. What's going on?"

"You..." Cole blinked. "You're not real."

"I am real." Klaus pinched her arm. They left her in her underwear but her thighs were red from punishment, arms scratched up, face flush. "What the hell did they do to you?"

"The same... as... you..."

"Can you stand? This is our chance to get out of here or die trying, girl. We do not want to stay here. Even if we can't escape, we gotta go down fighting. You ready?"

"Yes." Cole nodded. "I think so. But you... can't be... real..."

"I am. I'll take you to where they stored my clothes."

"Cut mine..." Cole shook her head. "They cut them off."

"Then we'll get you a jumpsuit or something. Come on!" Klaus hoisted her to her feet then dragged her out.

"No! No!" Cole screamed but she didn't fight. "Please don't take me back there!"

"Relax," Klaus replied, "you're not going on that thing. You can wait in the hall. I promise."

"I don't want to see it, Klaus! I don't want to ever see it again! Please!" Cole closed her eyes, thrashing her head to the left and right. "I can't do it! I can't!"

"I know." Klaus clenched his jaw. "Just… stay here." He leaned her against the wall. "Try to walk it off. Let your limbs wake up. We'll be out of here in no time." He dashed inside, throwing the various lockers open. When he found some coveralls, he brought them out, then paused to take another weapon.

Cole leaned against the wall, but she hadn't sunk to the floor. That was a good sign. She bent her head, rubbing her eyes with the heels of her hands. The wounds were worse than his. They did something else to her. He couldn't tell what by the welts. Maybe whipped her? That didn't make sense.

"Do you want help?" Klaus asked. "I can help you get this thing on."

"I'll do it." Cole stepped into the garment then zipped it up. He handed her one of the pistols. "Thank you." She met his gaze. "I couldn't have taken much more, Klaus."

"Yeah, I get it." Klaus motioned behind him. "Pretty sure the hangar's that way. We can get out of here."

"What about Trildair?" Cole asked. There was a lot of steel in her voice. "We can't leave him here. He can't survive this."

"He's not our problem," Klaus replied. Though he wanted to go along with her. Until he located her, he figured he had to take the guy out. Now that they had the means to fly away, he changed his tune. Survival sounded better. Specifically far away from the destroyer without contending with a psycho."

"No." Cole growled. "No, he's going to die, Klaus. Besides, he'll just shoot us down if we don't take care of him. Where is the bridge?"

Klaus remembered the path from his time before. It wouldn't take much to get there. This time, he'd take a ladder if at all possible. The elevator proved problematic. He agreed with her conviction. Killing the guy probably made the most sense. And it would be damn satisfying to boot.

"Okay." Klaus nodded. "Let's go. We'll make it happen." He gestured. "It's this way." He moved to the end of the hallway, then peaked around the corner. The barrel of a rifle touched his forehead. "Whoa!"

"Don't move," a gruff voice came out sounding metallic through a helmet.

"Who the hell are you?" Klaus asked. "What's this about?"

"Lieutenant Commander Patrick Worthing of the JTF." The man pushed Klaus back into the hallway. "You don't seem like the others around here."

"We were prisoners, you asshole!" Klaus gestured to the weapon. "Can you take this away from my head? We just escaped!"

"Probably true," another armored guy said as he came out. "I think they're the ones abducted at the fuel depot."

Patrick lowered his weapon. "How did you escape?"

Klaus replied, "They were taking me for torture when they stopped moving abruptly. They hadn't done it before so I took my opportunity. Then I found my partner here. Saved her too. How did you yahoos even get here? Why didn't you come sooner? And if you're with the JTF, why should we trust you?"

"This Trildair guy nearly killed me and some friends," Patrick explained, "so we hunted him down. Chased this destroyer across the sector. We didn't know if any of his victims would still be alive. I'm grateful you're okay. But I need your help now. Do you know where he is? I can't leave here without him."

Cole said, "We were on our way to the bridge to kill him. I'm not leaving without him being dead. So don't even try to stop us." She pointed her weapon at Patrick. "I don't care who you are or who you call a boss. You have no idea what he did to me. Or what he intended to do. So this is happening. Understood?"

"Whoa." Patrick held up a hand. "We're on your side. And yes, I understand. Let's get along. We might be the only friendlies aboard this ship." She stopped aiming the gun. "Thank you. There's a ladder system in case of power failure. We just came up through it. The bridge should be next."

"Good." Klaus nodded. "Let's go. Lead the way."

"Alright," Patrick said, "Esher, take up the rear. You two with me. Let's move it."

He doesn't trust us. But I can't blame him. Klaus only believed these two because of their equipment. No one else aboard seemed to dress that way. Nor did they have the articulation to talk. If he understood how bad the occupants of this ship really are, he'd know we're good.

But until he proved it, they'd have the other soldier pacing behind them, ensuring they didn't suddenly turn into rampaging killers.

I got to Cole in time. We're safe. A little unfinished business and we'll be on our way. Unless the JTF guys had other plans. I can talk them down, I'm pretty sure. Maybe we've got some big mission we're on. Something classified. That should win over these militant bastards. They understand that kind of thing.

"Here." Patrick gestured. "The ladder is in that alcove." He held up his hand. "We've got contact rear. Less than ten seconds. Esher?"

"On it." Esher swung his weapon in that direction. "You two take cover. Get ready to climb. I can pin them down."

"I don't think so," Klaus said. "If they're anything like the guards we've been dealing with, then they don't necessarily feel pain. Headshots and heart shots. I just shot a guy in the ribs point blank and he didn't even wince. Be sure you aim high... and if you can't, then you might as well—"

"I'll be fine," Esher interrupted. "Now move!"

Klaus didn't like it. Arguing seemed pointless. He helped Cole onto the ladder first then followed her up. She moved faster than he anticipated. After what they put her through, adrenaline must've kicked in. They passed by two floors when she disembarked, offering him a hand.

"I'm good," Klaus said. Though he had to admit, he was a little winded. She panted, leaning against the wall. "You sure you're okay? We don't have to go through with this. We can—"

"Stop trying to talk me out of it." Cole leaned to look down the ladder. "Only one of them's coming."

Gunfire echoed from the passage below. Esher must've been fighting off some of the guards. Klaus shrugged. "I'm sure the three of us will be more than enough to take out Trildair." He motioned to her. "How're you feeling though? Do you think you've got this? I know you were—"

"Don't worry. When this is done and we're far away from here, I'll have a minute to freak out. Get some rest. But now... now, we have to focus on making sure this never happens to anyone else ever again." Cole glared at Patrick as he stepped off the ladder. "Can we go now? We're wasting time."

"Sorry to keep you," Patrick said. "We want this guy as much as you do. Seems like half his forces are down there though. Esher's holding them, but we should take care of Trildair as soon as possible. Maybe we can turn off the... I don't even know what to call them. Drones, I guess? Victims?"

"Sounds good." Cole marched away. She stopped. "Klaus, what direction?"

"Uh... this way." Klaus turned to Patrick. "You sure you want to leave your guy behind? Is that a good idea?"

"There were a lot of them," Patrick replied, "and if he didn't, they would've been shooting at us through the shaft. But they also weren't advancing on him for some reason. Not that they seem to have much in the way of self-preservation. Let's just do it. Before we run into them up here."

Klaus nodded. He led the way, moving swiftly down the hall toward the bridge. He remembered his last attempt. Moving through the door... taking a blow to the head... going down. That cost him a lot of suffering. Enough that he had no intention of making the same mistake twice.

This time Cole seemed ready to make a mad dash inside. Her determination exceeded his own. It made him wonder what sort of atrocities Trildair inflicted on her. Had he violated her? Or just beaten her along with the machine? Asking seemed inappropriate. She might talk about it later.

The only thing that seemed like it might help her at the moment was vengeance. Putting Trildair down felt like more of an obligation than a luxury. Klaus didn't want him to come back on them, or try to find them again. He reserved his ire for Colm still, though to be fair, he wasn't nearly as bad as Trildair.

Not by a long shot. Klaus never believed he'd meet someone worse than his nemesis. Colm's evil, so what's that make Trildair? The devil?

They drew close to the door. Klaus knew it from them dragging him out that way. The elevator on the inside was the reason he got in trouble. He looked at the others. "When we open that up, we'd better be prepared for action. You know he's kept back some people to protect him."

"Of course." Patrick stepped over to the panel. He leaned against the wall. "Stack up on me. Just behind."

Klaus stepped up first. "Take up the rear," he said. "I'll clear the area with him."

"He can't survive this," Cole said. "You hear me?"

"I know..." Klaus nodded. "We're ready, Patrick."

"On three." Patrick counted back then tapped the panel. He waited as people started shooting, flooding the doorway volleys of weapon fire. They stopped after a good thirty seconds. "Now!" He darted out, laying down a quick burst.

Klaus followed, opening up with his pistol. It dawned on him that Patrick's armor advantage made him ideal to go first, but it also meant he could take some punishment. Running into the enemy's line of fire seemed crazy. Enough that he wished they would've stayed back behind cover to provide support.

The men standing at the door were dead before he fired his weapon. He ended up blasting a console, sending sparks into the air. As they entered, two people stood beside the elevator. Klaus put one of them down. A strong hand grabbed his shoulder, shoving him to the ground a second before a beam of light would've cut him in half.

Patrick took the blow to the shoulder then killed the attacker.

"You okay?" Klaus stood. "That didn't—"

"I'm fine," Patrick interrupted. "Grazing shot. Clear the room!" He took the right. "Go left!"

Another of the mindless enemies poked up from near the viewscreen. Patrick put them down before they had the chance to fire. The elevator opened. Klaus spun, spraying into the section without a second thought. The people trying to enter danced back into the chamber, burnt flesh crisping off before they dropped.

Thank God that wasn't the Esher guy. Klaus doubted the soldier was stupid enough to try it. Still, that would've been bad. He scampered to his feet, hustling over to check the bodies. Cole did the same, giving each a shot to the head. She means it as much as she said. Damn. I wouldn't have given it to her.

"I'm clearing the space," Klaus said. "You okay here?"

Cole nodded. "I've got your back."

"Thanks." Klaus moved away. The area proved much bigger than he remembered with enough space to house half a dozen men. He got halfway through when he caught sight of someone cowering in the middle of the room near the captain's chair. Their dark clothes almost saved them from the first pass.

"Here!" Klaus aimed his weapon. "Get your ass up! Now!"

Trildair rose, holding his hands over his head. "Don't shoot! You've got me!"

"You son of a bitch." Klaus sneered. "Why the hell shouldn't I shoot you in the face right now?"

Patrick stepped closer, holding the rifle on the man. "You've got some serious questions to answer. Don't you dare move!"

"Of course not." Trildair cleared his throat. "I want to cooperate. I'll do whatever I have to for you.

Just... don't hurt me." He snapped his fingers twice, then clapped them together.

Klaus frowned. "What the—"

A weapon discharged. The chirp accompanied a burning sensation that started in Klaus's shoulder. He stumbled, turning as he leaned against a console. He stared at Cole, aiming her gun at him. The barrel shook. Her brows furrowed. Tears soaked her cheeks. She seemed to be in pain.

"What... the..."

"I'm sorry," Cole said. "I'm so sorry." She pulled the trigger again. Pain roared in Klaus's chest... left side. He fell to the cool, metal floor. Drifting. Distant sounds tried to keep him awake. But they faded into nothing as blackness settled over him like a thick, weighted blanket.

Printed in Great Britain
by Amazon

33016513R00185